Ruth Erskine's Son

Pansy

Copyright © 2017 Okitoks Press

All rights reserved.

ISBN: 1976562767

ISBN-13: 978-1976562761

Table of Contents

CHAPTER I 3
CHAPTER II 6
CHAPTER III 10
CHAPTER IV 14
CHAPTER V 17
CHAPTER VI 23
CHAPTER VII 26
CHAPTER VIII 30
CHAPTER IX 34
CHAPTER X 37
CHAPTER XI 41
CHAPTER XII 45
CHAPTER XIII 49
CHAPTER XIV 54
CHAPTER XV 58
CHAPTER XVI 62
CHAPTER XVII 65
CHAPTER XVIII 69
CHAPTER XIX 73
CHAPTER XX 76
CHAPTER XXI 80
CHAPTER XXII 83
CHAPTER XXIII 87
CHAPTER XXIV 90
CHAPTER XXV 94
CHAPTER XXVI 98
CHAPTER XXVII 101
CHAPTER XXVIII 107
CHAPTER XXIX 111
CHAPTER XXX 115

CHAPTER I

WHIMS

As a matter of fact the name of this story should be: Ruth Erskine Burnham's Son. But there are those living who remember Ruth Erskine and her memorable summer at the New York Chautauqua; and that name is so entirely associated with those four girls at Chautauqua, and their after experiences, that it seems natural to speak of her boy, Erskine, as Ruth Erskine's son; although, of course, he was also Judge Burnham's son.

The day on which she is again introduced to her friends was a dull one in late autumn; the afterglow of sunset was already fading, and the shadows were gathering fast. It was the hour that Erskine Burnham liked best for the piano. He was at that moment softly touching the keys, bringing forth harmonious sounds with the air of one not even hearing them.

He was a handsome boy. The promise of his early life,—during which time the exclamation, "What a beautiful child!" was being continually heard,—was being fulfilled in his boyhood. Friends of his father were fond of assuring Ruth that the boy was his father's image; while her friends were sure that no boy could be more like his mother.

As for Ruth when she saw her son bending over his books, a lock of hair continually dropping over his left eye and being continually flung back with a gesture peculiar to Judge Erskine, she would say:—

"He is very much like his grandfather."

As the boy grew older he laughed at all these opinions, and asked his mother if she did not think it would be difficult for a fellow to have any individuality who was strikingly like three people who were all, as nearly as he could make out, strikingly unlike one another.

This remark was one of the memories that came back to her as she looked out at the swift-falling night, and listened to that musical strain which was being played over and over and *over*. She seemed to be watching the people who were hurrying homeward, glancing apprehensively now and then at the sky; for despite the glow of sunset there were premonitions of a coming storm, and already a few advance snowflakes were beginning to fall. But Mrs. Burnham saw neither people nor snowflakes; or rather she saw them without seeing. Her eyes were swimming in tears that she did not intend to let have their way. Not as girl or woman had Ruth Erskine Burnham been given to tears, although there had been reason enough in her life for them. Since she had not indulged them then, she did not mean to begin now that she was middle-aged and her hair was being sprinkled with gray.

She had been going over the story of the years with herself, that afternoon, which might account in part for the dimmed eyes. It seemed to her, looking back, that her chief mission in life had been to minister at dying beds and follow as chief or almost chief mourner in funeral processions. She had gone away back to the betrothed of her youth, and added one more heavy sigh to the multitude that stood for a lost opportunity. How entirely Harold Wayne had been under her influence! how utterly she had failed him! And she had felt it only when she was following him to the grave. Then those other graves, her father's and Judge Burnham's daughters', Seraph and Minta, what strange sad memories she had connected with both those graves that were not a year apart in their making. And then their father had been laid beside them and they two were left alone in the world, she and Erskine.

3

He was not yet eighteen, but there were times when it seemed to his mother that he was much older, and that he and she had been alone together always. All these memories that, because it was an anniversary of one of her bereavements, had been more vivid with her than usual that day, trooped again about her as she stood in the waning light, apparently intent on watching the outside world, in order to escape being watched by her world, inside.

To people who were acquainted with the girl, Ruth Erskine, it will not seem strange that a look backward over her checkered life brought sombre thoughts that were close to tears.

Of the four girls who, years and years before when they were young and full of courage, went to Chautauqua together and lived their eventful summer and began their new lives together, hers had had the strangest, saddest story; it had been marked by experiences so unlike the commonplace that the world had stopped to look, and express its astonishment.

The unusual began with her father's strange revelations about that new mother who yet was not new, but had been her stepmother for years. Was ever daughter before called upon to receive a new mother in such way as that? But why go over all that ground again? She too had been followed to the grave, and no one of all Mrs. Burnham's friends had been more sincerely missed and mourned. Then there was her sister, Susan Erskine. Was ever heavier cross or greater blessing thrust into a life than that girl represented to the girl Ruth Erskine? It had been one of her later trials to give Susan up to China. She was sorely missed, but it had been good for Erskine to have such a missionary Auntie as she made. And those two strange girls Seraphina and Araminta Burnham. Could some writer put into print the story of those two lives as it interlaced with hers, the foolish world would call it fiction, and criticise it as unnatural.

Over the early days of her widowhood Ruth Burnham knew better than to linger. Though so many years had intervened that the little boy he left had grown to young manhood, she still missed his father so sorely that she could not trust herself to stay among those few precious months before he went suddenly from her.

She had been left, without even the warning of an hour, to bring up their boy alone! It was from this form of her bereavement that she had shrunken back most fearfully. Judge Burnham, with his life consecrated to God, had seemed eminently fitted to guide the life of just such a boy as theirs; but God had planned differently.

And now, what people call the anxious years were gone, and she had kept her boy.

Yet the tears which she did not mean to shed were, in part, for him. She knew better than most mothers seem to understand that there were still "anxious years" to be lived through.

They had lingered over the breakfast table that morning, discussing certain questions that had been discussed before.

"Mamma," the boy had said as he served her to fruit, "how came you to have pronounced ideas about all sorts of things? Were you always so?"

His mother laughed genially.

"What a definite question for a lawyer to ask!" for Erskine had already announced his intention of being a lawyer like his father and grandfather.

"What 'things' are supposed to be under consideration?"

He echoed her laugh.

"I was thinking aloud then," he said. "It often seems to me as though you and I knew each other's thoughts. But just now I am thinking of one of our argumentative subjects. In spite of the horror in which you have brought me up of those bits of pasteboard called cards, I find that I cannot feel precisely as you would like to have me, concerning them. I used to. As a child nobody could be fiercer than I in their denunciation; but I find that that was merely a reflex influence, and not judgment. In spite of me nowadays they look meek and harmless; and I was wondering how you and they came to be in such fierce antagonism. Was my father of that mind?"

"Am I fierce, Erskine?"

He gave her a half-quizzical, wholly loving smile as he said gayly:—

"That of course is not the word to apply to the most charming of women, but you know, dearest, that you are very much in earnest about all such matters. Were you brought up in that way?"

Mrs. Burnham shook her head.

"No, when I was of your age, and younger, we played cards at home; and I went to card-parties in our set very often. It was your Aunt Flossy who set a number of us to thinking and studying and praying about such matters."

Erskine shook his head with pretended gravity.

"I might have known it, mamma. Aunt Flossy isn't like people; in fact she always seems to me a trifle out of place on earth."

"I thought you were very fond indeed of your Aunt Flossy."

"So I am; and I think I should be very fond of an angel from heaven; but you see, when a fellow has to live on the earth, it is a trifle more convenient to be like the other earth worms. All of which was suggested by the fact that the Mitchells are to give a card-party next week. Very select, you understand, only the choice few are bidden and I happen to be one of them."

Then, although his mother shrank from it, feeling that it did harm rather than good to go again over ground that was familiar to both and that was so clear to her and did not convince her son, he persisted in arguing, and in trying to prove that her position was narrow and untenable in these days. Throughout the interview he had been courteous and winsome, as he always was with her, and had laughingly complimented her more than once on her skill in argument; but for all that, she knew he was entirely unconvinced, and felt that her hold on him was weaker than when they had gone over the same ground before. The fact was, and this mother knew it well, that the world and all the allurements for which that phrase stands was making a hard fight for her handsome son even so early in life, and there were times when she felt fearful that in a sense it would win. It was not that she believed he would ever be sorely tempted by any of the amusements or frivolities of life; he was strong-principled and strong-willed, and certain, that might be called main, points had been settled by him once for all. Yet none knew better than did this woman of long and peculiar experience that it was possible to maintain a high standing in the world and in the church and yet have almost as little knowledge of that life hid with Christ in God which was the Christian's rightful heritage as did the gay world around him. She craved this separated life for Erskine, yet he was social in his tastes and fond of being looked upon as a leader, and his mother knew it already irked him to feel that in certain social functions he must always be counted out.

"There are so many of them!" he had said to her once, with as much impatience in his tone as he ever gave to her.

"A fellow could manage to indulge one or two whims, but you know, dearest, you have at least half a dozen, and to humor them all will make a rather conspicuous wallflower, I am afraid."

Something very like that he had repeated that morning, and it had colored his mother's day. She knew that the Mitchells were fond of Erskine and would make vigorous efforts to secure him for their party. It was hard, she told herself, that one so fitted to shine in cultured circles of young people must so often be made to feel embarrassed and out of place, and she wondered for the dozenth time that season if ways of thinking about these things had changed, along with other changes. Was she herself what Erskine, if he had made use of the modern slang, might call a "back number"? "Still, his father, who had no such prejudices as mine to deal with, grew very positive in his objection to cards," she reminded herself, and sighed. If his father had lived, he would have known just how to manage Erskine; this, at least, she pleased herself by believing, ignoring the fact that in their son's early boyhood the father had had many ways of managing, of which she did not approve. This is a habit which we all have with our beloved dead.

It was the memory of their morning talk that had led Mrs. Burnham to appeal, that afternoon, to Mr. Conway when he dropped in for a social chat. Mr. Conway was their new pastor; a brilliant, scholarly man, much admired by old and young. Erskine in particular had been attracted to him, and was decidedly of the opinion that in the pulpit he was a great improvement on Dr. Dennis, even. Of course his mother did not agree with this verdict, but she was wise enough to remember that the friends of her girlhood could not be expected to be to her son what they were to her. Yet Erskine was eminently fair and thoughtful beyond his years for her. At the very time when he had so heartily indorsed Mr. Conway, he had made haste to say:—

"Of course, mamma, there is a sense in which no one can ever equal Dr. Dennis to us, and as for Aunt Marian her loss is irreparable." He held carefully to the boyish custom of claiming his mother's girl friends as aunts, and she liked it in him:—

"Nevertheless," he had added firmly, "as a preacher Mr. Conway is far superior to Dr. Dennis."

Despite his careful courtesy Erskine was at the age when wisdom is at its height, and opinions as a rule are delivered autocratically without any softening "I think." His mother, having often to make objections from principle, had learned the art of being silent when she could, and she had made no objection in words to his estimate of Mr. Conway. To a degree she was in sympathy with it. She liked Mr. Conway and was glad that he was so young that Erskine, being old for his years, could find him almost companionable, and at the same time could be helped by him.

Because of all these reasons she had been glad that Erskine was in, that afternoon when Mr. Conway called. He was fond of calling there, and playfully accused the two of being responsible for many neglected families in his parish. She had kept herself almost quiet while Erskine and their guest discussed books and music and men. They had many tastes in common. Then Erskine had been urged to play, and his selection from one of the great masters had chanced to be Mr. Conway's special favorite; and then, Mrs. Erskine having studied how to do it in an unstudied way, had skilfully turned the conversation into the channel of her morning talk with Erskine; and before two minutes had passed would have given much to be able to take back what she had done.

CHAPTER II

"NEVER MIND, MOMMIE"

Yet in thinking it over, this course had seemed to Mrs. Burnham eminently wise. Mr. Conway was quite as much in touch with the fashionable world as a clergyman could well be; he had been brought up in its atmosphere and had turned from what were supposed to be very alluring prospects to live the comparatively straitened life of a minister of the gospel. His undoubted scholarship commended him especially to a young fellow like Erskine who came of a scholarly line. If, without being directly appealed to for advice, the minister could be drawn into an expression of opinion about these questionable matters, it would certainly help; and under her skilful management he expressed himself; but behold, he was on the wrong side! At least he was not on the side that Ruth Burnham, having been for years accustomed to the pastorate of Dr. Dennis, had taken it for granted that he would be.

There was, he assured her, something to be said on the other side of that question. Of course he was opposed to all forms of gambling, but a social game of cards in the parlor of a friend was innocent amusement enough—much better than certain others he could name that seemed to have escaped the ban of the over-cautious. He was really in earnest about this matter. He considered that there was positive danger in drawing the lines too taut. He knew a fellow in college who had been very carefully reared in one of those very narrow homes where a card was never allowed to penetrate, and where they looked in holy horror upon the idea of his touching one elsewhere; but he hadn't been in college an entire year before he spent half his nights at cards! and he went to the bad as fast as he could. That, the clergyman believed, was what often happened when young people were held too closely. That was by no means the only instance which had come under his personal knowledge, and indeed he believed that, of the two extremes, he feared the narrow the more. Human nature was such that there was sure to be a rebound from over-strictness, and the clearer, keener brained the victim was, the more fear of results. There was much more of the same sort. Poor Ruth, who had not meant to argue, and who had wished of all things to avoid anything that would look in the least like a personal matter, tried in vain to change the subject. Erskine, with an occasional mischievous glance for her alone, led his pastor on to say much more than he had probably intended at first. Not that he differed from him in the least; on the contrary he took the rôle of an eager youth to whom it was a vital matter to have the "narrowness" of his surroundings immediately widened.

Mrs. Burnham, disappointed and hurt, became almost entirely silent, and when she finally walked down the hall with her departing pastor, felt no wish to consult him about a matter on which she had intended to ask his advice at the first opportunity. She had a feeling that it made little difference to her what his advice was on any subject; yet she knew that that was real narrowness and that she must rise above it. Such was the condition of things on that evening in late autumn when she stood looking out of the bay window at the swiftly gathering night and appeared to be watching the passers-by through a mist of unshed tears, while Erskine played exquisite strains of harmony. His mother, listening, or rather letting the music melt unconsciously into her being, felt peculiarly alone with her responsibilities. Who was she that she should hope, alone and unaided, to battle successfully with the temptations of this great wicked world full of yawning pitfalls especially prepared for the feet of young men? How was she ever to hope to guide a boy like Erskine successfully through its snares, without even a pastor to lean upon? What if Erskine should be like that college boy Mr. Conway had taken such pains to describe graphically and insist upon going to the bad as soon as he was away from her influence? She could see that that was just what was being feared for him; it was probably what Mr. Conway meant.

Wait, must her boy, her one treasure, be away from her influence? Yes, of course he must; everybody said so. Why, there were people who were certain that she was ruining her son by keeping so close to him even now. Not only now, but away back in his young boyhood. She recalled with a shiver of pain how her husband had once said to her:—

"Have a care, Ruth; you don't want to make a Molly Coddle of the boy, remember."

Later, she had heard of one of the Mitchells as declaring that "Mrs. Burnham was making a regular 'Miss Nancy' of that boy of hers, and if somebody did not take him in hand, he would be ruined."

Then, her intimate friends had been as plain with their cautions as they dared. Had not Marian Dennis pleaded earnestly for a famous boys' school fifty miles away? "It would be so good for him, Ruth; he would learn self-reliance and patience; two lessons that a boy never can learn at home, when there is but one." And Dr. Dennis had added his word: "As a rule, my friend, a boy learns manliness by being compelled to be manly and to depend upon himself."

There was her old friend Eurie, with four rollicking, romping boys of her own, always looking doubtfully at Ruth's fair-haired, fair-skinned, rather quiet, always gentlemanly boy.

"Let him come and spend a summer with us, Ruth," she urged, "and row and swim and hunt and get almost shot and quite drowned a few times; it will do him good, body and soul. Boys learn manhood by hairbreadth escapes, you know." She had laughed at Ruth's shudder and had told Marian privately that "Ruth was simply idiotic over that poor boy."

Only Flossy, their dainty, gentle, still beautiful Flossy, had seemed to understand. Had she too meant a caution? As she kissed Ruth good-by, the four girls of Chautauqua memory having spent a never-to-be-forgotten week together at Ruth Burnham's home, she had said gently:—

"The best place in the world for a boy, dear Ruth, is as close to his mother as he wants to be, just as long as he plans to be there. I have studied boys a good deal, and I think I am sure of so much."

Ruth's face had flushed over this murmured word. She had been half vexed with the others, but it had been given to their little Flossy, as often before, to give her a new thought. She studied over it; she took it to heart and let it color all her movements. More and more after that, although Erskine was still quite young, she kept herself in the background and pushed him forward. On their little trips to the larger city and in any of their outings indeed, she compelled herself to sit quietly in the waiting-room, while Erskine went to buy tickets and check baggage. It is true that every nerve in her body quivered with apprehension until he was safely beside her again, yet she held firmly to her purpose.

Very early in their life alone together she ceased any attempt to drive the ponies that were Erskine's delight, and sat beside him outwardly quiet and inwardly quaking until she had learned her lesson—reminding herself continually that the boy's father had taught him to love and to manage horses when he was too small to touch his feet to the carriage floor.

She gave up early, and with a purpose, the taking Erskine to town with her for a round of shopping or pleasure-seeking, and learned to say meekly and in a natural tone of voice:—

"Can you take me to town on Saturday, dear? I have many errands to do, and I don't like to go alone."

She had lived through all these things, and it was not in any such directions that either she or her friends had fears any more. Erskine was self-reliant enough; in fact he was masterful, though so courteous in his ways that few beside herself suspected it. He had inherited much from his father. Still, the mother knew that there was a strong sense in which she dominated his life. That he went to certain places and refrained from going to certain others simply to please her and not at all as a matter of principle. She was far from being satisfied with this, and was always asking herself: "How long will he do this?" and "Are such concessions worth anything in the way of character?"

She had many questions, this anxious mother of one child; there were days, and this was one, when they pressed her sorely.

The music flowed on; now soft and tender as a caress, now breaking into great waves of sound that meant energy, and possibly conflict.

Suddenly it ceased with a great crash of keys, still in harmony, and the boy wheeled on his stool, looked at his mother, and laughed.

"You woke up the wrong chap that time, didn't you, mother?" he said. "It was as good as a play to hear him go on and to watch your face. I haven't enjoyed anything so much in a long time."

He laughed again over the memory. His mother did not join in the laugh; just then she could not. Those tears that she had managed, not allowing them to fall, had somehow got into her throat. She felt that she should choke if she attempted to speak, and she could not summon at the moment more than the ghost of a smile.

Erskine wheeled back to the piano for a moment, played a few bars of a popular song with one hand, humming it softly; then, in the midst of a line, arose and strolled over to the window where his mother stood.

"Never mind, mommie," he said, bending his tall form low enough to kiss the tip of one ear—a whimsical little caress peculiar to himself. "She mustn't go and look at the clouds and the storm and the dark as though there wasn't any sunshine anywhere. I am not intending to go to the dogs as soon as I go away from home, merely because my mother did her level best all her life to keep me right side up with care; and in my opinion it would be a poor sort of chap who would do any such thing. And I don't feel the need of a social game of cards now and then as a safeguard, either. I don't feel especially 'taut,' mommie, honestly; and I don't care a straw for the Mitchells' card party. Did you really think I cared for it on that account? How absurd! Don't you worry one least little mite, mamma, there is absolutely nothing to be troubled over except that you have a pastor who doesn't know enough to talk a little bit on the side that you want talked, or else keep still. Wasn't it funny?" He laughed once more, then added, a trifle more gravely:—

"When that man is older, he will understand people better, perhaps. Don't you hope so? Shall I read to you, mamma, a little while? I have a delicious book here that I know you will enjoy."

Did he understand, would he ever understand, what a mountain weight he had suddenly lifted from his mother's heart? What a gracious, sweet-spirited, self-sacrificing boy he was! Had there ever been one just like him? She knew he was fond of the Mitchells, and that they were eager to have him with them in their social life; they had brought as much pressure as they could, and he had resisted it for his mother's sake.

It was sweet, but—She could not keep back one little sigh. She was a devoted mother; but she would, oh, so much rather it had been for Christ's sake.

There was an unexpected outcome from that interview with Mr. Conway. In a very short time it became evident that he had lost his hold upon Erskine. Not that the boy turned against him seriously; but he smiled over some of his words and purposely misquoted others in a spirit of mischief. Occasionally there was a curve to the smile that suggested a sneer; and the strongest feeling he evinced for him might be called indifference. In his secret heart Erskine knew that he was being unreasonable, and was really resenting his mother's having been made uncomfortable; but he could not get away from the feeling that Mr. Conway, having been weighed in his mother's balance and found wanting, was not to his mind, however much he himself might differ from her. Of course all this was mere feeling, not principle.

Nevertheless, the clergyman, who prided himself on his influence with young men and who puzzled anxiously over Erskine Burnham's changed attitude which he vaguely felt and could not define, might have been helped if some one had been frank enough to explain the situation. Nobody did. The boy scoffed in secret, assuring himself that a minister who could not be a comfort to a woman and a widow when she tried to lean on him was a "poor sort of chap." As for the mother, she told herself that if she had not been weak and foolish in carrying her anxieties to others, Mr. Conway would not have lost his influence over Erskine; and the minister remained perplexed and anxious; he was sincerely eager to be helpful to young men.

Outwardly they all went on as before. The Mitchells and others of their kind made their card parties and their social dances and their theatre parties and continued to invite eagerly Mrs. Burnham's handsome young son, who cheerfully declined all invitations and stayed with his mother. But he argued no more; in fact he declined to do so, setting the whole matter gayly aside, with a cheerful—

"Don't let us argue about these things any more, mommie. We shouldn't agree, and they are not worth disagreeing over. I don't care a copper for the whole crowd of entertainments that you think of with interrogation points attached, and I don't care two straws about what others think of me in connection with them; so let us taboo the whole subject and enjoy ourselves."

His mother would have liked something very different. She would have been glad if he had given himself to the study of such matters, and settled them from principle. She harassed herself by imagining what an unspeakably happy mother she would be if instead of his gay, kind words he had said:—

"I have been looking into this matter carefully and I understand why you take the position that you do. In fact I do not see how a Christian could do otherwise. I shall take it with you, and you may consider that the question is settled with me for all time."

However, it is something, indeed it is a great deal, for a lone and lonely mother to have a boy go her way, and go smilingly, merely to please her.

CHAPTER III

MAMIE PARKER

On a bright winter day more than a year after Mr. Conway's deliverance with regard to cards, Mrs. Burnham's next very distinct milestone was set up. She was away from the old home and Mr. Conway and all the associations of her past. She was spending her second winter in a lively college town, and Erskine was a sophomore.

The lonely mother of one son had been through much anxiety and perplexity before the plans for this change in their life were fully formed. Erskine's gay rendering of the situation was that not only did every adopted aunt and uncle and grandmother that he had in the world know best how to plan their life for them, but had each a pet college to ride as a hobby. He gave this as a reason why it was just as well to break all their hearts at one fell swoop and choose for himself—which was what in effect he had done; at least he had gone quite contrary to the urgings of his other friends and had compromised with his mother. But he had made quite a compromise. His very first choice had been one of which she entirely disapproved; nor could she be persuaded despite his arguments to change her point of view. In vain he held her quite into the night in a close and eager debate, setting forth his important reasons with skill and eloquence. In vain he assured her that conditions had very much changed since his father had expressed disapproval of this particular centre of learning, and as for his grandfather, why there was nothing left of his times but the name.

His mother urged that her opinion, or her feeling—he might call it feeling if he chose—was not based on his grandfather's or even entirely on his father's views, but was the result of her own reading and inquiry, and was unalterable. If he selected that college, it would be in direct opposition to her strongly expressed wishes. She had been tempted to add that if he did so, his money, left in her charge and subject to her decisions until he was of legal age, would not be forthcoming. She was mercifully preserved from making this mistake. Had she said so, he would probably have gone to the college of his choice even though he had to go penniless. As it was, his eyes flashed a little. But his mother's voice had trembled as she added those last words, "And I suppose I need not try to tell you how such a course would hurt me."

It was that which held the boy. He sprang up suddenly, took two or three hasty turns up and down the room in a manner so like his father's that Ruth could hardly bear it, then his face had cleared.

"You shall not be hurt, mommie," he had said in his usual cheery tone. "You shall never be hurt by me. I want that college more I presume than I could make you understand, and the more I think about it the more I feel that I should like to choose it. But I am not a baby who must have everything he wants; and I do not care enough for anything on earth to get it at the expense of hurting you. You know that, don't you? I'll tell you, mother, we will compromise; this is an age of compromise. I will drop my first choice from this time forth if you will unite heartily with me on the second one and help me stop this clamor of tongues."

It had not been by any means her second choice, but she felt that having been treated so well she must meet him halfway; so the vexed question was settled.

There had been another anxiety. Marion Dennis had written to her not to make the mistake of following her boy to college; and Dr. Dennis had added a few lines to the same effect, saying that in nine cases out of ten he believed such a course to be a mistake, and even in the tenth, separation would probably have been better. Moreover, an only son and an only child needed, as a rule, more than any other to be thrown on his own resources. All the old arguments over again, and numberless plans for the disposal of the mother. She was to come to the Dennis home for a visit of unlimited length; she was to spend the winter with Flossy; she was to go abroad with Grace and her husband. Eurie, the outspoken, wrote:—

"Now, Ruth, don't, I beg of you, tie that dear boy to your apron-string. I am the mother of five, and I know all about how they talk, and how they feel when they don't talk. Besides, I need you this winter as never before; let me tell you something." Then had followed revelations intended to prove that it was Ruth's imperative duty to spend the winter with her old friend.

Mr. Conway added his courteous hint, and suggested plans. Mrs. Conway wondered if Mrs. Burnham would not like to join her sister Helen and their mutual friends, the Hosmers, on an extended Western trip, now that she was to be alone. The winter was an ideal time for such a tour as they had planned; and it would be pleasant for Erskine to think of his mother as travelling with friends instead of being at home alone. Poor Ruth! her heart turned from them all in almost rebellion. If she must be separated from Erskine for the first time in his life, couldn't she be let alone in her own home? To go visiting or sight-seeing without him she felt would be unbearable. She kept most of these anxieties and advices to herself, feeling that she must not cloud Erskine's last days at home with them. Still, she wondered not a little,—and sometimes it hurt her,—that he had not spoken of her plans at all, but seemed to be so absorbed in his own as to have forgotten her. At last, when she felt that some positive decision must be reached, she told him of Mr. Conway's proposition, and showed him Eurie's letter. He glanced it through, smiling serenely:—

"Aunt Eurie is cool, as usual," he remarked. "They can all save their time by planning for somebody else, can't they? Of course I am going to take you with me, mommie. Do they think I would leave you in this big house alone, or let you go travelling without me!"

It was all so easy to arrange after that. It sounded so different from the wording in those letters when Erskine himself replied to them.

"I am very grateful for your thoughtful kindness about my mother, but I am going to take her with me; I had not a thought of doing otherwise. I should not be comfortable to have her away from my care in winter, even though she were with you. I have so long made her first in my thoughts and look upon her so entirely as my father's precious charge to me, that no other plan is to be thought of. I shall find pleasant rooms for her, and I think she will enjoy the change."

Ruth smiled proudly as she made her verbal explanations. "Thank you very much, but Erskine says I am to go with him; he cannot think of trusting me to myself; he has taken care of me for a long time, you know." There was not a thought of sarcasm in this suggestion. She knew that the assumption of authority sat well on her handsome son who could look down on her from his splendid height; it seemed quite in keeping with his appearance and character that he was going to take his mother with him in order to take care of her.

The scheme had worked well. He "took" his mother and took excellent care of her, and incidentally she did much, of course, for his comfort, and they were happy. Early in his college career she had sometimes overheard explanations like this:—

"No, boys, I can't join you to-night. You see, I have my mother with me and I feel bound to give her what time I can spare. It will never do to have her feel lonely and deserted after bringing her away out here among strangers, on purpose to take care of her."

It was all very pleasant. But she had learned something from those letters and that volume of advice. She tried steadily not to dominate her son; indeed, so far as a carefully-watched-over mother could, she effaced herself, or tried to. Erskine had no thought of such a thing, and was openly and serenely happy in his mother's society.

"I pity the other fellows," was a phrase often on his lips. "Most of them live in pokey rooms all by themselves or with only each other; no woman to speak to but a cross-grained hostess, and nothing homelike anywhere; while here it is almost as nice as being at home."

And he would glance complacently around the handsomely furnished suite of rooms that showed everywhere the touch of his mother's hand. But of course there were evenings that were not spent with his mother. It was in connection with one of these that she reached that distinct milestone of which mention has been made. Erskine in explaining about it had shown an unaccountable embarrassment.

"It is just a kind of spread that one of the boys is getting up in honor of his sister; she has come to spend the winter with him. It is rather new business to him and I have promised to help him through, so I must go early and stay late—not very late, though. Parker's landlady will look out for that; she is one of the grim and surly kind. I should have the shivers if I had to get up a spread, with her in charge. Yes, Parker is the curly-headed one that you don't quite fancy. I don't know why, he is a good fellow. Haven't I spoken before of his sister? She has been here for three weeks. Didn't you notice Parker last Wednesday at the concert? He sat just across from us and had her with him. Yes, she is at his boarding-house, and the spread is in his room. He has the downstairs room, mother, in fact it is the back parlor; there is a folding-bed that does duty as a sort of sideboard during the day. It is very nice, really. One wouldn't imagine that there was a bed anywhere around. Parker is one of the fellows who has a good deal of money, I think, but not the culture that generally goes with such a condition. Sometimes I fancy that his father must have made his money lately and suddenly; but, of course, I don't know. Still, everything is very nice and proper about this spread; of course you know that, or I wouldn't be in it. The sister? Oh, yes, she is young—younger than Parker. He is older than most of us, you know. No, there are no women in the house except the landlady and her sister, a maiden lady. That's a pity; it must be rather lonely for Ma—for Miss Parker."

The color flamed in his face and he laughed in an embarrassed way and spoke apologetically:—

"Parker has 'Mamie' so constantly on his tongue that the rest of us are in danger of forgetting. He is very proud of his sister. Why, no, mother, of course he could not very well make any other arrangement; why should he? Of course it is a perfectly proper thing for a young lady to be in her brother's boarding-house. She isn't obliged to have any more to do with the other young men than she chooses. Parker wants her to stay with him all winter. Their father is a mining man, and he and his wife have gone to the mountains somewhere among the mines to look up some more of their money, I suppose."

He spoke almost contemptuously; for some reason the evidence of abundance of money in the Parker family seemed to annoy him. He went on quickly with his labored explanations:—

"Of course it would be pleasanter for M—for his sister if Parker were in a house where there are ladies, but he has been there for several years and has a room that suits him; he doesn't seem to think he can make a change. Oh, yes, there are to be ladies to-night. Some of the other boys have sisters, and cousins, or intimate friends; it is a very informal affair. I fancy that Miss Parker herself is to be hostess. As for a chaperon, I don't think they have thought of her." He laughed in a half-embarrassed way as he said that, and added hastily:—

"It is really just a frolic, mother; they are not formal people at all, under any circumstances, I fancy. Is it possible that that clock is striking seven! I must be off at once; Parker will think I have forgotten my promise to see him through from beginning to end."

What had he said to cause his mother to sit, for an hour after his departure, as still as a stone, her hands clasped over the neglected book in her lap? What was making that strange stricture around her heart as though a cold hand had clutched her and was holding on?

He had kissed her good-by with almost more tenderness than usual, if that were possible. He had called her "mommie," his special pet name for her, and had inquired solicitously as to whether there was any special reason for his getting home early. If there was, why of course—or if for any reason she would rather not be left to-night, he could excuse himself to Parker,—of course he could. All his friends knew well enough that his mother came first.

But how relieved and pleased he had looked when she made haste to assure him that there was not, and that she would be quietly happy with her book all the evening, and there was no need at all for his hastening home. And besides—she paused over that connecting phrase and tried to formulate her fears. How had her son conveyed to her heart the feeling that the time to which it seemed to her she had always looked forward—the time when he would look upon some other woman with eyes that were no longer indifferent, had come?

She could not have put it into words; but though she arose, at last, and put away her book as something that seemed to have failed her, and sat down at her desk to spend an hour with Marian Dennis, and abandoned her, presently, for Flossy Shipley, and gave them both up after the second page, and selected another book with the firm determination to compel herself to read it, the simple truth is that she spent the entire evening, and a large portion of the night as well, with one Mamie Parker.

CHAPTER IV

WOULD SHE "DO"?

The next morning Mrs. Burnham came into her pretty parlor, where a dainty breakfast table was laid for two, prepared to be as wise as a serpent over the new situation. She was genial, sympathetic, and not too penetrative in her questions. Erskine had come home late, much later than he had ever been before; yet apparently his mother had not noticed it.

She did not even ask at what time he had come. In truth she needed no information, but how was Erskine to know that?

Did he have a pleasant evening, and was the occasion all that it should have been? He was not enthusiastic. It was pleasant enough, he said. In some respects very pleasant; only—well, a few of the boys were noisier than was agreeable, and two or three of them did not apparently know how to treat ladies.

"Oh, nothing objectionable, of course," he said quickly, in response to her startled look.

"They are so used to being alone that they grow loud-voiced and careless about the small proprieties, or at least courtesies; I fancy some of their ways must have seemed peculiar to Miss Parker."

"The other girls? Oh, they are used to such things; they were the sisters and cousins of the boys, and the ways of a lot of fellows accustomed chiefly to their own society would not seem so strange to the others; but Miss Parker is—at least I hope, I mean I think she—" He caught himself and left the sentence unfinished save by a half-embarrassed laugh, which changed into a slight frown.

While his mother rang her table bell and gave low-voiced directions to the maid, she pondered. What was it that Erskine hoped? That Miss Parker was by nature more refined than the other ladies? And was the hope well founded? She was slightly acquainted with some of the sisters and cousins who were probably at this gathering. At least she had met them once or twice and had felt no fear as to their influence over Erskine. Was this Mamie Parker different? She felt her face flush a little even over her thoughts. Must she learn to say "Mamie"? One thing was certain: she must make the acquaintance of the girl at once. She ventured a move.

"Is this Mr. Parker so much your friend, Erskine, that he will expect your mother to call on his sister, or is that unnecessary?"

Her heart beat in steady thumps while she waited for his answer. If only he would say in his pleasant, indifferent tone:—

"Oh, it isn't necessary, mother; Parker and I are not especially intimate, and he has no reason to expect such attentions from you." But there was no indifference in the quick response.

"Mommie, you know just what, and how, always, don't you? I was wishing for that very thing and not wanting to trouble you. Parker and I cannot be said to be inseparable; but he is a good fellow, and I think you would like him better on closer acquaintance. His sister is very much alone here; none of those girls who were there last night have homes or mothers; I mean of course that they are away from home; though I must admit that some of them acted last night as though they had no mothers anywhere, worthy of the name. It would mean very much to Miss Parker, mother, if she could know you; and of course Parker would appreciate it more than anything else that could be done for her. You don't know how much the boys admire my mother."

His mother managed to smile cheerfully, and assure him that she would make the proposed call. When he went away to his recitation he kissed her fervently and told her she was the dearest mother in the world; and as she watched him out of sight, she turned from the window and said with a kind of strange gravity:—

"I think it has come: I must pray for grace to do right."

For several days thereafter the hours that Mrs. Burnham spent alone were unusually thoughtful and prayerful. The feeling grew upon her that her son had reached a critical point in his life. It is true he was very young, not yet twenty; but none knew better than she that boys of twenty sometimes glorify and sometimes mar all their future by reason of their interest in one young woman. Also, she knew that a single false step on her part, just now, might spoil all her future with her son and hasten a condition of things that she longed to postpone for him. But she could not plan her way, could not indeed see a single step before her until that first one was taken: she must make that call on Mamie Parker. While she allowed one triviality after another to delay her, the conviction grew upon her that the step was important. Erskine's interest was keen; despite the sympathy there had always been between them he had never before shown such a lively desire to hear about each moment of his mother's time while they were separated. That he chose not to ask in so many words whether or not she had yet made that call but emphasized the situation. When, before, had he hesitated to urge what he desired? Moreover, he was often absent-minded and constrained; seeming to be almost embarrassed over his own thoughts. He could not mention the girl's name without a heightened color, yet he evidently planned ways of introducing it that would sound accidental.

All things considered, Mrs. Burnham, as she dressed carefully for calling, gravely admitted to herself that she was evidently about to meet one who, for good or ill, had taken a strong hold upon her son's life.

As she waited in the large ugly parlor, where the wall-paper was gaudily angry over the colors in the carpet, and where every article of furniture or ornament—of which last there were many—seemed ready to fight with every other one, she wondered what Erskine the fastidious thought of this room. It seemed almost profane to think of meeting one's ideal in such a room. Yet she must be reasonable; of course the girl was not to blame for the taste, or want of taste, displayed in her brother's boarding-house.

She had to wait an unreasonable length of time, and despite her furs she felt the chill of the half-warmed room. There were a few books on the table, but she tried in vain to find one that would hold her thoughts. Perhaps no book could have been expected to do that under the circumstances.

Presently she became aware that some one else had entered an adjoining room where there had been brisk moving about ever since her arrival. With the coming of another, a sharp little voice could be distinctly heard:—

"Oh, say, Lucile, do come here and fasten this waist; I'm scared to pieces and my fingers all feel like thumbs. Don't you think 'Ma' has come to look me over and see if I will do! Oh dear! can't you hook it? It's awful tight, but I've got to be squeezed into it somehow; I'm keeping her waiting an awful while. I had on that fright of a wrapper when she came, and my hair in crimps. I didn't get up to breakfast this morning; we were so horrid late last night, I couldn't."

"'Ma' who?" said another voice. "Not Erskine Burnham's mother? You don't say so! My land! I should think you would be scared. They say she's awful particular who she calls on. You must mind your p's and q's, Mamie, or you'll never see that handsome boy of hers again. They say she keeps him right under her thumb all the time."

Mamie's response was in too low a tone to penetrate into the next room, but it was followed by explosive giggles from both talkers. Meanwhile, the caller's face was glowing, not only with shame for them, but with indignation. What might *not* those coarse girls—she was sure they were both coarse—be saying about her son!

The door opened at last and a mass of fluffy hair entered; behind which peeped a pert little face with pink cheeks and bright, keen eyes.

The girl was dressed in the extreme of the prevailing style,—quite too much dressed for morning, though the material of which her garments were made was flimsy and cheap-looking. Plainly if she had money she had not learned how to spend it to advantage. Still the clothes were worn with an air that hinted at her ability to learn how to play the fine lady if she were given the opportunity.

Her manner to her caller suggested a curious mixture of timidity and bravado. She chattered incessantly and showered slang words and phrases about her freely; yet all the while kept up a nervous little undertone of movement and manner that showed she was not at ease.

"Oh, indeed, she was having an awfully good time. Brother Jim was doing the best he could to give her a lark. She had never been much away from home and they lived in a stupid little village where there was nothing going on. Oh, Jim was an elegant brother; he wanted her to stay all winter and look after his buttons and things."

"I expect you have heard a good deal about Jim, haven't you, from your son? Only he calls him 'Parker' instead of Jim; the boys all do that, you know. It's 'Parker,' and 'Burnham,' and all the rest of them. Ain't it funny, instead of using their first names? I s'pose that's the college of it; but your son has such a pretty name it seems a pity not to use it. Don't you think Erskine is an awful pretty name? I do. It has such an aristocratic sound. Ma says I ought to have been born with a silver spoon in my mouth, I like aristocratic things so well. Not but what we've got money enough;"—this with an airy toss of the frizzed head. Then, in a confidential tone: "But I may as well own to you that it didn't pan out until a little while ago."

Mrs. Burnham, as she took her thoughtful way home, too much exhausted with this effort to think of making another call, studied in vain the problem of her son's enthralment.

The girl was pretty, certainly, with a kind of garish, unfinished beauty, not unlike that of a pert doll; and her chatter, if one could divest one's self of all thought of interest in the chatterer save in the way of a moment's diversion, was rather entertaining than otherwise, when it was not too much mixed with slang; but what Erskine, her cultivated and always fastidious son, could find in the empty little brain to attract him was beyond the mother's comprehension. But he must have been pronounced in his attentions. Had she not been reported as having called to see if the girl would "do"? Ruth's sensitive face flushed over the memory. Should she tell that to Erskine? What should she tell to Erskine? How should the place and the interview and her impressions of the entire scene be described? It required serious thought. The more the mother considered it, the more sure she felt that much of Erskine's future might turn on the way in which she, his mother, conducted herself just now. She puzzled long and reached no clearer conclusion than that until she saw her way clearer she would take no steps at all, and would be entirely noncommittal in her statements. This she found hard; Erskine was curious, more curious than she had ever before known him to be. He cross-questioned her closely as to her call, and was openly regretful, almost annoyed, at her having so little to tell. In the course of the next few days the watching mother, who yet did not wish to appear to watch, knew of at least two social functions that included her son and Miss Parker. One was a sleigh-ride which fell on the evening of the mid-week prayer-meeting in the church they were attending. Erskine had been scrupulous in his attendance on this meeting, declining for it social and business engagements alike, sometimes to his own inconvenience.

"There was no use in compromising about these matters," he said. "Busy people can find something important to detain them every week of their lives if they once admit an exception. The only way is to set one's face like a flint and march ahead."

But he came to her with profuse apologies for this exception; Parker had planned, without knowing anything about the prayer-meeting; he had not been brought up to think of such things, and it was going to embarrass him very much if he declined. He wouldn't have had it happen in this way for a great deal, and he should take care to let Parker know in the future that Thursday evening belonged to his mother and to no one else. He himself arranged for her to have agreeable company to and from the church, and she had grace to be sweet and cheerfully acquiescent in all his plans. Nevertheless she owned, quite to herself, that she felt in a strange, new sense alone. She was more straitened in her praying that evening than she had been for months, almost for years. There was a miserable undertone question hovering about each petition: Could it be possible that she must teach herself to pray for Mamie Parker, not as a passing acquaintance but as one of her very own? and could she learn such a lesson? She had by no means settled it that such a catastrophe must come upon them, but she could not keep down her forebodings.

It was two days afterwards that Mrs. Burnham, having at last reached a decision, made another very careful move. It was discussed over the cosey breakfast which she and Erskine took together in her parlor.

"Would he like to have her ask Mr. Parker and his sister in to dinner on some evening soon? or would that indicate a greater degree of intimacy with the young man than he cared to live up to?"

There was a sudden stricture at her heart over the flash of pleasure on her son's face.

"Mommie, you are a jewel!" this was his first outburst. "Parker would be everlastingly obliged to you for such an attention. You see he knows very few people here of the sort that he would care to have his sister visit. Most of his friends are just college boys away from home, and Parker has ideas about his sister's associates. He is a real good fellow, Mommie; if he had had one-third of my opportunities, he would have made more of them, I believe, than I have."

His mother did not choose to argue that question. She felt a wicked temptation to say that she would be glad if she need never hear his name again; but she restrained herself and asked another question.

CHAPTER V

THE OLD CAT!

"Would he like to have one or two young people asked to meet them? Alice Warder, for instance, and her cousin. How would they do?" Did his face cloud a little?

"I don't know," he said slowly, and his voice suggested a cloud, or at least a diminution of his pleasure.

"Is that necessary, do you think, mother? It is not as though we were at home, of course. Several guests at one time would hardly be expected at a boarding-house."

His mother reminded him of their hostess's cordial offer of a separate table for themselves and three or four guests whenever they cared to give her a half-day's notice; and added that Alice was so used to being called upon to help entertain their guests, that to count her out would seem almost strange to her. Besides, wouldn't this be a convenient time to show her cousin some attention? He was not to be with her long.

Apparently Erskine had no more arguments to offer.

"Oh, very well," he said. Those were matters for her to settle, and it must all be just as she thought, of course. Then he kissed her, lavishly, and went away; but she felt that she had destroyed much of his pleasure in the proposed visit. And he used to be so fond of Alice!

During the next two days she spent much time and thought over her little boarding-house dinner-party. She had adhered to her resolve to include Alice and her cousin among the guests, although she had given herself time to look steadily in the face the reason why she was so insistent about this when Erskine evidently desired it otherwise.

Alice Warder was Flossy Shipley's dear friend, and being introduced by her to the Burnhams was at once established on the footing of an old friend. It had taken but a very short time to learn to love her for herself. Even the careful mother of one son of marriageable age would have found it hard to find flaws in Alice Warder. She was beautiful to look upon, with regular, well-modelled features and a complexion that was faultless. Perhaps her great brown eyes were what a stranger noticed first; they were certainly very expressive. But she was much more than beautiful. There was about her a charm of manner and movement that are difficult to define and impossible to describe, but that made their invariable impression even on those who met her casually. Ruth Burnham, who in her womanhood was, as she had been in her girlhood, fastidious to a fault with regard to young women, had yielded to the subtle charm of this one at their very first meeting; and as the intimacy between them deepened into friendship she had found graces of heart and mind that fully harmonized with the lovely exterior.

The Warders bought a home very near to the Burnham place, and so far as social life was concerned the two families speedily became as one.

Mrs. Burnham, singularly enough, as she reflected afterward, had not once, during the early days of their friendship, coupled the names of Alice and Erskine in her thoughts, congenial as they were. Although they were almost to a day of the same age, Alice, who had been for several years the nominal head of her father's house, appeared much the older, and more like a mature young woman than a girl still in the charge of a governess. It might have been this apparent disparity in their ages that helped Mrs. Burnham to take the girl to her heart and think of her as the daughter she had often wished for; not by any means as Erskine's wife, but as his sister.

Erskine had been from the first of their acquaintance drawn to the young woman in the frank and brotherly way that his mother desired. When the plans for college were matured, one of the loudly spoken regrets on the part of both mother and son was that they must be separated from the Warders.

It came to pass, however, in the course of their second year of absence that Mr. Warder had occasion to make the college town his headquarters for several months; so Alice and her former governess were installed in one of the hotels for the winter, that her father might have as much of her company as possible; and the Burnhams rejoiced greatly thereat.

Yet here was Erskine, barely six weeks afterwards, considering it not necessary to invite Alice to dinner! The poor mother sighed over the perversity and the blindness of young manhood, and knew for the first time that if Erskine had developed the peculiar interest which Miss Parker seemed to have awakened, for Alice Warder, instead, she could have rejoiced with her whole heart.

They came to dinner, Alice and her Boston cousin, a Harvard student of marked ability, and Miss Parker and her brother. And Alice was fully as marked a contrast to the other young woman as Ruth had believed that she would be. First, in the matter of dress. Alice Warder was an artist in dress. She wore at this quiet little dinner party a cloth gown of olive-green, so severely plain in its make-up that its richness of texture and faultless workmanship were apparent. And Miss Parker appeared in an elbow-sleeved white dress badly laundered and profusely trimmed with a quantity of lace that was startling rather than fine. Moreover, she was adorned with a mass of hothouse blooms to which she referred so significantly that the little company were at once made aware that Erskine was the giver.

But the dress was perfection compared with the poor girl's manner. She gayly and unblushingly appropriated Erskine to herself and rallied her brother on the situation.

"Poor Jim! you haven't any girl at all, have you? Since Miss Warder—must I call you 'Miss Warder'? it sounds ever so much more friendly and cosey to say 'Alice.' You must look after your cousin, I suppose. Are you sure he is your cousin? You know that is a dodge girls have when—Oh, well, never mind; I won't bother you. This is good for Jim; he always has half a dozen strings to his bow and can never decide which one of them he wants the most; so this will be excellent discipline for him, leaving him out in the cold. Dear me! What am I talking about? Here is Mrs. Burnham looking young enough this minute to be one of us."

All this, while they were making their way through the boarding-house halls and large dining-room to a cosey little alcove, where a table had been set for the Burnhams and their guests. Erskine's face had flushed deeply during the outburst, and he had darted an annoyed look at his mother to see if she was hearing it. He led the way across the dining-room much to the irrepressible Mamie's disappointment, though she chose to seem to ridicule it.

"Dear me!" she said in a stage whisper to Alice, "do look at that ridiculous boy walking off alone. Where I come from, the fellows take the girls out to supper. Can't I borrow your cousin for this evening, and get even with him?"

Mrs. Burnham felt the color rising in her face, but Alice was gracious and lovely. She laughed pleasantly as though used to such jokes, linked her arm in the girl's, and said merrily:—

"We will give them all the slip, my dear, and go in together."

"We will give them all the slip, my dear."—*Page 61.*

Throughout that embarrassing and long-drawn-out dinner Alice was a help and comfort at least to her hostess, and did steadily and patiently what she could to cover the blunders of the girl beside her. Utterly unaccustomed to even the formalities of a fashionable boarding-house table, Mamie made constant blunders with forks and spoons and other instruments of torture for the uninitiated; but these were trifles compared with the blunders of her tongue. She made evident attempts to cover her ignorance with regard to table formalities by much gay talk. She laughed incessantly, and told many jokes at her brother's expense. She said: "him and me," and "her and I," and "you folks," and a dozen other provincialisms. When they returned to Mrs. Burnham's parlor, it was almost worse—for then Mamie sang; and it was hard for her hostess to determine of which she was most ashamed, the bad taste of the girl's selections or the less than mediocre execution.

Still, the music was by no means the worst feature of that memorable hour. Mamie's next startling venture was a pretence of being offended by what she called Erskine's desertion of her at dinner-time.

"Oh, you needn't come around," she said rudely, as he rose to arrange her music. "I can fix things myself, thank you, and Mr. Colchester will turn the music for me, I know; won't you, Mr. Colchester?" with a jaunty little smile for the stately Boston cousin. "You can't make up for rudeness to me, sir, as easy as you think. I make fellows who want my company mind their p's and q's, don't I, Jim?"

The stalwart brother thus appealed to replied only by a slight embarrassed laugh, and the hostess had time out of her own embarrassment to bestow a swift glance of pity upon him. He had already seen enough of another sort of world to realize that his pretty, pert little sister, the idol of his country home, was not making as good an impression on these new friends of his as he wished she were. If the ladies had but known it, the poor young fellow was at that moment saying to himself:—

"Why can't Mamie act more like that Miss Warder, I wonder? There's an awful difference between them, and she doesn't catch on, somehow."

Throughout the interminable evening, Alice Warder proved not only the excellent foil that Mrs. Burnham had foreseen, but a faithful and efficient coadjutor. Not a lift of her eyebrows or a stray glance of any kind betrayed a second's surprise at the character of the guests invited to meet her dignified cousin and herself. She was gracious and friendly to such an extent that before the evening was over, Mamie, who was frankness itself, said admiringly:—

"How long you going to stay in this place? Dear me! I wish you was going to be here all winter; I can see that you and me would be real cronies."

In the privacy of Mrs. Burnham's bedroom, whither Alice was taken to put on her wraps, the girl bestowed her closing touch of sweetness and balm upon her hostess.

"I had quite a little visit with Mr. Parker while you were entertaining the others with those pictures; I was much interested in him; he is a young man of good principle, isn't he? One on whom education will tell. It is lovely in you and Erskine to open your home to him in this way; it will be sure to mean much to him; and it ought to help the little sister, too. It is pleasant to see how fond he is of her."

"You helped," said Mrs. Burnham, significantly. "I am more grateful for your help to-night than the mere words will express."

She kissed her as she spoke, and felt in her heart that she was willing that Erskine should marry this girl to-morrow, if he would.

"I was glad of the opportunity," the girl said simply. "And so, I am sure, was Ranford. He is very much interested in young men of this type."

21

For a full half hour after "Jim" had carried off his pouting sister,—whose parting shot had been that she considered it "awfully pokey" for a girl to go home from a dinner-party with "nothing but her brother"—spoken in a pretended confidence to him, but loud enough for all to hear,—silence reigned in the Burnham parlor.

Erskine had a desk in one of its corners, where he kept certain of his books, and studied, whenever he chose to remain with his mother. He flung himself down before it the moment the door closed after their guests, as though work pressed hard.

His mother took a book and sat silent and apparently absorbed, although as a matter of fact, instead of reading, she was studying the half-averted face that was drawn in almost stern lines, and the eyes that stared at the open page as though they did not see its words. She did not believe that Erskine was studying Latin.

What had this terrible evening done for him, and for her? Had that pretty-faced, ill-dressed, ill-bred girl secured in some unaccountable way a permanent hold on her son's heart? Might it not be possible that in giving him this awful view of her in sharp contrast with Alice Warder she had but alienated him from herself? Perhaps she had blundered, and perhaps the consequences of her blunder would be fatal to them both. Why had she done it? Why had she not waited, and watched, and understood better before she attempted anything? What should she do now? How was she to bear this silence? And yet, what might not Erskine say when at last he broke it?

A half-hour passed and neither mother nor son had turned a page. Suddenly he wheeled his chair around so that she could get a full view of his face, and smiled a half-sad, half-whimsical smile, and spoke his word:—

"I don't believe we can do it, Mommie. It was good in you to try, and you did it royally, as you do things, but—she can't be assimilated. She doesn't belong. We shall have to wait until she goes home before we can do much for Parker. All the same, mother, you understand that I thank you for the effort. Alice was superb to-night, wasn't she?"

Then Ruth Burnham understood that it was her business to understand that her son's interest lay solely in the young man Parker, and that in the desire to help the brother the sister must be thought of as simply tolerated. Already Erskine had put away his first illusion so utterly that he did not propose to own it to himself, much less to his mother.

Poor Mamie Parker spent her fruitless winter in the college town, and tried by many innocent and a few questionable ways to win back to interest and special attention her brother's handsome friend, whose sudden defection she could not understand. She tortured herself in a vain effort to discover what could have happened on that evening which she had expected to be memorable to her for other reasons than now appeared. Why had it so utterly changed the attitude toward her of the young man who, she had confidently assured Jim, was "caught, all right," she "knew the signs"?

By degrees, without any clearly defined reason for doing so, she came to associate the defection with the young man's mother, and called her "that old cat!" with a bitterness that had more than mere anger behind it; there was a lump in her throat and a curious stricture about the little organ that she called her heart, which was new to the frivolous girl.

Jim's handsome college friend had afforded his sister Mamie a glimpse into a new, strange world, one that she felt she could have loved, and in which she believed that she could have shone; and in some way, she did not understand how, his mother had closed the door.

"The old cat!" she said. "I should like to get even with her!" And then she cried.

CHAPTER VI

IDEAL CONDITIONS

Erskine Burnham's lesson was short, but sharp, and he seemed to have learned it thoroughly. He gave himself more persistently to study than before, and was even more devoted to his mother than ever, if that were possible. He let the visiting sisters of freshmen and sophomores dignifiedly alone, and resisted without a sigh numerous attempts to draw him into local society circles.

"Haven't time for society just now," was his invariable excuse. "Nor inclination," he would add privately for his mother's benefit.

Occasionally the mother urged the acceptance of an invitation and begged him not to make a recluse of himself for her sake; but he met her suggestions with his whimsical smile and the gay retort that a society composed of two entirely congenial people met all his present requirements. She was not insistent. Why should she be, when Erskine was undeniably happy in the life he had planned?

Certainly it was an ideal life for the fond mother; for both of them, perhaps. It had been unique from the first of Erskine's college course. They had been settled but a few weeks in their new home when Mrs. Burnham, finding much time at her disposal, proposed to Erskine that she take up some of her long-ago-dropped studies and let him introduce her to modern college ways. The young man laughed as he gave her an admiring glance and assured her that she knew more than other women, already. Nevertheless it pleased him to go into careful detail about his work, and on the following day it surprised as well as pleased him to find that his mother was quite as well prepared with some of his studies as he was himself. From that evening a new order of things was established; Mrs. Burnham, without matriculating as a college student, and without letting it be known, save to the choice few who were their very intimate friends, became nevertheless a student. How much of Erskine Burnham's acknowledged success in college was due to the fact that his mother studied with him throughout the entire course is something that will never be known; but her son gave her full credit for the help that she was to him. From the first he recognized her as a stimulant; he discovered that he must have his points very fully in his grasp in order to explain them satisfactorily to his pupil. She always insisted on being his pupil and kept carefully the subordinate place, although her keen questionings more than once led him to change his view of a subject under discussion.

Altogether, it was a life replete with satisfaction to both mother and son. Not that they shut themselves away from society. Such of his friends as Erskine thought his mother would enjoy or could help he brought freely to their rooms, and between several of the students and herself there was built up by degrees that kind of friendship which one occasionally sees between self-respecting young men and certain middle-aged women. It was a very pleasant experience, and it made Ruth feel, as she expressed it to Erskine, that she had several sons always ready to serve her.

Neither did they wholly neglect the outside world. Both mother and son held carefully to their resolve not to let college or any other functions interfere with their Sunday and mid-week engagements in the church of their choice, and through this channel they made certain acquaintances that ripened into friendship. But there came a time in the mother's life when she wished, not that she had enjoyed her studies with Erskine less, but that both of them had given more time and thought and enjoyment to distinctively religious themes and duties.

Meantime their friendship for Alice Warder ripened and deepened, although there had been an interim during which its very life had seemed to be threatened. Following that painful episode with Mamie Parker, Erskine had seemed to shun even Alice Warder. He had not from the first been entirely sure that he cared to see much of her Boston cousin, and presently made him an excuse for seeing little of Alice, for the cousin seemed to be staying indefinitely. This state of things lasted until the college year closed and they went home, and became again next-door neighbors to the Warders. At first, it seemed to Mrs. Burnham that the old friendship was lost. Something very vague and intangible, but distinctly felt, seemed to have come between them. Then, suddenly, whatever it was, it passed. On a certain evening that stood out plainly afterward in the mother's memory Alice had appeared at her window with an air of decision, and a question.

"Has Erskine come in yet, Mrs. Burnham? When he comes, will you ask him if he can give me an uninterrupted half-hour this evening for something special?"

Later, the mother wondered, and often wondered what that something special was, but she had not been told. It was something that made a marked difference in Erskine's manner. From apparently avoiding Alice Warder's society as much as possible, he frankly sought it; proposing her as a third on occasions when his mother would have hesitated, and in every possible way proclaiming that the old cordial relations were reestablished. From that time on, the young woman next door became so entirely identified with the daily life of the Burnhams that the intimate friends of the family said "Alice and Erskine," quite as a matter of course.

In the fall they went back to college, mother and son. At least that was Erskine's way of putting it.

"Why not?" he said, laughing at his mother's protest. "You are as much in college as I am. They ought to give you a diploma. I believe I'll divide mine; have the sheepskin cut exactly in two, and your name inserted. Half of my honors belong to you, anyhow."

During his senior year Erskine and Alice Warder were more inseparable than ever. Mr. Warder went abroad on an extended business trip, which was so entirely business that he would have little or no time for Alice, and she chose to be left behind. But her friend who had lived with her as a companion, since she had ceased to be a governess, wanted the winter for her personal friends, so it was decided that Alice should secure rooms at the same house where the Burnhams boarded and be chaperoned by Mrs. Burnham. This made them practically one family, though each adhered to his own programme. Alice gave much time to correspondence, and interested herself at once in special church work; while Mrs. Burnham continued to study with her son. But in all social functions, and indeed, in all their leisure time, they were together quite as a family.

It was during this winter that Mrs. Burnham took up a study quite by herself and made diligent effort in it. This was the study of adjusting herself to new relations. She was getting acquainted with and growing used to her daughter, she told herself hopefully; for by this time she had fully decided that Alice Warder was the one who was to share through all their future Erskine's love and care. She grew more than reconciled; she told herself that she was perfectly happy in Erskine's choice; that of course she wanted him to marry, she had always wanted it; and where in all the earth could he have found a more lovely character or a more entirely acceptable person in every way than Alice Warder? It really seemed as though a special Providence had planned and created them each for the other.

As the intimacy deepened, so that the three seemed to think in unison, the mother told herself cheerfully that it was almost as though the two were married already; there would be no strange chasm to bridge over when that time came; nor would they have to readjust themselves in any way. Alice had not known a mother's love and care since childhood, and she turned as naturally to Mrs. Burnham for mothering as though they were really mother and daughter. It was all ideal.

There were times, of course, when Mrs. Burnham could not help sitting in secret judgment on certain ways and words of this daughter of hers. She would allow herself to wish that this or that had been different, and then would bring herself to order with severity, assuring herself that she had no right to expect perfection, and where, on this earth, could there be found another girl so near it as Alice?

Over one phase of the girl's life this mother in all sincerity rejoiced. Alice was unquestionably and deeply religious. Her Christian life was deep-rooted and pervasive, and the perfume of its flowering filled her days. To come in contact with her for even a short interview was to discover that religion with her was not merely a duty, but a joy.

"Alice is very unusual in this respect," Ruth said to Erskine. "It isn't simply that she is regular and methodical in her Christianity as in everything else. I have seen girls before who went to prayer-meeting, for instance, regularly, from a sense of duty; but with Alice it is this, and something more. She looks forward to it as a pleasure; and she comes from it uplifted and advanced in her Christian experience."

Erskine was hearty in his response.

"Yes, Alice takes hold of life generally with a kind of joyful enthusiasm that is delicious. And there is contagion in it; I enjoy the mid-week meetings better myself, since I have learned to plan for them as she does."

Everything considered, that last year of college life passed all too quickly, at least for Mrs. Burnham. There were times when she realized that the peculiarly close relations which she and her son had sustained for four beautiful winters could not, in reason, continue, and she shrank from any change. Yet for the most part she was strong in her gratitude that her son's college life had been what it had been, and that the most censorious could not discover any evil results from this long, close fellowship with his mother. There were still years of study for him. It had been decided that he would study law in the city where his father had practised it, and live at the old homestead, making daily trips to and from the larger city. In due course of time, therefore, they were once more settled at home for an indefinite period. Alice Warder had gone to the coast of Maine for a long-promised visit among her mother's relatives, but on her return, the Warders were again to become next-door neighbors.

Already in her letters to Mrs. Burnham, which were quite as frequent as those to Erskine, Alice Warder was planning certain functions in which "You and father, and Erskine and I" were in evidence.

There was one feature of the situation that troubled the mother. As the days passed the question which it involved grew more and more insistent. Why did not Erskine, at least, confide in her? Had he not from his very babyhood been in the habit of bringing to her not only every joy and sorrow, but every passing emotion or fancy, however trivial, until she had believed them as nearly one as it was possible for two people to become? Why then, in this supreme decision of his life, had she in a sense been counted out? No hint as to his new hopes and plans had been put into words for her; she had simply been left like the rest of the world to take things for granted.

There were times when this question probed her keenly. She struggled to discover whether she had been in fault. Despite her earnest efforts to hold herself well in check and give no sign of certain emotions which every true mother must feel at such an hour, had she failed? Had she appeared cold, or indifferent, or, worse than either, jealous? Despite her careful cross-examination of herself she could not lay her finger upon any word or act that she could make different; and she was obliged to content herself with redoubling her efforts to show her entire acceptance of Alice as one of them; but so far as any special confidences were concerned she did it in vain. Both Erskine and Alice were entirely frank in their manifest interest in each other, acting at all times as though they had nothing to conceal. They had even reached the stage when they claimed each other's time and attention as a matter of course, and so expressed themselves.

Erskine, for instance, would glance at a note that had been laid on his desk a short time before, and explain to his mother:—

"I shall have to defer my call on Dr. West, mother, until some other evening. Alice has to meet her committee at the hall, and wants me to take her over."

Could anything, argued the mother, indicate more surely that they two had already passed the early stages of sentiment, and begun to realize that they belonged to each other for convenience as well as for love? Then why did they not confide in his mother, *their* mother?

No comparatively small matter had ever troubled Ruth Burnham more than did this one. There were times when she felt almost indignant, and was on the verge of saying to them both that she did not think she deserved such careless treatment at their hands. Why, her very intimate friends were almost asking when the wedding was to be! There were other times when she told herself that she would not be the first to speak, even though they kept silence until the wedding day was come.

Matters were in this state when she reached another distinct milestone in the singularly marked journey of her life.

CHAPTER VII

"MOTHERS ARE QUEER!"

It was but the week before Alice's expected return, and Mrs. Burnham was out paying afternoon visits. She had confessed to Erskine that she wanted to get them off of her mind before Alice came, and be able to give undivided attention to her for a while.

"I don't suppose you can imagine how I have missed her," she added in a voice that she intended to express archness, but which was almost wistful. He felt the wistfulness and mistook its cause, and said tenderly:—

"Poor little mother! you need a daughter, don't you?"

She had turned from him abruptly to hide the glimmer of tears; and she had told herself almost angrily afterward that it was time she had learned self-control.

At the home of one of her friends she met a Mrs. Carson, with whom she had also a calling acquaintance. Mrs. Carson had been spending some weeks in Boston, and had no sooner exchanged greetings with Mrs. Burnham than she brought out with eager hand from her news budget a choice morsel.

"And what do you both think I heard just before I left the city? At first I could scarcely believe my ears; in fact, I did not credit the news at all; I said it could not be so; I am sure, dear Mrs. Burnham, you will understand why. But afterward it was so signally confirmed that I was obliged to accept it."

"Dear me!" said the hostess, "this is quite exciting. Do enlighten us, Mrs. Carson. We have been so humdrum here this fall that news is thrice welcome."

"You would never guess my news, I am sure, that is, you would not, Mrs. Webster; but there sits our dear Mrs. Burnham, looking as calm and unconcerned as usual, though I presume she has known all about it this long time."

"Now you arouse my curiosity, certainly," that lady said with a quiet smile. "I don't recall any special news from Boston, of late."

"Oh, well, I don't suppose it is late news to you, but it certainly was to me. Why, Mrs. Webster, I have it on excellent authority that our friend Alice Warder is engaged to her cousin, Ranford Colchester, and the marriage is to take place very soon. Now do you wonder that I was simply amazed over such an announcement?"

Mrs. Burnham took her startled nerves into instant and stern check, and was entirely silent while Mrs. Webster exclaimed and expostulated.

"I told you you wouldn't be able to believe it," said the gratified news-dealer. "Such a surprise to us all! and yet you see this naughty woman doesn't express any, and hasn't a word to say for herself! Dear Mrs. Burnham, it isn't necessary I suppose for us to confess that we have been waiting these many weeks for the formal announcement of her engagement to an entirely different person? Her cousin, indeed! why I thought they were the same as brother and sister. I was never more surprised in my life. At first I simply disputed it and assured my friends that Alice Warder was as good as married, already. But it came to me too straight to be disputed. It's this way. My aunt has a young niece living with her this year who is a very intimate friend of Miriam Stevens, and she, you know, is Mr. Colchester's stepdaughter; and she told her all about it. It seems, although they have been engaged for a very long time, years and years, Miriam said, the engagement has just been announced. Mr. Colchester, the father, of course, has opposed the match, because it interfered with some of his pet plans. There was an old love story connected with it, don't you know, and a good deal of sentiment and obstinacy on the part of the old gentleman, who has always thought that the world was made for his convenience. But he found that his son could be obstinate too; he was willing to marry Alice Warder, and he would never, no never, marry anybody else. Then Alice decided that she would show a little spirit, and she refused to come into the family so long as there was a breath of opposition. Nobody knows just what has happened, at least Miriam doesn't; but she says that her stepfather has not only withdrawn his opposition, but seems quite as eager as his son to have the marriage take place. Miriam did not think that the day had been fixed yet, but she felt sure it would be not later than Christmas. Now, isn't that a romantic story, and a startling one? Just think how that girl has stolen a march on us when we thought we understood all about her future, and were breathlessly awaiting our invitations to the wedding! And here sits our dear Mrs. Burnham, looking as unconcerned as possible; though all this while she has been helping deceive us into the belief that Alice Warder was almost her daughter!"

How Ruth Burnham got away from their volubility and their playful accusations and their congratulations she was never afterward able to clearly explain, even to herself. She knew that her brain felt on fire, and every nerve in her body seemed to be quivering, but she also knew that she had one supreme determination, not by word or glance to betray consternation or surprise or indeed feeling of any sort. Since these women believed that she had deceived them, let them by all means continue to do so, at least until she could determine what she thought, or what she was to say.

She knew that she preserved her outward calm, and made some commonplace reply to the eager questioning exclamations showered upon her. She remembered murmuring something about young people's secrets being sacred to themselves, and then she got herself away and walked the seven squares between her and her home, and wished that there were more of them, that she might have time to steady herself and plan what step to take next. How, for instance, was she to break this terrible piece of news to Erskine?

To her astonishment she found that she was giving full credit to the story. Although the details had been too minute and the source of information too terribly reliable to admit of reasonable doubt, yet her reason told her that she ought to be able to turn in contempt from such a story. How was it possible for Alice Warder to be guilty of such long-drawn-out unpardonable hypocrisy as this? Alice Warder of all women in the world! How had it

27

been possible for her to deceive Erskine in this way? Why had she done it? What could have been her motive? Had she simply and deliberately flirted with him, to show that insufferable old man that there were others besides his son who wanted her? Poor Erskine! poor trusting, deceived heart! What could his mother do or say to soften such a revelation as this! Finally she walked quite past her own door, adding several more blocks to the already long distance, before she had herself under sufficient control to meet her son. For the first time in her life she was glad that he was not in when she reached home; and glad again that when he came a friend was with him, who remained to dinner. This enabled her to watch Erskine closely, without his observing it, and to determine whether he might have heard from some other source the strange news.

She decided that he had not; he was even more full of good cheer than usual, and referred several times to Alice, as his guest was also her friend.

Mrs. Burnham's unusual quiet finally called forth solicitous inquiries from her son. Had she overwearied herself that afternoon? Had there been any accident or detention that had worn upon her? She made haste to reassure him, and struggled to appear at ease; while all the time her mind was busy with the problem of how to break her news to Erskine. The more she thought about it, the more strangely improbable it seemed. Alice Warder engaged to be married to any one but Erskine! As for the cruel wickedness of the girl whom she had loved and trusted as a daughter, the woman who felt herself betrayed could not trust her thoughts just yet in that direction. She must give all there was of her to Erskine.

When their visitor had gone, Erskine gave himself in earnest to anxiety about his mother.

"I cannot remember ever to have seen you look so wan and worn. Is it simply the making calls that has exhausted you? I remember I used to notice that that was an exhausting function for you. I wouldn't do it any more, Mommie; let people come to you. Where did you go? and what was said to tire you so? or was it what they didn't say? I have noticed that ladies when making calls never seem to really say anything. They talk a good deal, but then!—"

If he only knew what they had said that day! How should she tell him?

They went to the library; Erskine bemoaning the fact that he had some work which must be done, and could not read to her. But he would establish her among the cushions where she could rest, and he could look at her occasionally. So she lay there, outwardly quiet, looking steadily at him as though she must see his very soul, and going on with her problem. Was she being cruel, too, lying quietly there concealing a weapon with which she was presently to stab him? If she could only decide upon the least terrible way of telling him what she had heard! She planned and discarded a dozen forms of speech, and finally plunged headlong into the baldest and most commonplace of them.

Erskine had risen to close a door, and then had come to adjust her cushions and ask if she were comfortable. And then—should she like him by and by, when he had run over two or three more pages, to read to her? There was a magazine article he had been saving up to enjoy with her. Or was she too tired to-night for reading?

And she had caught his hand and held it in a nervous grip while she exploded her news.

"I heard something very strange this afternoon, Erskine; something that I do not in the least understand. I don't know how to credit it, yet it came to me very straight. Mrs. Carson has just returned from Boston, and has it, she says, from one of the family that Alice Warder is soon to be married to her cousin."

She felt breathless. She did not know whether to look at her victim or to look mercifully away from him. He was leaning forward in the act of tucking a refractory cushion into place, and he persisted in conquering the cushion before he spoke. Then he said cheerfully:

"That is out at last, is it? Alice must feel relieved."

His mother pushed all the cushions recklessly and sat upright.

"Erskine," she said eagerly, "what do you mean? You don't mean, you *can't* mean that you knew it all the while!"

"Why not, mother? have known it for months, might say years. It had to be a profound secret, though, on account of old Mr. Colchester's state of mind; he had other plans, you see, and at first he utterly refused to side with the young people; then Alice refused to enter the family so long as there was any objection to her, and also refused to have her engagement made public; it has been a long, wearisome time; I am glad for both of them that the struggle is over. I have served them to the best of my abilities, but I can see that the new order of things will be a comfort to both; to all three of us indeed."

He laughed a little over that last admission, but his mother had not yet recovered from her first amazement.

"Erskine, why didn't you tell me?"

He laughed again and bent over to kiss her.

"Mommie, you speak as though at the least I had committed forgery. How could I tell you, dearest? It was another's secret. Alice was absurdly sensitive, it is true, but of course I had to respect her wishes. She is not accustomed to being objected to, you know. There was a sense in which I came upon their secret at first, by accident, which served to make me doubly careful; I did not feel that I could speak of it even to you; though I will own that I thought it extremely foolish in Alice not to do so.

"Do you feel like being read to, mamma, or would you rather be entirely quiet to-night? Do you feel a little bit rested?"

"Yes, indeed," she told him eagerly. She was very much rested; in fact she did not feel tired at all; she would like exceedingly to be read to; or she was ready to do anything that he wished.

He looked at her curiously, and a trifle anxiously. There was something about his mother this evening that he did not understand. A few minutes ago she had looked pale and worn to a degree that was unusual; now her cheeks were flushed and her eyes were very bright. Could she be feverish? he wondered. And he mentally vowed vengeance on all formal calls.

It was nearly a week afterward that Erskine and Alice, walking home together from some society function, lapsed into confidential talk.

"How did you find my mother?" Erskine asked. "Was she able to be as glad over it all as you could wish?"

"She was lovely," said Alice, enthusiastically. "An own mother could not have shown more tenderness and lovingness. I have missed my mother all my life, Erskine, but I shall miss her less, even during this time when a girl needs her mother most, because you are so kind in lending me yours."

"And yet, do you know, I think she has lately suffered a shock and a disappointment? I am nearly certain that she had cherished hopes which included us both. I did not realize until very lately indeed that she too was being deceived; else I must have insisted on her being taken into confidence."

Alice's merry laugh astonished and almost vexed him, her first words were more surprising still.

"So you thought she was disappointed? What bats men are, to be sure!"

"What do you mean? Do you not know that to my mother you are the one young woman?"

"Oh, indeed I do, and rejoice in it. But I know also, my dear simpleton, that she is almost deliriously happy at this moment over her late discovery. I know she loves me almost as she could a daughter, and I also know that she loves me more, oh, far more, because her son Erskine is a brother to me instead of—something else."

His puzzled look made her laugh again.

But after that he studied his mother from a new standpoint. Certainly she was very fond of Alice and was about to lose her; yet certainly she was happy—happier than he had ever known her to be.

"Mothers are queer!" was his grave conclusion.

CHAPTER VIII

A SPOILED MOTHER

It had been an ideal October day: one of those ravishing days that come sometimes in late autumn when, though the air is crisp with the hint of a coming winter, it is at the same time balmy with the memory of the departed summer. The hills in the near distance had put on their glorified autumn dress, and the flowers in the gardens were all of the gorgeous or deep-toned colorings that tell of summer suns and autumn crispness. It was, in short, one of those days when it is, or should be, a delight simply to live.

The Burnham place had never looked more lovely than it did that afternoon, bathed in the soft glory of an unusually brilliant sun-setting. It was customary to speak of this as the old Burnham place; yet nothing in Ruth Erskine Burnham's changeful life showed more markedly the effect of change than did this.

The long, low, rambling, old-fashioned house, much in need of paint, that Ruth had come to as a bride, was there still, but so altered that even she had all but forgotten the original. The house and the grounds had been, like many other things and persons, transformed. No spot anywhere, for miles around, was such a source of pride and pleasure to the old friends of that region as the Burnham place. There were those still living who could tell in minutest detail the story of its transformation, when the Judge's new wife came out there to live, and astonished the country by her doings. Some of them had been more than half afraid of Ruth in those early days; they all believed in her now.

She had come out to the upper porch for a moment, not so much to get a view of the wonderful sunset as to get her breath. The house was full of flowers, and they had seemed to stifle her.

A handsome woman still was Mrs. Burnham. Stately was one of the words that people had been wont to use in describing her; she was stately yet, though her son Erskine would soon celebrate his thirtieth birthday.

These later years had touched her lightly. They had been spent, for the most part, in the cheerful quiet of their old home, which, although the city had grown out to it, had yet not absorbed it, but allowed its favored residents to have much of the pleasures of country life, with a rapid transit into the heart of the great city as often as life of that kind was desired.

Erskine had for several years been admitted to the bar, and the old firm name that had meant so much in legal circles had once more the strong name of Burnham associated with it. That her son was a legal success was not a surprise to his mother. With such antecedents as his how could it have been otherwise? She had not kept up with his legal studies as she had almost done through his college course, but she had kept in touch with them, and could copy his notes for him, giving him just the points he needed—better, he told her, than he could do it himself.

"We will take you into the firm if you say so, dearest," he said gayly one evening, after a spirited argument between them with regard to a point of law in which Mrs. Burnham had vindicated her side by an appeal to an undoubted authority. "I told Judge Hallowell, yesterday, that it was easier to consult you than to look up a point, and did just as well. He would agree to the partnership, mother, without hesitation; he considers you a wonderful woman."

At which the happy mother laughed, and told him he was a wonderful flatterer; and then—Did he want her to look up the evidence in that Brainard case for him? She could do it as well as not. She had been reading up about it that morning.

An ideal life they had lived together all these years, this mother and son. More than once in the years gone by Mrs. Burnham had overheard some such remark as: "It will be hard on that mother when Erskine marries, will it not?" It used to annoy her a little. She was conscious of a feeling very like resentment that people should consider it necessary to discuss their affairs at all; especially to intimate that there would ever be anything "hard" between them.

There had been other talk, too, that she had resented. It had been noticed that Judge Hallowell, Judge Burnham's lifelong friend, came often to the old Burnham place, and somebody got up a very sentimental reason for his never having married; and somebody else objected that Mrs. Burnham did not believe in second marriages; she had been heard to go so far as to say she thought they were actually wrong. Then somebody else looked wise and smiled, and said she had heard of people, before this, who changed their opinions about such things, on occasion. And— How would such a masterful young man as Erskine get on with a stepfather? This bit of gossip had floated about the Burnhams for a year or more, while Erskine was studying law, without their having been the wiser for it. The day for the wedding had almost been set, still without reference to them, when Judge Hallowell, sixty years old though he was, suddenly brought home a wife; and that, without an hour's break in the friendship between himself and the Burnhams.

By degrees, the form of the question which the talkers asked each other slightly changed, and they said they were afraid it would be hard on Mrs. Burnham if Erskine should ever marry, and they added that it wasn't probable that he ever would. They even ventured, one or two of the more intimate, or the more rude, to express some such thought to the mother herself. When they did, she laughed lightly and bade them not be sure of anything. Her son might astonish them all, yet. She was sure she hoped so. She was sincere in this. As each year passed she told herself more and more firmly that of course she wanted him to marry. Why shouldn't she want him to find that lovely being who must have been foreordained for him? She was sure now, after all her long years of experience with him, that she should know the very first moment when he discovered her. Of course she had not been through the years since Alice Warder was married without more than once imagining that she had been discovered. They had numbered some very lovely young women among their friends. There had been a certain Miriam whom she had admired and liked and almost loved, and had meant to love in earnest if Erskine really wished it. And she had gone about the finding out very cautiously. Didn't he think Miriam was pretty?

"Very pretty indeed," he had answered promptly.

And she was so sweet and winsome, so thoughtful of her elders, so gracious to everybody; quite unlike many others in that respect.

He was quick to agree with this, also.

Didn't he think her delightful in conversation? She seemed able to converse sensibly on any subject that was under discussion, as well as to talk the most delicious nonsense, on occasion.

"Well," he said cheerfully. In that respect he must differ from her. He could not say he thought the young woman especially gifted in conversation; it seemed to him to be her weak point. If she could talk as well as her grandmother, she would be charming.

Mrs. Burnham had argued loyally for her favorite; had assured her son that Miriam was a charming talker when she chose, and that it was ridiculous to think of comparing her with her grandmother! But she had laughed light-heartedly at his folly, and had confessed to her secret self that she was glad he liked the grandmother better.

There were several other temporary interests, and then the mother settled down to restfulness. Erskine was a boy no longer, but a full-grown man, doing a man's work in the world; she could trust him. He had always confided in her and of course he would not fail to do so when this supreme hour of his life came to him. She still wanted him to marry; she believed that he would, some day. She promised herself that she would be, when the time came, a perfect mother. She would love the chosen one with all her heart; she should be second only to Erskine himself. And she would give herself to helping them both to be so happy, anticipating their wishes and aiding and abetting all their plans, that they would be glad to have her with them always. And always she closed these hours of planning with a long-drawn sigh of satisfaction that they were all in the dim future.

Erskine Burnham had passed his thirtieth birthday before he had been separated from his mother for more than a few days at a time. It was early in the May following the thirtieth anniversary when the break came. He went abroad then, on legal business of importance.

"Shall you take your mother over with you?" Judge Hallowell had asked, but a short time before he started; and he had answered quickly: "Oh, yes, indeed; I couldn't think of leaving mother alone, with the ocean between us; she is too much accustomed to my daily care for that. Moreover, I think a sea voyage will be good for her."

But his mother met him at the door, that afternoon, open letter in hand, and the grave announcement that she had bad news for him.

"What is it, dearest?" he had asked composedly, as he bent to kiss her. It occurred to him then there could be no very bad news for either of them so long as they stood there together, safe and well.

"It is Alice; she is ill, very ill they are afraid, and her husband writes that she wants me immediately. They think, Erskine, that there will have to be an operation, and she feels that she cannot go through it without me. I fill the place of mother to her, you know, dear."

Erskine did not take his disappointment easily. He was used to having his own way, and he had planned a delightful outing for his mother. He argued the question strenuously, and was loath to admit that his mother's duty lay elsewhere, and that he must go abroad without her.

"It is hard on my mother," he said discontentedly to Judge Hallowell. But he admitted to himself that it was quite as hard for him; he hated travelling alone.

For Mrs. Burnham the summer had dragged. For thirty years she had lived for her son. Why should life without him be called living? It was harder for her because her sacrifice proved to be unnecessary. The surgical operation was, after all, postponed; there was some hope that it would not have to be at all; and Alice herself had gone abroad with her husband: not by Erskine's route, but on a sailing vessel, making the ocean trip as long as possible.

Mrs. Burnham had stayed to do the thousand and one little things for the invalid that a mother would naturally do, and to see her fairly started on her journey, and then had come back to her lonely home: what might-have-been crowding itself discontentedly among her thoughts. She had lost her summer with Erskine for nothing, she told herself. Still, the summer was going; it would not be long now.

Erskine had written to her daily, mailing his letters as opportunity offered. At first the letters were long, very long and full; it was almost like seeing the old world with him. Then, as business matters pressed him, and social functions growing out of business relations consumed more and more of his time, they shortened, often to a few hurried lines.

Sometimes there was only the date at a late hour, and "Good night, mother dear. This has been my 'busy day.' Interesting things have happened. Heaps to tell you when I get home, which I hope now will be soon. Perhaps in my very next I can set the date."

She had lived on his letters, watching for each as eagerly as a maiden might watch for word from her lover. Was he not her lover? All she had in all the world, she told herself proudly, and was satisfied, and smiled over that word, "Dearest," that fell as naturally from his pen as from his lips.

That next letter in which perhaps he would set the date of his return was waited for in almost feverish impatience. There was so much she wanted to do just before he came. She had planned to set the house and grounds in festive array as for the coming of a conqueror. Actually his first home-coming of any note in which she was there to greet him! Always before they had come together.

The watched-for letter was delayed. There occurred a longer interval by several days than there had been before, between letters. Mrs. Burnham allowed herself to grow almost nervous over this, and watched the newspapers hourly, glancing over foreign items in feverish haste. She talked about the strangeness of this delay with her friends, until the most sympathetic among them laughed a little and told each other that that spoiled mother was really absurd! And at last it came.

She remembered—she will always remember that October evening when, the shades being drawn close and a brisk fire burning in the grate, she had seated herself near it in a luxurious reading chair and, merely for company, had pushed Erskine's favorite easy-chair just opposite and laughed a little at her folly, and tried to assure herself that young Ben had returned long ago with the evening mail, which had to be sent for, if one could not wait until morning. And then—Ben's step had crunched on the gravel outside, and she had held her breath to listen, and—in another minute it lay in her lap! A thick letter, when she had expected only a few hurried lines. It was almost like the steamer letter that he had written her on going out. It couldn't be a steamer letter! not yet! She seized it eagerly and studied the postmark. Could he be coming so soon that this was really her last letter?

How silly she was! her hand trembled so that the thin foreign paper rattled in her grasp. There were many sheets written fine and full.

But it was not a steamer letter; he was still in Paris.

She made herself wait until she gave careful attention to Ellen, who appeared just then, answering all her questions, directing her in minute detail as to a piece of next morning's work, having her add another block to the fire and rearrange the windows before she finally dismissed her.

At last she was fairly into her letter. She read rapidly at first, devouring the pages with her eyes. Then, more slowly, stopping over one page, re-reading it, a third, a fourth time;

staring at it, with a strange look in her eyes. Suddenly she dropped them, all the thin rustling sheets, and covered her face with both hands.

It seemed to her afterward that she spent a lifetime shut up with that foreign letter.

CHAPTER IX

SENTIMENT AND SACRIFICE

The woman on the upper porch who had come out to get her breath had in a short time passed through so many phases of feeling as to be hardly able to recognize herself. She had lived ten days since that bulky foreign letter had seemed to change the current of her life and set it flowing—when indeed it flowed again—in another channel.

In truth, Ruth Erskine Burnham, as she stood there ostensibly watching the sunset, was reviewing the days in a half-frightened, half-shamefaced way. She had always, even in young girlhood, been self-controlled. Why could she not hold herself in better check even though her world had suddenly turned to—stop! she would not say it! What had happened to her, after all, but that which fell to the lot of mothers? It was not as though some terrible calamity had overtaken her, and yet—could she have done differently if it had been? She went back in thought to that evening ten days away and looked at herself as though she were another person looking on. She even smiled faintly at the absurdity of that foolish woman's first action, before she had finished reading the letter. She had risen suddenly and turned off the light, and pushed up every window to its highest, and rolled back the curtains and let in a whirl of wind that had made the foreign sheets fly about as though they were things of life. Then, aided only by the firelight, she had stooped and clutched after them and held them for a second to her breast and then, suddenly, had thrown them from her with a low cry of pain. The woman on the upper porch looking at the sunset smiled at that half-insane woman of ten days ago and wondered that she could have so far forgotten herself. Why should there have been any such outburst as that, when Erskine was well and—and happy. She shivered a little even now over the word, and drew her wrap closer and told herself that as soon as the sun disappeared the chill came. Then she went back to her review and reminded herself firmly that there had been no calamity to any one; there was nothing but joy. Erskine was not only well and happy, but he was coming home. He was coming to-night! No, she must not say "he" any more; *they* were coming. Forever and ever after this it must be "they": her son and daughter. That to which she had looked forward for so many years with varying emotions had come upon her. Erskine was a married man; and to-night he was bringing home his bride. She had said over the words aloud, that day, when she was quite alone, trying to make herself feel that she was speaking of her son. It was all so sudden, so utterly different from any imaginings of hers, and she thought that she had gone over in her imaginings the whole wide range of possibilities.

That long letter over which she had spent a strange night, believed that it was giving her the minutest particulars of this strange thing.

Erskine had met the woman who was now his wife on his first evening in Paris, and from the very first had been attracted to her by his sympathy with her unprotected condition. Her only friend and companion in a strange land was a maiden aunt who was an invalid. Indeed it was for her sake that they were lingering in France, because she was not able to travel; she had been made worse by the ocean voyage, instead of better as had been hoped. Irene had been very closely confined with her for many weeks, and welcomed a face and voice from home as only those can understand who have themselves been cast adrift among foreigners. He had been able to do a few little things for the comfort of the invalid, and the gratitude of both ladies was almost embarrassing. They were staying at the same hotel, and as they chanced at that time to be almost the only Americans, at least the only ones belonging to their world, they naturally saw much of each other. As the aunt grew more and more feeble and Irene became entirely dependent on him not only for what little rest and recreation she got, but for all those offices which members of the same family can do for each other in a time of illness, their friendship made rapid strides. Then, when her aunt was suddenly taken alarmingly ill, and after a few days of really terrible suffering died, leaving Irene alone in a strange land, her situation was pitiable. He would have to confess that he did not know just what she would have done, had he not been there to care for her.

"Of course, mother, you do not need to have me tell you that long before this I knew that I had met the one woman in all the world who could ever become my wife. The reason that I had not mentioned her in any of my letters was that I could not, even on paper, speak of her casually, as of any ordinary acquaintance, and I had no right to speak in any other way. Then, when I had the right to tell you everything, it was so near my home-coming that I determined to leave it until you and I were face to face, and I could answer all your questions and look into your dear eyes and receive from you the sympathy that has never failed me and I know never will. Nothing was farther from our thoughts at that time than immediate marriage. Indeed it would have seemed preposterous to me, as it would have been under any other circumstances, to be married without your knowledge and presence. But when this unexpected blow came, I realized the almost impossibility of any other course, although, even then, I had the greatest difficulty in persuading Irene to take such a step. She had to be convinced through some annoying experiences of the folly of her hesitation. I do not know that even you, with your long experience, realize the difference between this country and ours in matters of etiquette. Things which at home would be done as a matter-of-course are so unusual here as to be almost, if not quite, questionable; and the number of purely business details that loomed up to be managed by that lonely homesick girl simply appalled her. She sank under them, physically, and I plainly saw that she simply must have my help and care day and night. Why, even the nurse who had attended her aunt, deserted us! that is, she was summoned away by telegraph. In short, mamma, there was literally no other course for us than the one we took; although it had to be taken at the sacrifice of a good deal of sentiment on the part of both. It is a continual relief to me to remember that I am writing to a sane and reasonable woman, who is in the habit of weighing questions carefully, and who, when she decides that a thing is right, does it without regard to sentiment or adverse opinion. But oh, mommie, it was hard not to have you with us."

There was more in the letter, much more. Erskine had exhausted language and repeated himself again and again in his effort to make everything very clear and convincing.

He had been skilful also in his attempt to make his mother see the woman of his choice with his eyes.

"She will appeal to your sympathies, mamma," he had written. "Although she is so young, barely twenty-six, she has been through much trouble and sorrow. She is an orphan, and has been for four years a widow. I need hardly add that her short married life was unhappy and so sad that she can scarcely speak of that year even to me. Of course it is an experience that I shall do my utmost to make her forget; and I need not speak of it again. I wanted you to know, dear mother, that you and I have much to make up to her. She was made fatherless and motherless in a single day, when she was a child of sixteen. I like to think of what you will be to her, dearest mother; a revelation, I am sure, of mother-love; for besides being so young when she lost hers, there are mothers, and *mothers*, you know, and I am sure Irene does not understand it very well; Do you know, she is half afraid of you? She has read a few of your letters, and has caught an idea of what we are to each other, and talks mournfully about coming between us! as though any one ever could! I have assured her that I am simply bringing to you the daughter for whom your heart has always longed."

It was at that point that Ruth Burnham had flung the sheets away from her and buried her face in her hands.

But ten days had passed since then, and she had long known, by heart, all that that letter could tell her.

And now, in less than another hour, they would be at home! her son and daughter!

She had not gone to New York to meet the incoming steamer, as had been arranged, or rather, as it had once arranged itself, quite as a matter of course.

"Think how delightful it will be, when you stand on the dock watching the incoming steamer, and straining your eyes to discover which frantically waved handkerchief is mine!"

This was what Erskine had said as he gave her one of her good-by kisses.

She had replied that she would recognize his handkerchief among a thousand.

In the earlier letters much had been said about that home-coming, and elaborate plans had been made as to what they would do together in New York. But in that last long letter, on the margin of the last page, as though it had been an afterthought, were these words:—

"On the whole, mother, we believe that it would be better for you not to try to meet us in New York. Irene has no love for that city; it was the scene of some of her sorrows. She wants to stop there only long enough to call upon her cousins; and we are both in such frantic haste to be at home that we shall make the delay as short as possible; so we think it would be less fatiguing to you to avoid that trip and be at home to welcome us."

Ruth Burnham said over that sentence as she stood on that upper veranda, waiting to welcome them. She had said it a hundred times before. What was there about it that jarred? She could not have told, in words; yet the jar was there.

Could it be that continually recurring "we"? Was she going to be a jealous woman, with all the rest? So meanly jealous as that? "God forbid!" she said the words aloud, and solemnly.

She knew that she needed the help of God in this crisis of her life; since the news of it came to her she had spent hours on her knees seeking his strength. She wanted Erskine to say "we" and think "we" and to be supremely happy,—not only in his married life, but to have that life all that it could be to two souls. And yet—Would it have been wrong for him, in that first letter, to have remembered that she had been used all his life to being the "we" of his thoughts, and to have said simply "I" once or twice? Of course she could never any more be "dearest"—his special name for her; but—was he never again for a little while to be just himself, to her? And must she learn to think "they" and never "him"?

Oh, she didn't mean any of this, she told herself nervously, and she must get her thoughts away at once. Of course she would say "Erskine and Irene" now, always, and forever. Or should she put it, "Irene and Erskine"? Could she? Perhaps that would help. Did other mothers, waiting for the home-coming of their married sons, have such strange thoughts as haunted her?

There was Mrs. Adams, for instance, whose three sons had all been married within a few years. And Mrs. Adams had not seemed to care. Well, as to that, neither would she seem to; and she drew herself up instinctively. But Mrs. Adams had four boys; five, indeed; the youngest of them was almost as tall as his mother, while she—"The only son of his mother, and she was a widow." The words seemed to repeat themselves in her brain like a dull undertone refrain.

Other words that had nothing whatever to do with the situation, but that had been familiar to her girlhood, came back and stupidly repeated themselves:—

"Dead! One of them shot by the sea in the east." But that was wildness, and utter folly! Erskine would be ashamed of her and with reason, could he know—which he never should—that such fancies had been tolerated for a moment.

Outwardly Mrs. Burnham was irreproachable. So was her home. In the ten days following that letter she had given time and thought to its adorning. She was a model housekeeper, and to have Erskine's rooms always in spotless order had been one of her pleasures. But they had been very thoroughly gone over, and whereever it was possible to add a touch of beauty, it had been done.

Already she had drawn the shades and lighted up brilliantly, for at this season the twilights were very brief. She had paused, on her way to the veranda, to take a final critical survey, and had told herself that she did not know how to make an added touch. And then she went swiftly to her own room and brought therefrom a vase of roses and set them on the dressing-table of the bride. The vase was a costly trifle that Erskine had brought her just before he went abroad, and the roses were his special favorites. She had kept that vase filled with them on her table ever since she reached home.

For herself, she was dressed in white: Erskine's favorite home dress for her, summer and winter. Indeed he was almost absurd about it, never quite liking to see her in any other attire. "I suppose you will want me to dress in white when I am eighty!" she had said to him once, laughingly. His reply had been quick. "Of course I shall. What could be more appropriate for a beautiful old lady? You will be beautiful, dearest, but I cannot think that you will ever be old."

So, on this evening, although she had taken down a black silk and looked at it wistfully, she had resolutely hung it away again, and brought out a white cashmere richly trimmed with white silk. This was a festive evening and she must honor it with one of her prettiest dresses.

All at once as she stood there, waiting, her heart seemed for a moment to stop its beating. She clutched at the railing to prevent her falling, and made a stern and effectual protest. "This is ridiculous! I will not faint, and I shall do nothing to mar his home-coming, or to give him occasion to be ashamed of me."

But she stood still, although the carriage that had gone to the station to meet the bridal party was whirling around the corner, was turning in at the carriage drive, was stopping before the door. They were getting out. They were on the porch, they were in the hall; she could hear her son's voice:—

"Where is my mother?"

And she was not there as she had meant to be to welcome them! she was still on the upper veranda, steadying herself by the railing and feeling it impossible to take a single step.

CHAPTER X

"SENTIMENTAL" PEOPLE

Erskine came up the stairs in quick leaps. "Mother!" he was calling. "Mother! Where are you? Why, mommie!" and he had her in his arms.

"I thought I should be sure to see you the moment the carriage turned the corner! Are you ill, mother? What is the matter?"

Was there reproach in his voice? There was something that gave back his mother's self-command.

"It is tardiness," she said lightly. "The carriage came sooner than I had thought it possible. O Erskine, it is good to hear your voice again."

He kept his arms about her and was half smothering her in kisses while he talked. Yet his tones had that note in them which held her in check.

"Irene will think this a strange welcome home, I am afraid; I had to leave her in the hall with the maids while I came in search of you."

"We will go down at once," said his mother; and she withdrew herself from his arms and led the way.

"She is very pretty." This was Mrs. Burnham's mental tribute to her new daughter, as they stood together on the side porch after breakfast. It was the morning after the arrival of the bride and groom. They had been drawn thither by Erskine, who had walked back and forth with an arm about each, bewailing the fact that he could not spare even one day for his wife in her new home, but must get at once to business. In the midst of his regretful sentence his car was heard at the crossing above, and he had hurried away, calling back to them to take care of themselves, and get well acquainted while he was gone.

The two ladies had each returned a gay answer, and then had watched their opportunity to glance furtively at each other, uncertain how to begin the formidable task set them.

Ruth Burnham had it in her heart to be almost sorry for the younger woman, left thus without Erskine to lean upon, her only companion in this new, strange home, a woman to whom the place had been home for a generation. Did this give her a special advantage? Ought she to do something to make the other woman feel at home? What should it be? What ideas had they in common? There was Erskine, of course. It was not hard for the mother to understand why this woman had been attracted to him. How indeed could she help it? But what was it in her that had won him?

"She is certainly very pretty," she said again, as she studied the shapely figure leaning meditatively against one of the porch pillars; she was looking down into the garden gay with autumn blooms.

She was rather above medium height, with a fair skin and a wealth of golden brown hair and eyes that were very blue. Ruth did not like her eyes. That is, she would not have liked them if they had not belonged to her daughter-in-law. In the solitude of her strangely solitary room, the night before, she had fought out again one of her battles, and had resolved anew that there should be nothing about this new daughter that she would not like.

Certainly she was pretty; so was her dress. She was all in white; not a touch of color anywhere. Was that her taste, or Erskine's fancy? Could his mother make it a stepping-stone to conversation?

"You dressed for Erskine, this morning, I fancy," she said with a winsome smile. "I presume you have already discovered how fond he is of white?"

"Oh, yes, he has held forth to me on that subject. Some of his ideas are absurd, but they serve me very well just now. All white answers as a substitute for mourning, under the circumstances. I hate black, and I am glad that Erskine did not want me to wear it."

This was the first reference that had been made to her bereavement. Mrs. Burnham had not known how to touch it. Neither had her daughter's words suggested what should be said. She murmured some commonplace about the peculiar hardness of the situation.

"Yes, indeed," said the younger woman. "It was simply dreadful! Aunt Mary had been an invalid always,—ever since I knew her, at least,—but nobody supposed that she would ever die. She was one of the nervous kind, you know, full of aches and pains; a fresh list each morning, and a detailed description of each. I did get so tired of it! If it hadn't been for Erskine, I don't know what I should have done. Poor auntie was very fond of him, and no wonder. He bore with all her stories and her whims like a hero. I used to tell him that he had not lived with his mother all his life, for nothing."

"Her sudden death must have been a great shock to you."

The new mother made a distinct effort to keep her voice from sounding cold. Something in the words or the tones of the younger woman had jarred.

"Oh yes," she said, and sighed. "You cannot imagine what a perfectly dreadful time it was! You know when people are always ill and always fussing, you get used to it, and expect them to go on forever. If I had had the least idea that she was going to die, I should have planned differently, of course. What I should have done without Erskine, as things turned out, it makes me shudder to think. What a queer old place this is, isn't it? Erskine tells me that he has always lived here and that the garden looks much as it did when he was a child. Is that so? It seems so strange to me! I have moved about so much that I cannot imagine how it would be to live always, anywhere. I don't believe I should like it. The everlasting sameness, you know, would be such a bore. Don't you find it so?"

Ruth tried to smile. "I am very much attached to the place. I came to it, as you have, a bride; and now I am afraid I should have difficulty in making any other place seem like home."

"Yes, that is because you are old. Poor auntie was forever sighing for home. Nothing in all France or Italy was at all to be compared to the delights of her room at home with four south windows and long curtains that she had hemstitched herself."

She laughed lightly and flitted away from the subject.

"Is that an oak tree over there by the south gateway? Don't you think oaks are ugly? They haven't the least bit of grace. I like elm trees better than any other; every movement of their limbs is graceful. There isn't one about the place, is there?"

"Oh, yes, indeed, the other entrance from the east is lined with them the entire length of the carriage drive. Was your aunt compelled to remain abroad on account of the climate? It seems sad to think that she had to be away from her home when she missed it and mourned for it." Ruth could not keep her thoughts from reverting to the aunt who had been so large a part of the younger woman's life for many years and had been so recently removed from it.

"Oh, I suppose she could have lived at home. In fact she was worse after leaving it, or thought she was; I didn't see any great difference. It was a lonesome, poky old house where she lived. Older than this, and awfully dreary in winter. I couldn't have stayed there a winter, after I once got away, to have saved her life. It was back in the country, you know, two miles from town; think of it! I hate the country. Little cities like this one are bad enough, but the country! Deliver me from ever having to live in it again. I thought I should die when I was there as a girl.

"Is Erskine very much attached to this place, do you suppose, or has he stayed here just for your sake? I should think it would be much better for him to live where his business is. Think how much of his time is consumed in going back and forth! and then, too, it is so disagreeable for him to never be within call when one wants him."

"As to the length of time it takes to go back and forth, that is no more than is taken by those who live in the best residence portions of the large city; we have rapid transit, and all the business men who can afford to do so, keep their homes out here. Erskine has never known any other home than this, and it would be strange indeed if he were not attached to it. Of course it is associated with his father as no other place can ever be."

This time it was not possible for the elder lady to keep her voice from sounding cold and constrained. The thought of Erskine in any other home than this one that had been improved from time to time and made beautiful, always with his interests in view, had not so much as occurred to her. She recoiled from the mere suggestion, and also from the easy and careless manner in which it was made.

The young woman's manner was still careless.

"Oh, of course; but young people do not feel such attachments much; it isn't natural. We talk a great deal about sentimental youth, but I think it is the old who are sentimental, don't you? Auntie was an illustration of that. She had the greatest quantity of old duds that she carried about with her wherever she went, just because they were keepsakes, souvenirs, and all that sort of thing. They were of no real value, you know, the most of them, and some were mere rubbish. I had the greatest time when we were packing to go abroad; she wanted to lug ever so much of that stuff with her! I just had to set my foot down that it couldn't be done; and it was fortunate that I did, as things turned out. We had a horrid time getting packed; if Erskine had had all that rubbish to see to with the rest, I don't know what would have become of him. I don't believe he has sentimental notions; he is too sensible. He ought to be in the city; that is the place for a man to rise; and you want him to rise, don't you? Aren't you ambitious for him? I am. I want him to stand at the very head of his profession. I tell him that if he doesn't, it will not be for lack of brains, but on account of a morbid conscience. Don't you think he is inclined to be over-conscientious, sometimes? What an odd, old-fashioned plant that is beyond the rose arbor; it looks like a weed."

She had a curious fashion of mixing the important and the trivial in a single sentence. The mother, whose nerves quivered with her desire to answer that remark about over-conscientiousness, restrained herself and explained the plant that looked like a weed.

"It is a very choice variety of begonia and has a lovely blossom in its season. It is the first thing that Erskine planted quite by himself. He was a tiny boy then, with yellow curls."

The mother's voice trembled. A vision of her boy in his childish beauty, in the long-ago days when he was all her own, came back to her, bringing with it a strange new pang.

The wife laughed carelessly.

"And you have kept it all these years, ugly as it is, on that account? I told you it was old people who were sentimental."

Mrs. Burnham turned abruptly away, murmuring something about household duties. She went to the kitchen and gave the cook some directions that she did not need; then went swiftly to her room and closed and locked her door. Then she passed through to her sitting room, the door of which was opposite her son's, and stood always open, inviting his entrance, and closed and locked it. She had a feeling that she must be alone. More alone than closed and locked doors would make her. She must shut out something that had come in unawares and taken hold of her life. But could she shut it out, or get away from it?

"I must pray," she said aloud, clasping both hands over her throbbing forehead. "I must pray a great deal. I am not alone; God is with me; and nothing dreadful has happened, or is about to happen. There is nothing and there must be nothing but peace and joy in our home. I must be quiet and sensible and not sentimental. Oh, I must not be sentimental at all!"

She laughed a little over that word—the kind of laugh that does not help one; but it was followed immediately by tears, and they relieved a little of the strain.

Then she went to her knees; and when she arose, was quiet and ready for life. The thought came to her that it was well that she was acquainted with God and did not have to seek him at this time as one unknown. He had kept his everlasting arms underneath her through trying years, certainly she could trust him now.

She went out at once in search of her daughter, intending to propose a drive; but Ellen met her in the hall with a message.

"I was to tell you, ma'am, that young Mrs. Burnham has gone to lie down and doesn't want to be disturbed. She doesn't want to be awakened even for luncheon; she says she has been on a steady strain for weeks, and has a lot of sleeping to make up; she shouldn't wonder if she slept all day."

"Very well, Ellen, we will keep the house quiet and let her rest as long as she will."

The mother's voice was quietness itself, yet, despite that phrase "young Mrs. Burnham," which, some way, jarred, her heart was filled with compunction. Had the poor young wife, a stranger in a strange home, shut herself up to sleep, or to cry? She had been through nerve-straining experiences so recently; death and marriage coming into one short week; and now, a new home, and Erskine away for the day, and no one within sight or sound whom she had ever seen before. Would it be any wonder if the tears wanted to come? Could not her new mother have helped her through this first strange day? Why had she not put tender arms about her and kissed her, and called her "daughter," and said how glad she was to have a daughter? That was what she had meant to do. This morning when she came from her night vigil, she had almost the words on her lips that she meant to say as soon as they two were alone. She had meant the words in their fulness; so at least she believed. They had come to her in answer to her cry for help. What had kept her from saying them?

Even while she asked herself the question, a faint weary smile hovered about her lips.

Had she done so, would she have been thought "sentimental?"

CHAPTER XI

"PLANS FOR A PURPOSE"

The Burnhams were still seated at their dinner table, although Mrs. Erskine Burnham had just remarked that the evening was too lovely to spend in eating.

"Let us take a walk on the porch in the moonlight the minute we are through dinner," she said to her husband. Apparently she paid no heed to the slight dry cough which came so frequently from Erskine that his mother's face took on a shade of anxiety. Erskine's coughs had been his mother's chief anxiety concerning him through the years; he had never been able to tamper with them; but his wife laughed at her fears and frankly told her that Erskine was too old now to be coddled.

To all outward appearances the Burnham dining room was exhibiting a perfect home scene. The day had been balmy, with a hint of summer in the air, and although the evening was cool enough for a bright fire in the grate, the mantle above it had been banked with violets, whose sweet spring breath pervaded the air.

To Erskine Burnham who had been all day in the rush and roar of the great city, the lovely room with its flower-laden air, and its daintily appointed dinner table with the two ladies seated thereat in careful toilets, formed a picture of complete and restful home life. He glanced from wife to mother with eyes of approval and spoke joyously.

"I don't suppose you two can fully appreciate what it is to me to get home to you after a stuffy, snarly day in town. I sit in the car sometimes with closed eyes after a day of turmoil, to picture how it will all look. But the reality always exceeds my imagination."

His wife laughed gayly.

"That is because you come home hungry," she said. "You want your dinner and you like the odor of it and make believe that it is sentiment and violets. In reality it is roast beef and jelly that charm you."

He echoed her laugh. He thought her gay spirits were charming. "The roast beef helps, undoubtedly," he said. "Though it was violets I noticed first, to-night. Aren't they lovely? Did you arrange them, Irene? Hasn't it been a perfect day? Too pleasant for staying in doors patiently. I hope you have both been out a great deal? Oh, it is Friday, isn't it? Then you have, mamma, of course. What have you been about, Irene?"

"I went to the lake this morning with the Bensons; and we spent an hour or more with the Langhams; they are here for a month. It is lovely out there, Erskine, and there are some charming cottages for rent. Two simply ideal ones, either of which would suit us. Darling little bird's-nests of cottages, not a great staring room in one of them. I wish we could go there for the summer."

Erskine laughed indulgently, but at the same time shook his head.

"Too far away, dear. I couldn't get out there at night until seven, or later. Besides, you wouldn't find it so pleasant as you fancy. Life in one of those bird's-nest cottages is ideal only on paper. Nothing could be pleasanter, I am sure, than our own home; and it is a delightful drive to the lake whenever we want to go there. So the Langhams are down."

"Oh, yes, and came to lunch with me. You should see Harry! he has shaved his mustache, and it changes his face so that I hardly knew him."

"Oh, Harry is here, is he? His face could bear changing. What did you think of him, mamma? He is the young man of whom I wrote you, who went over on the same steamer that I did, last spring."

Before Mrs. Burnham could reply, his wife's voice chimed in. "She didn't meet him. I went off with a rush, this morning. I heard through the mail that the Langhams were down, and I was in such a hurry to see Nettie that I thought of nothing else. I ran away, don't you think! Never said where I was going, or anything; and then came back to luncheon so late that I supposed of course mother had lunched long before, and was lying down, so I wouldn't have her disturbed. And don't you think she had waited, and so lost her luncheon altogether."

Erskine laughed genially and waited to hear his mother say that of course that was of no consequence; but she did not speak. The cheerful voice of his wife went on:—

"Nettie Langham has the sweetest little home, Erskine. If you could see it, you would never say again that cottages were only nice on paper. I'm sure I long to prove to you how perfectly charming one could be. And we have such a host of pretty things that would fit into it. Will Langham says he saves ten minutes night and morning by being at that end of the town instead of this."

Erskine chose to ignore the cottage.

"You had an afternoon of calls, had you not? I met the Emersons and the Stuarts down town and both spoke of having been here."

"Oh, yes, they were here, with the Needham girls; and Mrs. Easton and her daughter Faye were here. We met them in New York, you know. And oh, don't you think, Mrs. Janeway's niece that we used to hear so much about called this afternoon with a letter of introduction from Mrs. Janeway. She is lovely, Erskine. I was prepared to dislike her because we heard such perfection of her; but really she is charming. And she is going to be at one of the lake cottages for several weeks; that is another reason for our being out there, you see."

She seemed bent on holding his attention, but Erskine turned to his mother with a question.

"Mamma, don't you think Mrs. Stuart is looking ill? I was shocked at the change in her. Isn't it marked, or is it because I haven't seen her lately?"

"I did not see her to-day, my son. I did not even know she had been here."

Mrs. Erskine Burnham pretended to frown at her husband.

"What a stupid boy you can be when you choose!" she said. "How many times must I tell you that I thought mother was resting, this afternoon, and did not disturb her with callers? I'm sure the Stuarts are not such infrequent guests that one must make a special effort to meet them. I'll tell you some other people who were here. The Hemingways, don't you think! The last time we saw them was just as we were leaving Paris. They came back only last month, and Mrs. Hemingway says she is already homesick for Paris. That is the worst of living abroad for a time; one is never afterward quite satisfied with this country."

"Mamma," said Erskine. "Do I understand that you have not been out, to-day, Friday, though it is? Aren't you feeling well?"

There was tender solicitude in his tones, but his mother's voice was cold.

"Quite well, Erskine. May I give you some coffee?" This he declined, and almost immediately his wife made a movement to leave the table. She linked her arm at once in her husband's and drew him toward the door.

"Come out on the porch, Erskine, do; this room is stuffy to-night. One can't breathe in a house with a fire, on such charming days as these. Why, of course, it's prudent. The air is as mild as it is in midsummer. Don't go to housing yourself up because you have a tiny little cold; it is the best way in the world to make it cling. Dear me! don't I know all about that? Poor auntie was forever hunting about for draughts, and closing doors and windows and putting shawls on herself and everybody else. If I had to stay in the house with another invalid of that kind, I should die."

They were on the porch by this time; she had overcome Erskine's half-reluctance and had closed the door behind them. But the window was open and the mother could distinctly hear the slight dry cough, more frequent now that they were in the open air. She stood irresolute for a moment, then turned and went swiftly up to her own rooms and closed and locked her door. Then she went hurriedly to the front windows and drew the curtains close; she had a feeling that she must shut out the outside world very carefully. But she had no tears to shed; on the contrary her eyes were very dry and bright and seemed almost to burn in their sockets, and two red spots glowed on her cheeks.

It was a little more than six months since that October evening when Erskine Burnham had brought home his bride, and they had been months of revelation to his mother.

During that time she had tried—did any woman ever try harder?—to be, in the true sense of the word, a mother to her daughter-in-law. Her son's appeal during their first moments of privacy had touched her deeply. He had ignored any necessity for a further explanation of his sudden marriage, accepting it as a matter of course that his mother would fully appreciate the simple statement that, however hard it was for all three, it seemed to be the only right solution of their difficulties; and went straight to his point.

"I want you to be a revelation to Irene, mommie. She knows very little about mother-love, having had chiefly to imagine it, with, I fancy, rather poor models on which to build her imaginings. She is singularly alone in the world, and she doesn't make close friends easily. It is a joy to me to think how a part of her nature that has heretofore been starved and dwarfed will blossom out under your love and care."

Then his mother had kissed him, a long, clinging, self-surrendering kiss, while she vowed to her secret soul never to disappoint his hopes. What had she not done and left undone and endured during those six months in order to try to keep that vow! What an impossible vow it was! How utterly Erskine had misunderstood his wife in supposing that she wanted to be loved by his mother! that she wanted anything whatever of his mother except to efface her.

By slow degrees Mrs. Burnham was reaching the conclusion that such was the policy of her daughter-in-law. It had come to her as a surprise. Whatever else in her checkered life Ruth Erskine Burnham had been called upon to bear, she had been accustomed to being recognized always as an important force. Mrs. Erskine Burnham had not planned in that way. She did not argue, she never openly combated any thing; she simply carried out her own intentions without the slightest regard to the plans or the convenience of others; or at least of one other.

From the first of her coming into this hitherto ideal home she had assumed that her mother-in-law was a feeble old woman on whom the claims of society were irksome, and the ordering of her home and servants a bore. At first, Ruth, with her utterly different experience from which to judge, did not understand the situation. When her new daughter assured her that it was too windy or too damp or too chilly or too warm for her to expose herself, she laughed amusedly and explained that she was in excellent health and was accustomed to going out in all weather. When callers came and went without her being notified, she attributed it at first to forgetfulness, on the part of a bride, or to her ignorance of the customs of the neighborhood; then to her over-solicitude for an older woman's comfort, then to carelessness, pure and simple, and finally, by closely contested steps, to the conviction that it was a deeply laid, steadily carried-out plan, for a purpose. This day, at the close of which she had locked herself into her room and vainly tried to shut out the sounds of laughter on the porch below, had given her abundant proof of the truth of this conviction.

It was Friday, the day which, ever since Erskine was graduated and they were permanently settled in their home, she had devoted to making a round of calls upon people who had been long ill, or who for any special reason needed special thought. She took one or another of them for a drive, she did errands for certain others, she carried flowers and fruit and reading matter to such as could enjoy them; in short she gave herself and her carriage and horses in any way that could best meet the interests of those set apart. So much a feature of their life had this morning programme become that Erskine was in the habit of referring to it much as he did to Sunday.

"We must not plan for guests at luncheon on Fridays, Irene; mamma is much too tired for social functions after her strenuous mornings."

"We could not have the carriage for that day, dear; it is Friday, you remember."

Numberless times since the advent of the new member of the family, had such reference to the special custom been made; the mother's eyes being now opened, she recalled instance after instance in which there had been in progress some pet scheme for Friday, that would interfere with her disposal of it. More than once she had tried to enter a protest; had urged that she could wait until another day, or she could order a carriage from the livery for that time; but Erskine's negative had been prompt and emphatic.

"No, indeed, mamma; we don't want you to do anything of the kind. We are interested in the Friday programme, too, remember. I consider it almost in the light of a trust. Why, the very horses would be hurt, Irene, if they were not allowed to go their Friday rounds, carrying roses, and jellies, and balm. Nothing not absolutely necessary, mommie, must be permitted to interfere with that."

Yet, on that Friday morning when Mrs. Burnham, having studied the barometer and the sky, had sent word to an especially delicate invalid that she believed she could safely take a drive, and had come down at the appointed hour dressed for driving, with a couch pillow in hand and an extra wrap over her arm, Ellen had met her at the foot of the stairs with a flushed face and eyes that had dropped their glance to the floor for very shame, as she said: "The carriage has gone, ma'am; I was coming to ask you if I should 'phone for another, right away."

"Gone!" echoed her mistress, standing still on the third step, and staring at the girl. "What do you mean, Ellen? Gone where?"

"To the station, ma'am. Jonas said Mrs. Erskine had ordered him to take her there to meet a friend."

"Oh," said Mrs. Burnham, reaching for her watch. "Some guest just heard from who must be met, I presume. Then they will be back very soon, of course."

Again the maid's indignant eyes drooped as though unwilling to see her mistress's discomfiture as she hurried her story.

"I guess not, ma'am. She ordered luncheon to be late; not earlier than two or half past, and said there would be company; two anyway, perhaps more. Will I 'phone for a carriage, ma'am?"

CHAPTER XII

ACCIDENT OR DESIGN?

Mrs. Burnham had stood for a full minute irresolute; then she had spoken in her usual tone, explaining to Ellen that the friend she had intended to take out would not be able to go in a livery carriage. She would herself make plain to her why the drive must be deferred until another time. The mistake had occurred by her neglecting to explain to her daughter the morning's plans. Then she had turned and slowly retraced her steps. She had seen and been humiliated by the flush on Ellen's face and the flash in her eyes. It was humiliating to think that her maid was indignant over the way she was being treated by her daughter. It is probably well that she did not hear the maid's exclamation:—

"The horrid cat! If I only dared tell Mr. Erskine all about it!"

Ruth Burnham had gone downstairs again after a time. She had changed her street dress first, and made a careful at-home toilet. She had given certain additional directions to the cook, with a view to doing honor to their unexpected guests. She had made a special effort to have Ellen understand that all was quite as it should be, and had sternly assured herself that such was the case. If she could not sympathize with the sudden movements of young people on hearing of the coming of friends, she deserved to be set aside as too old to be endurable. It was absurd in her to be so wedded to an old custom!

just as though any other day in the week would not do as well as Friday. Then she had gone to the living room which was Erskine's favorite of the entire house.

"It is such a home-y room, mamma," he used to say, away back in his early boyhood. When it had been refurnished, or at least renewed, with a view to Erskine's home-coming, his mother had taken pains to preserve the sense of homeiness, and had seen to it that his pet luxuries, sofa pillows, were in lavish evidence.

It was a charming room. Very long and many windowed, with wide, low window-seats, and tempting cosy-corners, piled high with cushions so carefully chosen, as to size and harmony of color, that they were in themselves studies in art. There was a smaller room opening from this and nearer the front entrance, which was used as a reception room, and was furnished more after the fashion of the conventional parlor; but guests who, as Erskine phrased it, really "belonged," were always entertained in the living room.

In the doorway of this room the mistress of the house had stopped short and looked about her in astonishment. It wore an unfamiliar air. The easy-chairs, each one of which she had made a study, until it seemed to have been created for the particular niche in which it was placed, had every one changed places and to the eyes of the mistress of the house looked awkward and uncomfortable. But that was foolish, she assured herself quickly. Chairs, of course, belonged wherever their friends chose to place them. There were other changes. The window-seats had been shorn of some of their largest and prettiest cushions, and a little onyx table that had occupied a quiet corner was gone. It had held a choice picture of Erskine's father, set in a dainty frame, and near it had stood a tiny vase which was daily filled with fresh blossoms. Picture and vase and flowers had disappeared.

"Ellen," Mrs. Burnham had said, catching sight of the girl in the next room, "what has happened here? Has there been an accident?"

"No, m'm," said Ellen, appearing in the opposite doorway, duster in hand.

"It wasn't any accident, ma'am, it was orders. She didn't want such a lot of pillows here, she said. It looked for all the world like a show room, or as if it had been got ready for a church fair. Those was her very words."

"Never mind the pillows, Ellen." Mrs. Burnham had spoken hastily, and was regretting that she had spoken at all. "It is the table, and especially the picture about which I am inquiring. I hope the picture is safe? It is the best one we have."

"It's all safe, ma'am; I looked out for that; but that was orders, too. She said the room was too full, and looked cluttery; and she said that only country folks kept family pictures in their parlors. And she had me take the table and the picture and the vase up into the back attic. She said the vase was a nuisance; it was always tipping over and she didn't want it around in the way. Of course I had to take them; you told me to obey orders."

Ellen's indignation was getting the better of her usual discreetness. It was her tone and manner that recalled the elder woman to her senses. She spoke with decision and dignity.

"Certainly, Ellen. Why should there be occasion for mentioning that? Of course Mrs. Erskine Burnham's orders are to be obeyed equally with my own; or, if they conflict at any time with my own, give hers the preference. Especially should the parlors and sitting rooms be arranged just as she wishes. Young people care more about such little matters than we older ones do."

She knew that her voice had been steady, and she took care to make her movements quiet and her manner natural and at ease. Not for the world would she have had Ellen know of the turmoil going on inside. It was the picture that hurt her; or rather that emphasized the hurt. Erskine's favorite picture of his father; the one that as a child he had daily kissed good morning; the one that now after all these years he always stood beside in silence for a moment, after greeting her. And she could not recall that he had ever forgotten to select from the flowers he brought home, an offering for the tiny vase.

How was it possible for his wife to have spent six months in his home without noting all this? And noting it, how could she possibly have interfered with that cherished corner?

The morning had been a distinct advance on former experiences. The new daughter had evidently misunderstood the spirit in which small interferences and small slights had heretofore been accepted, and determined on aggressive effort. Long before this, and as often as she chose, she had made what changes pleased her in the more pretentious parlor, and Mrs. Burnham had openly approved some of them and been pleasantly silent over others. She had also given explicit directions to the would-be rebel, Ellen, that the "new lady's" slightest hint was to be obeyed.

There had been no pettiness in her thoughts about the changes. She was earnestly anxious to have her son's wife feel so entirely at home that she would not need to hesitate about carrying out her own tastes. But was it not to be supposed that a wife would consult her husband's tastes as well as her own? And his father's picture that he had cherished ever since he was a child! She had herself told Irene one morning, standing before that very picture, how Erskine had singled it out from all the others and said decidedly: "That one is papa." And his wife could banish it to the attic!

Ruth Erskine Burnham was used to mental struggles. There had been times in her life when her strong-willed feelings had got the upper hand and swayed her for days together; but it is doubtful if a more violent storm of feeling had ever swept about her than surged that morning. For a while the pent-up emotions of many weeks were allowed their way. But only for a little while. The Christian of many years' experience had herself too well in training for long submission to the enemy's control. By the time that delayed luncheon hour drew near she believed that she was her quiet self again; ready to receive and assist in entertaining her daughter's guests whoever they might be. As was her habit when under the power of strong feeling that must be held in check she took refuge with her absent friends, and wrote a long letter to Marian Dennis, ignoring the immediate present utterly and revelling in certain happy experiences of their past. When her unusually lengthy epistle was finished, she was startled at the lateness of the hour, and began to wonder how certain details of the dinner could be managed if luncheon were much longer delayed. Just then Ellen knocked at her door.

"They are 'most through luncheon, ma'am," was her message. "I heard you moving around and I thought I'd venture to tell you."

"Why, Ellen, how is this? I did not hear any call to luncheon."

"You wasn't called, ma'am. She said you was likely asleep, and she wouldn't let me come up and see. She thinks you don't do anything but sleep when you are upstairs!"

This last was muttered, and not supposed to be heard by her mistress. Ellen had evidently reached the limit of her endurance. Since the mistress said not a word, she ventured a further statement. "There's four of them, ma'am, besides Mrs. Burnham; and it's long after three, and they're on the last course. I thought you would be wanting something to eat by this time."

Outwardly, Ruth was herself again.

"Thank you, Ellen," she said. "Since I am so late, I think I will not go down until the guests have left the dining room. I am not in the least hungry; I think on the whole I should prefer to wait until dinner is served."

Her tone was gentleness itself; but there was in it that quality which made Ellen understand that she was dismissed.

Then Mrs. Burnham went back to her room and sat down near the open window. The sweet spring air came to her, laden with the breath of the flowers she loved, but their odor almost sickened her. She had thought that her battle was fought and victory declared, and behold it was only a lull! What was she to do? What ought she to do? Should she go down to the guests, apologize for tardiness, and act as though nothing had occurred to disturb her? That, of course, would be the sensible way; but,—could she do it well, with the closely observing and indignant Ellen to confront? It scarcely seemed possible; and she blushed for shame over the thought that she was afraid to meet the anxious eyes of her maid.

Even while she waited and considered, a carriage swung around the corner and stopped before her door. Three ladies alighted, evidently with the intent of paying an afternoon visit. Among them was Mrs. Stuart, her most intimate acquaintance. Now indeed she would have to go down; but she would wait for a summons, that would make it appear more natural. So she waited; but no summons came. The ladies, all of them her friends, made their call and departed. And others came—a constant succession of callers; the new spring day had tempted everybody out. Most of the people Mrs. Burnham knew by sight; some of them were comparative strangers, paying their first calls. What was being given as the reason why she was not there to meet them? The words of Ellen recurred to her, words that she had considered it wisdom not to seem to hear:—

"She thinks you don't do anything but sleep when you are upstairs." The matron's lip curled a little. She was not given to sleeping by daylight; a fifteen minutes' nap after luncheon was always sufficient, and even that was frequently omitted.

It was a strange afternoon, the strangest that she had ever passed. She kept her seat at the window, almost within view, if the guests had raised their eyes, and saw friends who rarely got out to make calls, and whom she had always made special efforts to entertain. What must they think of her, at home, and well, and not there to meet them? And why was she not there? What strange freak or whim was this? Could her daughter-in-law hope to make a prisoner of her in her own house? Why did she sit there in that inane way as though she were in very deed a prisoner? Why not go down, as a matter of course, and take her proper place as usual? But the longer she delayed and watched those groups of callers come and go, the more impossible it seemed to do this. With each fresh arrival she felt sure that she would be summoned, and waited nervously for Ellen's knock. But no Ellen came.

The day waned and the hour for Erskine and dinner drew near; and still Mrs. Burnham sat like one dazed at that open window. An entire afternoon lost. When, before, had she spent a day in such fashion?

She leaned forward, presently, and watched Erskine's car stop at the corner, and watched his springing step as he came with glad haste to his home, and received his bow and smile as he looked up at her window. Now indeed she must go down; and go before he could come in search of her, and question her with keen gaze and searching words. Her eyes told no tales, they were dry, and there were bright spots glowing on her cheeks. She had not known what she should say, just how she should manage his solicitous inquiries. She would make no plans, she told herself; things must just take their course. Matters had so shaped themselves that any planning of hers was useless.

Then she had gone down to that cheerful dining room, and listened to the chatter of her daughter-in-law, and replied to her son as best she could. Now she was back in her room, and Erskine and his wife were out on the porch in the moonlight, and that slight, frequent cough was coming up to her. Presently he would come, and she dreaded it. For almost the first time in her life she dreaded to meet her son. He would be insistent, and she was not good at dissembling. And yet, he must not know, he must never know how she had been treated that day. If only he would stay away and give her a chance to think, to pray, to grow calm. Should she lock her door?

Lock out her son? She could not do that! but she could not talk with him to-night; she would turn off her light and ask him not to light up again and not to stay, because she was tired. That at least would be true: she was tired. For the first time in her life she was tired of life! She must get into a different spirit from this. After Erskine had kissed her good-night she would have it out with her heart, or her will.

Hark! he was coming! they were coming upstairs together, and Irene was chattering. Out went the lights in the mother's room. She heard the wife pass on to her own room, she heard her son, stepping lightly, stopping a moment before her door, then he too passed on, to his own room, and closed his door.

CHAPTER XIII

WAS IRENE RIGHT?

If she could have heard some of the talk that had taken place on the porch in the moonlight, Mrs. Burnham would have better understood her son's consideration. They had taken but very few turns on the porch when Erskine said:—

"Mamma has gone upstairs. I think I must run up and see her a few minutes, Irene. She does not seem to feel quite well to-night; although in some respects I think I never saw her looking better; her eyes were very bright, did you notice? Perhaps she is feverish. Did she speak of having cold?"

"Not at all; I have no idea that she doesn't feel quite well."

"There was something peculiar about her. Didn't she really go out at all to-day? That is certainly unusual; you have seen how particular she is to keep her Friday programme. Irene, I am really afraid that she is ill."

"She isn't ill at all, you fussy boy; I think you are absurd about your mother. You fuss over her as though she were a spoiled child. That is just the word for it."

"Very well," he said good-humouredly. "I must go and 'fuss over' her, enough to know why she overturned her usual programme," and he moved toward the door.

His wife held to his arm and tried to arrest his steps.

"Don't go in, Erskine; it is stuffy inside, and I haven't seen you since morning. As for that programme which worries you so much, if you were not dreadfully stupid to-night you would understand that it is I who overturned it. I ran away with the carriage, I told you—almost as soon as you went yourself. I was so charmed with the idea of seeing the Langhams again that I forgot everything else."

Her husband turned then to look at her, his face expressing surprise.

"Did you take our carriage, dear? I supposed you ordered one from the livery."

His wife pretended to pout.

"You are cross to-night, Erskine. I don't see why I should. I thought 'Our' meant mine as much as hers. Why shouldn't she order one if she wanted it?"

He laughed, as though he was expected to understand that she was talking nonsense, but he spoke with an undertone of decision.

"Oh if it comes to that, the carriage as well as the horses are undoubtedly my mother's, but she and I have never drawn any hard and fast lines about 'mine' and 'thine'; I have

49

always found her too willing to give up her convenience for mine. For that reason, perhaps, I have been careful to plan systematically for her, and to anticipate and overrule her personal sacrifices as much as possible, and I know that you will delight to join me in it. I am afraid that she was much inconvenienced to-day; still, that cannot be why she did not see any of her friends. What reason did she give, dear, for not coming down?"

Irene pouted in earnest this time.

"Really, Erskine, you are strangely obtuse! I have explained at least three times that mother spent the afternoon in her room, and that I gave orders that she should not be disturbed. I thought I should be commended for it instead of blamed."

"I haven't had a thought of blaming you, Irene, but I am a trifle anxious about my mother, and what you say only increases the anxiety. She has never been given to sleeping much in the daytime."

"Oh what nonsense! as though you knew what she did all day, while you are in town! Of course she sleeps; old people always do."

"My mother isn't old, Irene."

"My mother isn't old, Irene."—*Page 167.*

"Why not, I wonder? you ridiculous boy! When should people begin to be called old, pray, if not at fifty? And she is more than that. She is within a few years of Auntie's age, and you thought she was an old woman, and were always preaching to me about how patient I must be with her on that account."

Her husband gave her a troubled, half-startled look. His mother nearly as old as the invalid aunt who had seemed to him old enough to be his grandmother!

"Are you sure?" he asked helplessly.

His wife laughed satirically.

"Sure of what, my beloved dunce? That your mother is fifty-three? Of course I am. It was only a few days ago that she showed me her gold-lined silver cup, that has the imprint of her first teeth and is dated for her first birthday."

Then her face sobered.

"And I'll tell you another way in which I know it, Erskine. She is growing nervous and over-sensitive, as old people always do. I can see a great difference in her, even in the short time that I have been here. It is nothing to worry about, of course; simply something to be expected as among the infirmities of age. You ought to have married me six or eight years before you did; it would have been easier for her. She simply cannot get used to your having a wife. 'My son' has 'lived and breathed and had his being' so many years for her sake alone, that to share him with another is a bitter experience. She doesn't love me one bit, Erskine, and it is not my fault. If I were an angel from heaven, it wouldn't make any difference, provided I had presumed to marry you. It makes it hard for both of us; and for that very reason it would be much better if you and I were in a little house of our own. She would get used to it much easier if she did not have me continually before her eyes."

If she could have seen distinctly the look of pain on her husband's face, as she got off these sentences with composed voice, it might have moved her to pity for him. When he spoke, his voice was almost sharp. "I am sure you are mistaken, Irene; utterly mistaken. My mother wanted me to marry; she has wanted it for years; at times she was actually troubled because I did not, and spoke of it very seriously."

Irene laughed lightly as she gave his arm some half-reproving, half-caressing pats.

"Blind as a bat, you are!" she said. "Despite all your supposed wisdom. On general principles your mother wanted you to marry, of course, because that is the proper thing for a man to do. But marriage in the abstract and marriage in the concrete are two very different matters. There! haven't I put that well? Those are lawyers' terms, aren't they? They sound learned, anyway."

He smiled in an absent-minded way at her folly. His thoughts were elsewhere. Something in the turn of her sentence had carried him suddenly back to a moon-lighted evening in which he had walked and talked with Alice Warder, and he could seem to hear her voice again as she said:—

"I know your mother loves me, Erskine, almost as she would a daughter; and I also know that she loves me a great deal better because her son is like a brother to me instead of being—something else." He remembered how he had puzzled over it all, and studied his mother's face, and half decided that Alice was right. Was Irene right, also? Was his mother grieved that he had married at all? Was it possible that she could have stooped to so small a feeling as jealousy!

His wife laid her head caressingly against his arm and said softly:—

"Don't worry about it, Erskine. We can't either of us help it now; and we must just make the best of it and do as well as we can."

For the first time in his life, as those low tremulously spoken words sounded in his ears, a feeling very like resentment toward his mother swelled in Erskine Burnham's heart, and a torrent of tenderness rushed over him toward the wife who had no one in all the world but himself. This was what she had often told him.

All things considered it is perhaps not strange that he did not visit his mother's room that evening.

It is true that when they went upstairs he paused before her door and listened, and told himself that she was asleep and he would not disturb her. But there had been nights before, many of them, in which he had waited at her door and listened, and murmured: "Mommie," and received a prompt invitation to enter. On this evening, though the hour was not late, he was not insistent. He made no attempt to knock or to speak. It was his concession to that new thought about her being an old woman. Or was it a slight concession, unawares, to that new feeling of resentment?

His mother, knowing nothing of what had been talked over in the moonlight, held her breath and waited. Of course Erskine would come to say good night. She forgot that she had wished he would not come! When his footsteps moved toward his own room, she waited a minute, then stepped into the hall.

"Erskine!" she said; but she said it very softly and he did not hear her. She could hear his voice. He was talking with his wife. The mother slipped softly back to her own room and locked her door. It was not late, and she and her son were only across a hall from each other; yet, for the first time in her life under like conditions, if she slept at all it must be without his good-night kiss. There is no true mother but will appreciate the situation. There are, it is true, mothers who are not accustomed to good-night kisses from their grown sons, and so would not miss them, but they are accustomed to a certain atmosphere, and they can understand what it would be like to be suddenly removed from it.

Mrs. Burnham went to her bed as usual, after a while, like the sensible woman that she was. That she did not go to sleep was not her fault, for she made earnest effort to do so. She told herself repeatedly and with a calmness which was itself unnatural, that nothing terrible had happened, and that she was above making herself miserable over trifles. Was her daughter-in-law's indifference to her only a trifle? She made a distinct pause over that word "indifference" and selected it with care; of course it was nothing more; and—yes, it was a trifle. How could one who knew her so little and had so little in common with her life be expected to be other than indifferent? Erskine had expected more, very much more, but Erskine was—was different from other people.

Then, suddenly, all her heart went out in a great swell of tenderness for Erskine. She did not stop to reason about it, she did not wait to ask herself why Erskine, who had everything, should be the subject of her shielding care; she simply took him metaphorically once more into her mother-arms and vowed to shield him from even a hint of solicitude on her account. She would rise above it all; she would treat Irene exactly as though she were at all times the loving and considerate daughter that Erskine believed she was; she would let him be blind to her faults, she would even help him to increased blindness. That was her work for him now; she would accept it and be diligent in it. The thought helped to quiet her, but it did not bring her sleep. She was broad staring awake. She told herself that sleep seemed an impossibility; she wondered curiously how she had ever slept.

A low murmur of talk came to her from the room across the hall. They were not sleeping, either. Could she have heard some of the talk in that room across the hall it would have made things plainer to her than they were.

"There is one thing, dear," Erskine Burnham was saying to his wife, "which we must look upon as settled. We can have no home apart from my mother's. You can plan for summer cottages if you will, and where you will, for a stay of a few weeks, but the real home must always be here. I have taken care of my mother, practically all my life; and now if she is, as you say, growing old, it is not the time to make any change."

"Not even though the change would be a benefit to her?" His wife intended her words to represent a playful sarcasm, but Erskine's face had clouded and he had answered quickly:

"No; not even under such an extraordinary supposition as that. Young as I was when my father died, he said that to me about my mother which has always made her seem to me as a trust; and I must be true to my trust in any case."

After a moment's constrained silence between them his face had cleared and he had laughed cheerfully.

"But we need not be so solemn over it, Irene. I know my mother, and I have no fears as to her wishes. Nothing that anybody could say would make me believe that she could be happier away from me than with me. I would almost not believe it if she said so herself. Quite, indeed. I should feel that she had over-persuaded herself in some spirit of sacrifice. There is material in my mother for martyrdom, Irene. It shall be your and my study to prevent her from indulging in it."

His wife made no attempt to reply. She was in some respects a wise woman and she understood that there was a time when silence was golden. When she spoke again, it was to ask if he did not think curtains lined with rose color would be an improvement on those now separating their dressing room from the main apartment.

CHAPTER XIV

THE GENERAL MANAGER

"Mother, don't you think that you are being rather hard on Irene to undertake to hold her to restrictions to which she has never been accustomed, and which to her seem narrow and unreasonable?"

Erskine Burnham had followed his mother to her room evidently with a view to speaking to her alone, his wife having gone on into her own room and closed the door. Even though she had not felt it in the tone of his voice, Mrs. Burnham would have known by her son's opening word that he was annoyed.

He rarely used the word "mother" when addressing her directly. As a rule the habits of his childhood prevailed, and "mamma" was the name in frequent use; or, oftener still perhaps, when they were quite alone, his special pet name for her, "mommie," came naturally to his lips. But of late she had heard, oftener than ever before, what was to him a colder term "Mother," and had learned to know what it meant.

She hesitated a moment before replying, and her hesitation seemed to irritate her son. He spoke quickly, with a note in his voice which she had never found in it before.

"I must confess, mother, that I am surprised and not a little disappointed at the course you are taking. When I brought Irene here, it was not only in the hope but the assured belief that I was bringing her to what she had never really had before—a mother,—and that you would become to her in time, what you have always been to me. I never for a moment dreamed of your standing coldly at one side, not only indifferent to her innocent devices for pleasure, but actually blocking her way! If I could have imagined such a condition of things, I would have better understood her feeling from the very first that we ought to go into a house of our own, where she would not feel herself an interloper."

Mrs. Burnham was ready then with her reply.

"Erskine, I do not think Irene could have understood me. I made no attempt to hold her to any restrictions. She asked a direct question about my own views, which, of course, I answered. But I ought not to have to explain to my son that I do not try to force my opinions upon any one."

He made a movement of impatience.

"That kind of thing is not necessary, mother, between us; but you know very well that there are ways of expressing one's opinions that effectually trammel others of the same household.

"The simple truth is that Irene has played cards, for amusement, in her own and her friends' parlors, ever since she was old enough to play games of any kind; and to her, our ideas concerning cards seem as absurd as though applied to tennis or golf. Personally, I see no reason why she should not continue to amuse herself in her own way. It is true I do not play cards; but she knows, what both you and I understand perfectly, that this is a concession on my part to the extreme views of my mother, who could hardly expect my wife to have exactly the same spirit. I have told Irene that out of deference to your feelings, I do not want her to entertain her friends with cards, in the parlors, but she certainly ought to be left free to do in her own rooms what she pleases."

At almost any other period in Mrs. Burnham's life, a formal and elaborate expression of her son's views upon any subject, given in a haughty and almost dictatorial tone, such as he was using, would have filled his mother with astonishment and pain. She was almost curiously interested in herself on discovering that she had passed that stage, and was occupying her mind for the moment with quite a different matter.

Why had Irene chosen just this line of attack? What did she hope to accomplish by such a singularly distorted representation of their talk together? It must have been sadly distorted to have moved Erskine to an exhibition of annoyance such as he had never before shown to her. Yet had he been present at the interview, his mother felt confident that it would not have disturbed him.

She went swiftly over the talk, in memory, while Erskine waited, and fingered the books and magazines on her table with the air of a nervous man who wanted to appear at ease. It had been a brief conversation, not significant at least to an observer, in any way. Irene had been looking over the mail, and had exclaimed at an invitation.

"The Wheelers are giving another card party; what indefatigable entertainers they are! it isn't a month since their last one. This time it is a very select few, in Mrs. Harry Wheeler's rooms. That is what Erskine and I must do, since you won't allow cards in the parlors. Have you really such queer notions, mother, as Erskine pretends?"

Mrs. Burnham remembered just how carefully she had watched her words, in reply.

"I don't play cards, Irene, if that is what you mean."

"Oh, I mean a great deal more than that. Erskine says you won't allow such wicked things in your part of the house. Is that so?"

"We have never had them in the house since Judge Burnham changed his views with regard to them."

"Oh, did he change? how curious, for a lawyer, too! I don't believe Erskine will get notional as he grows older. He isn't one of that kind." Whereupon the older woman had turned resolutely away, resolved to speak no more words on the subject unless they were spoken in Erskine's presence. It was this conversation, reported, that had brought her son to her in his new and lofty mood of guardian of his wife's liberties! Just as he tossed down the magazine with which he had been playing, with the air of one who meant to wait no longer, his mother spoke with gentle dignity.

"Erskine, of course your rooms are your own, to do with as you will. I made no restrictions and hinted at none. On my desk under the paper-weight is the quotation you wished looked up, and also the statistics about which you asked." Then she turned and passed out, to the hall.

All this was on a midsummer morning nearly three months removed from that moonlighted evening on which this mother had renewed her solemn pledge to be to her son and her son's wife all that they would let her be. In the face of steady resistance she had been fairly true to the pledge. It had now become quite plain to her that it was not chance, nor mere heedlessness, that was working against her, but that Mrs. Erskine Burnham meant to resist her, meant to look upon her as a force in her way, to be got rid of if possible; if not by persuading her son to leave her, then, perhaps by making her so uncomfortable that she would leave him. The plan was not succeeding. Ruth Erskine Burnham had lived through too many trying experiences before this time to be easily routed. She was in the home to which her husband had brought her as a bride, and she meant that nothing but a stern sense of duty should ever separate her from it.

Yet Mrs. Erskine Burnham, if she had but known it, had accomplished much. The mother no longer turned with a sickening pain from the thought of Erskine having other home than hers. There were times when she could almost have joined his wife in pleading for that "cunning little cottage." There were days wherein she told herself breathlessly and very secretly, that for Erskine to come home to her for a single half-hour, *alone*, would compensate for days of absence.

But if she had changed her point of view, so had Irene. His wife talked to him no more of a home by themselves. She was growing fond of the many-roomed, rambling old house whose utter abandonment to luxurious comfort was the talk and the pride of the neighborhood; and was the result of years of careful study on the part of a cultured woman accustomed to luxuries.

The new Mrs. Burnham developed an interest in the carefully-trained servants who had been a part of the establishment for so many years that they said "our" and "ours" in speaking of its belongings. She came to realize, at least in a measure, that servants like these were hard to secure, and harder to keep. She began also to like the comfort of proprietorship, without the accompanying sense of responsibility. The machinery of this house could move on steadily without break or jar, and without an hour of care or thought bestowed by her; yet her slightest order was obeyed promptly and skilfully.

Her orders were growing more and more frequent, and it was becoming increasingly apparent to those who had eyes to see that "young Mrs. Burnham," as some of them called her, was assuming the reins and being recognized as the head of the house.

Ellen, the maid who had been with Mrs. Burnham since Erskine's boyhood, and who was a rebel against other authority than hers, had openly rebelled, one day, and with blazing eyes that yet softened when the tears came, assured Ruth that she could not have two mistresses, especially when the one who wasn't mistress at all took pains to contradict the orders of the other; and if she had got to be ordered about all the time by Mrs. Erskine, the sooner she went, the better.

"Very well, Ellen," Mrs. Burnham had said, holding her tones to cold dignity. "I shall be sorry to part with you, but it is quite certain that so long as you remain in the house you must obey Mrs. Erskine Burnham's slightest wish. If you cannot do this, of course we must separate."

So Ellen went. In a perfect storm of tears and sobs and regrets, it is true; but she went. This arrangement pleased just one person. Erskine openly complained that her successor was not and never would be a circumstance to Ellen, and made his mother confess that she missed Ellen sorely, and asked her why, after being faithfully served for twenty years, she could not have borne with a few peculiarities. His mother was thankful that he did not insist upon knowing just what form her peculiarities took, and his wife's eyes sparkled. She had recognized Ellen from the first as an enemy, and had meant to be rid of her.

In short, Mrs. Erskine Burnham had settled down. She told her special friends with a cheerful sigh that she had sacrificed herself to her husband's mother, who was growing old and ought not to be burdened with the care of a house. So, much as they would have enjoyed a home to themselves, they had determined to stay where they were.

So steady and skilful were this General's movements toward supremacy that Ruth herself scarcely realized the fact that when she gave an order in these days, she did it hesitatingly, often adding as an afterthought:—

"Let that be the arrangement, unless Mrs. Erskine Burnham has other plans; if she has, remember, I am not at all particular." And she was never surprised any more by the discovery that there was a totally different arrangement. It was therefore in exceeding bad taste for Erskine Burnham to present himself to his mother in lofty mood and threaten her with a separate home for himself and wife. One of his mother's chief concerns at this time was to shield him from the knowledge that she sometimes prayed for solitude as the safest way out of the thickening clouds. That he did not realize any of this can only be attributed to the condition of which his wife often accused him; namely, that he was "as blind as a bat."

The proposed card-party at the Wheelers' came off in due time, both Irene and Erskine being among the guests. Within the month, Irene gave what the next morning's social column called "an exclusive and charming affair" of the same kind in her own rooms. It is true that she had schemed for a different result from this. She had meant to give a card party on a larger scale. Her careful rendering to her husband of the talk about restrictions had been intended to call from him the declaration that the parlors were as much theirs as his mother's, and that if she chose to play cards in them, no one should disturb her. She miscalculated. Instead of this, his deliverance was more emphatic than ever before.

"Remember, Irene, that my mother's sense of the fitness of things must never be infringed upon in any way that can disturb her. Our rooms are our castle and we will do with them as we choose; but no cards downstairs, remember, or anything else that will disturb her—"

"Prejudices!" his wife had interrupted in a manner that she had intended should be playful; but he had spoken quickly and with dignity.

"Very well, prejudices if you will. I was going to say traditions; but if you prefer the other word, it doesn't matter. Whatever they are, they are to be respected."

So Irene, having learned some time before this that such deliverances on the part of her husband were to be respected, took care to keep within the limits of their own rooms. But she took a little private revenge upon her mother-in-law, given in that especially trying would-be playful tone of hers.

"I am sorry that your prejudices—oh, no, pardon me, I mean your traditions—will not allow you to meet our guests this evening; but I suppose that would be wicked, too? Pray how is your absence to be accounted for? Must I trump up an attack of mumps, or dumps, or what?"

As for Erskine, he remained happily unconscious of all these small stings. He was much engrossed in business cares, and left home early and returned late, so that in reality he knew little of what took place during his absence. That all was not quite as he had hoped between his wife and his mother he could not help seeing, but he told himself that he must not be unreasonable; that two people as differently reared as they had been must have time to assimilate; probably they were doing very well, and it was he who was struggling for the impossible. So he straightway put aside and forgot the words of dignified reproach that he had addressed to his mother, and she became "mommie" again, and always his second kiss of greeting was for her. And the mother during these days thanked God that she was able to hide her disappointment and her pain, and meet him always with a smile.

CHAPTER XV

LOOKING BACKWARD

Mrs. Burnham came into the room with the air of one in doubt as to whom she was to meet. Probably it was some one whom she ought to recognize; and if she did not, it would be embarrassing.

"She would not give any name, ma'am," the maid had said. "She says she is an old acquaintance, and she wants to see if you will know her."

But Ruth did not know her. She had a fairly good memory for faces, yet as she advanced she told herself that this woman was mistaken in the person. There must be some other Mrs. Burnham whom she had known. But the lady who arose to meet her was apparently not disappointed, and was at her ease and eager.

"I hope you will forgive this intrusion, dear Mrs. Burnham. I could not resist the temptation to see if you had a lingering remembrance of the silly girl to whom you were once very good. It was foolish in me to fancy such a thing. I was just at the age to change much in a few years."

Mrs. Burnham was studying the fair and singularly reposeful face; taking in unconsciously at the same time the grace of the whole perfect picture, hair and eyes and dress and form, all in exquisite harmony.

"A perfect lady!" she told herself. "How rarely the phrase fits, and how exactly it applies here. Yet where before have I seen that face?" She was back in the old college town, away back, among the early years. What had suddenly taken her there? She was—this was not!—

"You are surely not," she began, and hesitated.

The fair face broke into rippling smiles.

"Yes," she said, "I am. Do you really remember Mamie Parker just a little bit?"

"I remember her, perfectly, but—"

"But I am changed? Yes, fifteen years make changes in young people. I was not much over eighteen then, and very young for my years. But you have not changed, Mrs. Burnham; I should have known you anywhere. Perhaps that is partly because I have carried you around in my heart all these years. It must be beautiful to be able to do for girls all that you did for me. If I could do it, if I could be to one young girl what you became to me, I should know that I had not lived in vain."

Mrs. Burnham was almost embarrassed. What did the woman mean!

"My dear friend, I do not understand," she said. "There must be some strange mistake. Have you not confused me with some other friend? What could I possibly have done for you in the few, the very few times that we met?"

Her caller laughed a low, sweet laugh, and as she spoke made an inimitable gesture with her hands that emphasized her words.

"You did everything for me," she said. "Everything! You gave me ideals, you refashioned my entire view of life; you were the means God used to breathe into me the spirit of real living. May I claim a little of your time to-day, and tell you just a little bit of the story, for a purpose? I had only this one day here, and I felt compelled to intrude without permission."

Mrs. Burnham heard her almost as one in a dream. She was struggling with her memories; trying to find in this fair vision, with her refined voice and dress, and cultured language and perfect manner, a trace of the singularly ill-bred, loud-voiced, outspoken Mamie Parker. How had such a transformation been possible?

"You have but one day here?" she said, remembering her duties as hostess. "What does that mean, please? Are you staying in the neighborhood, and will you not come to us for a visit?"

"Thank you, I cannot. I am about to leave the country, and am paying a very brief farewell visit to my friends the Carletons, who are at their summer home in Carleton Park. I have broken away to-day from the numerous engagements they have made for me, and run over here alone, in the hope of securing an interview with you; I have been planning for this a long time. Dear Mrs. Burnham, may I claim the privilege of an old acquaintance and ask to see you quite alone where there will be no danger of interruption? I want to talk fast and put a good deal into a small space, because my own time is so limited, and I do not want to take more of yours than is necessary. I have a purpose which I think, and I hope you will think, justifies my intrusion."

Still as one under a spell, Mrs. Burnham led the way to her private sitting room and established her guest in an easy-chair, from which she looked about her eagerly.

"This is charming!" she said. "I remember your other room perfectly, Mrs. Burnham, and I think I should have recognized this as yours without being told. Rooms have a great deal of individuality, don't you think? Do you remember that parlor in the house where my dear brother Jim boarded? No, of course you don't, but I do, and I thought it very elegant until I was admitted to yours. May I tell you very briefly just a little of what you have been to me? That winter when I met you and your son—it was my first flight from home. I was young, you remember, and unformed in every way; I was, in fact, a young simpleton, with as little knowledge of the world as a girl reared as I had been would be likely to have. Up to that time I had cared very little for study of any kind. My opportunities were limited enough, but I had made very poor use even of them. My chief idea of a successful life was to marry young, some one who had plenty of money and who would be good to me and let me have a good time. I was what is called a popular girl in the little country village where I lived, and was much sought after because I was what they called 'lively' and could 'make things go.' When my brother invited me to visit him, I went in a flutter of anticipation. I had grown rather tired of the country boys by whom I was surrounded, and I believed that the fateful hour of my life had at last arrived."

She stopped to laugh at her folly; then said, apologetically, "I am giving you the whole crude story, but it is for a purpose. I can laugh at that silly girl, now, but there have been times in my life when I cried over her. She knew so little in any direction, and there were such possibilities of danger, such imminent fear of a wrecked life. She needed a friend, as every girl does; and I can never cease to be thankful that she found one.

"Mrs. Burnham, I presume you have never understood what you did for me by calling on me and inviting me to your home, and opening to me a new world. We were very plain people with limited opportunities in every way, and my father's sudden financial success but a short time before had almost turned our heads; mine, at least, so that I was ready to be injured in many ways. Do you remember me sufficiently to realize the possibilities?"

"I remember you perfectly, my dear," said her puzzled and charmed hostess. "But I do not understand in the least why you think, or how you can think, that I—"

Miss Parker interrupted her eagerly.

"Mrs. Burnham, you were a revelation to me. I had never before come into close contact with a perfect lady. At first, I was afraid of you, which was a new feeling to me, and in itself good for me; and then, for a while, I hated you; I thought that you came between me and some of my ambitions, I called them; now I know that they were utter follies." There was a heightened color on the fair face, and for a moment her eyes drooped. Then she laughed softly at her girlish follies.

"I recovered from them," she said briskly, "and enshrined you in my heart; made you my idol, and, better than that, my ideal. I had discovered from you what woman was meant to be.

"And, dear friend, I learned another lesson also, deeper and more far-reaching than any other. Up to that time I had always thought of religion as a very serious but somewhat tiresome experience that came to the old, or the sick, after they had got all they could out of life. It was Mr. Erskine Burnham who first showed me my utter misunderstanding of the whole matter. I do not know that he understood at the time what he was doing for me, but he gave me a hint of what Jesus Christ was, not only to you, but to himself, a young man in the first flush of youthful successes. I could not understand it at first, and it half vexed me by its strangeness; but there came a time in my life, afterward, when I was disappointed in all my plans, and unhappy. Then I thought of what had been said to me about Christ, and, almost as an experiment, I tried it. Mrs. Burnham, He stooped even to that low plane and revealed Himself to me, and I have counted it all joy to love and serve Him ever since And for this, too, I have to thank you and yours."

"My dear," said Mrs. Burnham, the tears shining in her eyes, "thank you; thank you very much; it is beautiful, although I do not understand it in the least—my part of it; I did nothing, *nothing*! I thought of it afterward with deep regret; what I might have said, and did not."

"You did better than that," said Miss Parker, gently. "You *lived*. But now, believe me, I did not intrude upon your leisure merely to talk about myself. I wanted you to understand the possibility of saving a girl's life to her, because—"

She broke off suddenly to introduce what seemed an entirely irrelevant topic.

"Mrs. Burnham, I saw your daughter down town to-day, for a moment. I did not know her, and should not have imagined it was she, if I had not been told. She has changed very much since I saw her last."

"Were you acquainted with my daughter, Miss Parker? Is it Miss Parker, now? I am taking a great deal for granted."

"Oh, yes; I am still 'Miss Parker'; and expect so to remain. No, I cannot be said to have been acquainted with your daughter, though I knew of her; knew a great deal about her, in fact, when she was a young girl. They were the one great family in our little town, Mrs. Burnham—her uncle's family, with whom she lived; they had a fine old place, three miles from the station, and your daughter used to drive to and from the train in what seemed to me then like royal state. I watched her on all possible occasions and admired and envied her always, though I do not suppose she ever heard of me in her life. She was not so very much older than I, only three years, but I remember I was still counted as a little girl when her sudden marriage took us all by surprise and overwhelmed me with jealous envy."

"Pardon me," said Mrs. Burnham, sitting erect and looking not only perplexed but troubled. "I am somewhat dazed by this sudden return to the long ago, and I must be getting things mixed. I thought until a moment ago that you were speaking of my son's wife."

"So I am, Mrs. Burnham. She was Irene Carpenter when I was at the envious stage; and she became Irene Somerville in the autumn that I was fourteen. I shall never forget the vision I had of her on her wedding day. It was at the station and the train was late, so I had ample opportunity to admire and make note of and sigh over the glories of her bridal travelling outfit. Although I was only fourteen and accounted a little girl by others, I by no means considered myself such; and the wild and foolish visions I had already indulged with regard to my own splendid future, make me blush even now to recall. Girls are so foolish, Mrs. Burnham, and so easily led! If there were only always some wise, sweet one at hand to lead them safely!"

Mrs. Burnham arose suddenly and closed both of the doors opening into the hall. She knew that her son was in town, and that his wife had gone by appointment to meet him there; but it seemed to her that such extraordinary talk as this must be closed away from the hall through which they must presently pass. What could this woman mean? She but fourteen when Irene was married? Yet she was at least eighteen when she visited her brother in the college town, and that was nearly fifteen years ago! Irene a married woman seventeen or eighteen years ago! She could see a line in that fateful foreign letter from her son as distinctly as though she were reading it from the page, 'although she is so young, barely twenty-six, she has,' etc. Of course there was some absurd mistake. Irene could not have been more than eight or nine years old at that time when some one whom Mamie Parker fancied was the same person, was married.

"How old do you think my son's wife is?" she asked suddenly. A few statistics, such as she could furnish, would help to clear up this absurd blunder.

"Oh, I know exactly. I have a vivid recollection of the wonderful doings there were in honor of her sixteenth birthday. It happens that our birthdays fall on the very same month and day, the eleventh of November; so that on the day she was sixteen, I was thirteen. I remember how sorely I took to heart the contrast between the two celebrations. It was before my father had made his successes, and we were much straitened at the time."

Mrs. Burnham's pulses were athrob with her effort at self-control. It was true that Irene's birthday fell on the eleventh of November. It had been celebrated with much circumstance that very season; but instead of its being her twenty-seventh, Miss Parker's story would make it her thirty-seventh! That was absurd! And yet—how often had the thought occurred to her that Irene looked much older than her years! Her maiden name, too, was Carpenter, and her married name had been Somerville. Still, there must have been a cousin, or some near relative of the same name. It was an insult to the family to suppose for a moment that Irene could deceive her husband as to her exact age!

And then, Miss Parker made a remark before which all else that she had said sank into insignificance.

"Mrs. Erskine Burnham as I saw her to-day, seemed to me a very beautiful woman, though she does not look in the least as she did when a girl. But her daughter does. At seventeen, Maybelle is really the image of what her mother was at that age. I wish so much that you could see her just now, in all her girlish beauty."

CHAPTER XVI

FOR MAYBELLE'S SAKE

Mrs. Burnham stared at her guest with a look that was not simply bewildered, it was frightened. What *could* the woman mean!

"Who is Maybelle?" she spoke the words almost fiercely; but her bewildered guest kept her voice low and gentle.

"I must ask you to forgive me, dear Mrs. Burnham. I know that my words must seem very intrusive, perhaps unpardonable; but indeed I thought I was doing right, and it is for Maybelle's sake alone that I have ventured."

The repetition of that name seemed to irritate Mrs. Burnham. "Will you tell me who she is?" she asked imperiously.

"My friend, is it possible that you do not understand? or do you mean that it is your pleasure to ignore her? Of course you know that there was a child, a little daughter?"

"Whose daughter?"

"The daughter of the lady who afterward became your son's wife." Mamie Parker was growing indignant. However painful the subject might be to Erskine Burnham's mother, certainly the child was not to blame; nor could she, who was apparently the child's only friend, be quite beyond the line of toleration because she had ventured to try to awaken sympathy for her in the heart of a woman who certainly had reason to be interested in her story. Whatever had taken place to hurt them, surely the child ought not to suffer for it.

Mrs. Burnham struggled for composure. Even at that moment the thought uppermost in her mind was that she must shield her son; yes, and her son's wife, if possible. Something terrible had happened somewhere. A confusion of persons, probably, or—she could not think clearly, but there was something, some story, which she must ferret out to its foundation, and must at the same time hide from her son, unless—she would not complete that thought.

"You will forgive me I am sure for not being able to quite follow you." Her voice though cold and constrained was again self-controlled, and she even forced a smile.

"I think I must be unusually stupid this afternoon. There is some misunderstanding that I do not yet quite grasp. This—child? is she?—of whom you are speaking, she is not,—not alone in the world? Why does she especially need a friend?"

Miss Parker's bewildered look returned; they were not getting on. She hesitated a moment, then said firmly:—

"Her father is still living, Mrs. Burnham, but he is seriously ill, and she will soon be quite alone. At the best, the father, as you probably know, is not the kind of friend that one would choose for a young girl, though he has tried to be good to her, in his way."

Mrs. Burnham suddenly leaned forward and grasped the arm of her caller, and spoke with more vehemence than before, though this time her voice was low.

"What do you mean?" she said. "Isn't it possible for you to speak plainly? How should I know what you are talking about? Her '*father*'! Whose father? Who is she? What is she? And what are either of them to me? I do not understand in the least."

"Mrs. Burnham," said Mamie Parker, sitting erect, with a bright spot of color burning on either cheek, "do you mean me to understand that you are ignorant of the fact that your son married a woman who was divorced from her first husband in less than three years after her marriage, and left with him a little child not six months old, who is now a young woman?"

It was well for Ruth Burnham that she could do just what she did at that moment, although it was for her an unprecedented thing. Every vestige of self-control gave way; she covered her face with her hands and broke into a perfect passion of weeping. Not the slow quiet weeping natural to a woman of her years, but a tempestuous outburst that shook her whole frame with its force.

The distressed witness of this misery sat for a moment irresolute, then she came softly to Mrs. Burnham's side and touched the bowed head with a gentle, caressing movement such as one might give to a little child, and spoke low and tenderly.

"Dear friend, forgive me; I am so sorry! I did not for a moment imagine that I was telling you anything that you did not already know. I felt my rudeness in coming to you with matters about which I was supposed to know nothing, but I thought you had, perhaps, been misinformed, and that if you could once understand, poor Maybelle would—"

Then she stopped. There seemed nothing that she could say, while that bowed form was shaken with emotion.

It passed in a few minutes. The woman who was accustomed to exercising self-control could not long be under the dominion of her emotions. She raised her head and spoke quietly.

"I hope you can forgive me for making your errand so hard. My nerves do not often play me false in this way. You did right to come to me. Now, may I ask you to begin at the beginning and tell me all that you know about this matter? You are correct in your inference; there are some things that I have not understood."

It was rather a long story. Miss Parker, feeling herself dismissed from the place of comforter, went back to her chair and tried to obey directions and begin at the beginning; held closely to her work by keen incisive questions.

Yes, she had known Mr. Somerville before he married Irene Carpenter; or rather, she had known of him, as girls in country villages always knew about any people who came their way. He was an Englishman of good family, a younger son she had heard, though just what significance attached to that, she had not understood at the time. He had the name among the young people of being wild. They had heard that Irene's uncle disapproved of the match, and threatened to lock her up if she tried to have anything more to do with him. She, Mamie, knowing something of Irene's temperament, had always thought that this was what precipitated matters. She knew that Irene was married during her uncle's absence from home, and that there were some exciting scenes after his return.

The newly married couple went abroad very soon, but they stayed only a short time, and rumor had it that they quarrelled with Mr. Somerville's family and were not invited to stay longer. After that, they lived in New York in good style for a few months, and Mrs. Somerville went into society and was said to be very gay. Yes, she had heard a number of things about that winter, but the stories were contradictory and not reliable. Oh, yes, some of the stories were ugly, but gossip was always that; she could not go into details about that period; there was nothing reliable, and nothing that she cared to talk of. It was when the child was about six months old that her father and mother quarrelled and separated. Oh, yes, there was a divorce; she had made an effort to discover the truth about that, for the little girl's sake, and was sure of it. The mother went abroad with some friends and remained there for several years.

She had heard that she served as nursery governess in an American family who were living in Berlin, for the purpose of educating their sons. She knew that this was so, because she had met one of the sons, later, and he had told her about her; she went by the name of Carpenter—Miss Carpenter. After leaving that family, Miss Parker did not know what she had done; knew nothing of her for several years. Then she came back to the old homestead and lived there for some time with a maiden aunt who was all that was left of the family, and was an invalid. She had heard that Irene was not contented there, and knew that after a time she and the invalid aunt went abroad. It was while they were living in Paris that Mr. Erskine Burnham met them. Miss Parker had heard of his marriage almost immediately, because she had friends in Paris at the time who had met both Miss Carpenter and Mr. Burnham. Indeed all these items had come to her from time to time by a series of accidents or happenings. She had admired Irene Carpenter at a distance as a girl, and that had made it seem natural to inquire after her, as opportunity offered.

Oh, yes, she had known more or less of Mr. Somerville during all these years. He had remained in New York much of the time; though he had twice crossed the ocean, and once had gone to the Pacific coast, always taking Maybelle with him.

Her first meeting with him in New York had been at the studio of an artist friend for whom he was doing some work. She had seen the child first, a beautiful little girl who had charmed her; then he had come in and she had been shocked on recognizing him, to think that she must have been playing with Irene's little girl. He was an amateur artist, never working steadily enough to make a success for himself, but doing very good work, and earning his living in that way. Oh, yes, and in music also, it was much the same story. He was in frail health, was unsteady, and could not be depended upon; but could play divinely when he chose, and on occasion earned money in that way, playing the violin, or piano, or organ. He always took the child with him and seemed devoted to her, never speaking other than gently to her; and he seemed to try to train her wisely. It was pathetic to see him making an effort to fill the place of both father and mother. Oh, yes, she saw a great deal of him, or rather, of the child, in whom she had been singularly interested from the first, of course.

Her father had moved his family to New York about that time, and she was in school as a real student for the first time in her life. But she gave most of her leisure to the little Maybelle. Her mother became very fond of the child, and after a while they kept her with them much of the time, to the great comfort of the father, who owned that he often had to go to places where he did not like to take the baby.

Yes, she came to know the father quite well. Maybelle had been allowed always to suppose that her mother was dead. She never questioned, having taken that for granted. Her father, however, during one of his ill turns when he thought he was going to die, had revealed to her mother and herself the sorrowful story of his life, and had shown them Irene's picture. Miss Parker believed that he had a faint hope that when he was gone, the mother would see that their child was cared for.

Yes, he had told her only the truth. She had taken pains to corroborate that part of the story which she had not known before; had gone herself to see the woman with whom they had been boarding when his wife left him. The woman said that Mr. Somerville had come home intoxicated the night before; "not bad," the poor creature said, "only silly," but the next morning he and his wife had quarrelled, and she went away and never came back.

Being closely cross-questioned Miss Parker added, that the woman had further given it as her opinion that Mrs. Somerville meant all along to be "that shabby," and was only waiting for a good excuse; that she didn't care a "toss up" for her husband, nor the baby neither, though he "just doted" on both of them.

Yes, Miss Parker had talked with him more than once about his sad, wrecked life. She considered him a weak man rather than an intentionally wicked one. He had never spoken ill of his wife. He said frankly that their marriage was a mistake, and that it was his fault.

Irene was too young to be married to any one, but he was fascinated with her, and determined to win her at any cost. The truth was, he said, he cheated her. She was tired of her humdrum life in that dull village where her people spent much of their time; she longed to get away, to travel; above all she wanted to go abroad. She had inferred that, because he was from across the water, and belonged to an old family and could show her pictures of a fine old estate that had been in the family for generations, he was therefore wealthy; and he had let her think so. It was the discovery that she had been deceived in this respect, he said, that made her begin to really dislike him, he thought, instead of being simply indifferent to him, as she had been at first. He made no pretence of believing that she had ever loved him.

No, he could not say that she had ever seemed to love the child. At first she had been angry about it, looking at it merely in the light of a hindrance to the few pleasures she could have, cooped up in a boarding-house; and the strongest feeling she had ever shown for the helpless little creature was toleration.

When they quarrelled, and she threatened to leave him, he had told her that she could not take the baby, and she had replied that it was the last thing she wanted to do. But he had not believed her; he had not thought such a state of mind possible. The little thing, he said, had so wound itself about his heart that the thought of living without her was torture; and he had believed that the mother felt the same, but did not choose to own it. He had taken the baby to a friend of his for the day, and felt secure all day in the thought that Irene would be drawn homeward from wherever she went that morning, by the memory of the clinging arms and smiling baby face. But she had never come back.

At this point Ruth Erskine Burnham lost her studied self-control and said the only unguarded word that she had spoken since the interview began.

"That is monstrous! I cannot credit it. The woman who would do such a thing as that would be a fiend!"

"Oh, no!" said Miss Parker, startled at the feeling she had roused, and remembering that they were speaking of this woman's son's wife. "He did not feel it so, the father. He made excuses for her. Even while he was telling me the story, he stopped to say simply:—

"'You see I didn't stop to consider that she disliked and despised me, by this time, and that the baby was my child; that made all the difference in the world;' and of course it would, Mrs. Burnham."

CHAPTER XVII

BUILT ON THE SAND

"Your mother has had a very special guest of some sort and was closeted with her all the afternoon; I suppose she is tired out; she looked so when I met her in the hall."

This was Mrs. Erskine Burnham's explanation to her husband of his mother's absence from the dinner table. They had waited for her a few minutes, then sent a maid to her room, who had reported that Mrs. Burnham was tired and did not care for dinner.

Erskine, on hearing it, had made a movement to rise, a troubled look on his face, and then had waited for his wife's word.

"A guest in her own room? That is unusual for mother, isn't it? Who was it?"

"How should I know? I wasn't enlightened. When I reached home soon after luncheon, I asked Nannie who had been here, and among others she mentioned a young lady who had asked very particularly to see 'Madame Burnham,' and said that after a while she took the lady to her own sitting room, and she was there yet. She left but a few minutes before you came, a very stylish-looking person, indeed, and quite young. It is fortunate that she did not stay for dinner, as I supposed she would, having spent the day, or I might have been seized with a fit of jealousy."

"Did you say my mother looked worn? Were you in her room?"

"No, indeed! I did not presume; I all but ran against her in the hall, and thought she looked older than usual."

"She may have had some unpleasant news; I think I will run up and see her."

"Don't, Erskine! I am sure you annoy your mother by such watchfulness. Old people don't like that sort of care, it seems to them like spying upon their movements; they want a chance to do as they please. I found that out from auntie; she seemed really annoyed when I questioned her about her movements. She wanted to be left to come to her dinner, or stay away, as she pleased; and your mother is just like her."

Erskine opened his lips to speak, then closed them again. He was on the verge of saying that he could not think of two people more unlike than his mother and her aunt; then it occurred to him that to make a remark so manifestly in favor of his own relative would hardly be courteous. Of course Irene thought of her aunt much as he did of his mother, and besides, the aunt was gone.

But he did not go up to his mother. It is true that he told his wife, presently, that he could not think for a moment that his care of and solicitude for his mother would ever look to her like espionage; they understood each other too well for that; but he spoke in a troubled tone. Despite this perfect understanding, his wife's constancy to the belief that his mother was growing old, and more or less feeble, and whimsical, as she believed old people always did, was having its effect upon him; he was beginning to feel at times that perhaps he did not understand his mother, after all.

It was well for his peace of mind that he did not go to her just then; for the first time in his life he would have been refused admittance to his mother's room. Ruth Erskine Burnham had shut herself away as much as she could from her outside world, and was fighting the battle of her life. A wild temptation was upon her, so strong that in its first strength she could not have resisted it, had she tried, and she did not try. It was so transformed that it did not appear to her as a temptation, but as a duty. Erskine's wife had deceived him; not once, in a crucial moment, but steadily, deliberately, continuously. Not only had she posed for him as a widow, but she had given him vivid pictures of her girlish desolation in her widowhood. His mother knew this, for Erskine had reproduced some of them in a few delicate touches, with the evident object of awakening in her a tender sympathy for one who, though so young, had suffered much.

"Young!" indeed! she had even stooped to the low and petty deception of making herself out to be much younger than she was! could an honorable man condone such small and unnecessary meannesses as that? Especially in his wife! And Erskine was married to her. Erskine of all men in the world the husband of a divorced woman! And he was on record in the public journals as one who had denounced with no gentle tongue the whole system of legal divorce as permitted in this country; he had characterized it as unrighteous and infamous. Young as he was, he had made himself felt in legal circles along this very line, and was recognized as a strong advocate for better laws and purer living.

So pronounced had he been on this whole subject that certain of his brother lawyers who, in the main, agreed with his views, did not hesitate to tell him that he was too severe, and was trying to accomplish the impossible. His mother, in the light of her recently acquired knowledge, laughed, a cruel laugh, then shivered and turned pale over the memory of a recent conversation which had now grown significant.

The pastor of their church, Mr. Conway's successor, was dining with them, and the talk had turned for a moment on the recent marriage of one of the parties in a famous divorce suit. Erskine had declared that if he were a clergyman, he should consider it his privilege as well as duty to anticipate the law that was surely coming and refuse to perform the marriage ceremony for a divorced person.

"Oh, now, brother Burnham," the clergyman had said, good naturedly, after a brief, keen argument on both sides: "Don't you really draw the lines too closely? You are not reasonable. Do you think he is, Mrs. Burnham?"—the appeal was to Erskine's wife— "You see you have made no allowance for accidents, or misunderstandings of any sort. What would you have a poor woman do who was caught as an acquaintance of mine was, a year or so ago? She married a divorced man without having the remotest idea that he had ever been married before, and did not discover it until six months afterward. Where would those sweeping assertions you have been making place her?"

Erskine had not smiled as he replied:—

"I was not speaking, of course, of people who had been the victims of cruel deception; certainly if I believed in divorce, I should consider that the woman you mention had sufficient cause."

"Because she had been deceived!"

"For just that reason. At least it must be terrible for a woman to spend her life with a man whose word she cannot trust. I should think it would be just ground for separation if anything is."

His mother recalled not only the energy of his tones, but the suddenness with which his wife introduced another topic.

Then there flashed upon her the memory of the clergyman's next remark, addressed to her:—

"Mrs. Burnham, is your daughter always as pale as she is to-day, or has our near approach to a quarrel, just now, frightened her?" Whereupon the color had flamed into Irene's face until her very forehead was flushed; and Erskine, looking at her, had said gayly:—

"My wife always blushes when she is the subject of conversation." What terrible significance attached to all these trifles now!

But, worse than all else, the woman had deserted and disowned her own child! So impossibly preposterous did this seem to Erskine Burnham's mother, that although she had detained her guest until a late hour, and questioned and cross-questioned, and insisted upon yet more proof, and been shown that there was not a possibility of error, she still shrank from it as something that could not be.

"Can a mother forget her child?" It was the question of inspiration, designed to show the almost impossibility of such a thing; yet inspiration had answered, "Yes, she may!" and here, under their own roof, was a living proof of its truth.

"*How* could she! How *could* she!" The mother-nature continually went back to that awful question. Suppose she had not? Suppose she had taken the child away with her, and mothered it all these years, and, at last, Erskine had married her? Then he would have stood in the place of father to that girl, and she would have been taught to call him so! His poor mother shivered as though in an ague chill as the strange, and to her appalling, details of this life-tragedy pressed upon her. A tragedy all the more terrible and bewildering because they had been—some of them—living it unawares.

The possibility that Erskine might have knowledge of this appalling story did not, even for a moment, occur to his mother. She knew him too well for that. Erskine had been deceived, fearfully deceived! not only in great and terrible ways, as one under awful provocation, but in petty details,—as to her age, for instance; and that this was merely an instance, Ruth knew only too well.

By slow degrees the conviction had been forced upon this truth-loving woman that she had for a daughter one to whom the truth was as a trifle to be trampled upon a dozen times a day if the fancy seized her.

Numberless instances of this had been thrust upon a close observer. "Yes," she would say unhesitatingly and unblushingly to Erskine, when his mother knew that "No" would have been the truth. Even the servants had learned to smile over this peculiarity in their young mistress, and to make efforts to have witnesses for any of her orders that were important. With the outside world she was so unpardonably careless of her word that Mrs. Burnham was almost growing used to apologizing for and blushing over her daughter's society inaccuracies.

Given a woman like Ruth Erskine Burnham, belonging to a family in whom, generations back, there had been martyrs for the truth's sake, trained from her very babyhood to despise every false way, self-trained, through the years, to hold with almost painful insistence to whatever she had seemed to promise, perhaps no other fault would have been harder to condone in others. She was still struggling to try to love her daughter-in-law, but she knew that she had ceased to respect her.

It was this condition of things which had made it possible for her to credit Miss Parker's story. Since Irene's moral twist with regard to truth was most apparent, why should she be expected to spurn the thought of other immoralities?

It was while Ruth Burnham was at this stage of her mental confusion that the temptation of her life came to her, clad in the white robes of truth and honor. It came, of course, by way of Erskine. He must know the whole blighting story and must know it at once. He must be told that the woman whom he had blessed with his love and whom he was tenderly sheltering from a rude world was a woman who could trample upon marriage vows, desert her first-born child, and lie about it all in a colossal manner; not only once, at first, but through the years! The whole fearful structure of Erskine's later life, built as it was upon falsehood, must be made to tumble about him in ruins. What a cruel thing! Erskine, the soul of honor, with as keen a love for truth as it was possible for human being to have, must, in spite of himself, be involved in the meshes of this false and cruel life! And yet, underneath the groan which she had for his ruined home and his ruined hopes, was a faint little thrill of exultation.

When Erskine must cease to respect his wife, he could not continue to love her with the kind of love that he was giving to her now. At the best it could be only a pitying, protecting love, and there was a sense in which she, his mother, would have him back again, at least to a degree. No one knew better than herself that there was a sense in which she had lost him.

What would he be likely to do? Irene was his wife, and he would do his duty at whatever cost, but just what was his duty? She tried to settle it for him. There was the child, the young woman rather, Irene's daughter. Would he not insist that the mother should do her tardy duty toward the child? But what was the duty of such a mother toward such a child? And how could anything be arranged for now, under such strange, such startling circumstances? She did not know. She could not plan, could not think; Erskine would have to do the thinking; but in the meantime, where would a boy, trained as he had been, turn naturally for sympathy but to his mother? She would have him again! She exulted in the thought; even then, in her first recoil from sin and its consequences, she exulted.

And then—just in that moment of exultation—she began to realize what she was doing, and a kind of terror of herself came upon her. Was it possible that she was really that despicable thing, a creature so full of self, and selfish loves, as to be able to thrill with joy, in the very midst of a ruin that involved her best and dearest, merely because out of it she was to gain something?

It was a terrible night. Mrs. Burnham kept her door close locked, though Erskine came once, and again, to seek admittance and went away puzzled and pained: locked out from his mother's room for the first time. She called out to him, trying to speak reassuringly, that she was not ill, only unusually tired; she was in bed, and did not feel equal to getting up to let him in.

"But, mommie," he said, "I did not know that you ever locked your door at night—not when we are together. What if you should be ill in the night?"

She would not be ill, she told him, and she really could not get up now and unlock the door.

She knew that he went away with an anxious heart, and that he came on tiptoe several times during the night and listened; and she hated herself for her apparent selfishness. But she could not let him in, she was not ready yet for the questions he would be sure to ask. She had not been able to plan how to make known to him her terrible secret.

CHAPTER XVIII

JUSTICE OR MERCY?

It was just as the silver-tongued clock on her mantel was tolling one, that the suggestion was suddenly made to Ruth Erskine Burnham that she was planning wickedness. Instead of trying to arrange how to break the dreadful news to Erskine, ought she not to be planning how to avoid having him know anything about it? Two very unreconcilable statements were in her mind clamoring to be heard.

"Of course she must tell him!" "No, she must *not* tell him!" "He ought to be told!" "He ought *not* to be told!" These in varying forms repeated themselves in her brain until she was bewildered. And the contradictory argument continued:—

"That girl, that forsaken, disowned girl—justice to her demanded the telling." "Justice did no such thing!" "But Irene was her mother, and had duties toward her that could not be ignored." "Irene was her mother only in name; there was no sense in which she could, even though she wished to do so, take the place of mother to her now." "Do not you know," continued that other voice speaking to the stricken woman, "do not you feel sure that for a young girl to be brought under the direction and daily influence of such a woman as Irene, would be almost the worst fate that could befall her?" "But Erskine has a duty toward her; he ought—" "Erskine *cannot*! you know he cannot. Have you not daily proof of the limit of his influence over Irene? Do you not know to your grief that in some matters she dominates him?"

"But Erskine ought to know the kind of woman that he is harboring. It is horrible to have him go on loving and trusting her!"

"Such knowledge coming to Erskine now, could work only harm. He has done no wrong; his conscience is clear, his hands are clean. Simply to reveal to him the former sins of the woman he has promised to love and cherish, would be to plunge him into depths of misery, without accomplishing anything for either the girl or his wife."

"But Irene ought to be exposed; she ought to repent, and confess her sin; it is monstrous to go on helping her to cover it!"

"You have nothing to do with Irene's 'oughts.' You cannot make her either confess or repent. To 'cover' her sin, as you call it, will not change the moral conditions for her in any way, it will simply bring unutterable pain and shame upon your son."

"But ought not sin to be exposed?"

"Not always. Sometimes to cover sin is God-like. Think, if you can, of one helpful, hopeful result which might reasonably be expected to follow such an exposure as you contemplate."

It was a long-drawn-out controversy; as real to Ruth as though her soul had separated itself from that other mysterious part of her which was yet not her body, and stood confronting her, calm, strong, unyielding. She tossed on her bed from side to side, and turned and re-turned her pillows, and straightened the disordered bedclothing, and sought in vain for an hour of rest. At times she resolutely told herself that she would put it all aside until morning, and wait, like a reasonable being, until her brain was clear and she was capable of reaching conclusions; then she would compose herself for sleep, only to find that she was taking up each minute detail of the story that had been told her and living it over again. She could not even interest herself in any of the side issues save for a few minutes at a time. She tried hard to centre her thoughts about the woman, Miss Parker, and contrast her with that crude disappointing girl by the same name that she had met years before; it did not seem to her that they could be one and the same! What a beautiful woman in every sense of the word this Miss Parker was! What if she, Erskine's mother, had been gifted with foresight, in those early years, had been able to conceive of the possibilities hidden in that uncouth, silly country girl, and had encouraged in Erskine the interest which she then awakened? Or, failing in that, what if she had simply kept her hand off and let things take their course? Would this woman with her beautiful face and gracious ways and cultivated mind and heart have become Erskine's wife, and her daughter? How extraordinary that it should have been Mamie Parker who had touched her life again, when she had labored so hard to be free from her, and had succeeded! And it was Mamie Parker who had come to the rescue of a desperately friendless girl who ought at this moment to be sheltered in their own home! And then she was back in the meshes of it all again!

She arose at length and began to move softly about her room through the darkness. She must stay in the darkness, otherwise Erskine might discover a light and insist upon being admitted. Very softly she drew back her curtains and looked out upon the moonless night. There were countless stars, but they gleamed from far away and looked even more indifferent than usual to what was going on below them. Softly she drew a chair beside the open casement and sat down to try the effect of the cool night air upon her throbbing head. If she could only get quiet enough to think! But those two conflicting thoughts were still pounding away in her brain: "Erskine must be told." "Erskine must *not* be told!"

Yet she made progress, and a discovery. It was beginning to humiliate her to the very dust to discover that there was a sense in which she wanted to tell him! No, not that, either; but she wanted him to know; and she wanted this because she desired to have Irene dethroned!

There were no tears shed during those hours. The victim had gone beyond tears. Her throat felt dry and parched and her eyes burned, as one in a fever. She was beginning to realize that this might be a conflict between right and wrong, and that her own personality was engaged in it. The clock struck two, struck three, and still that mother sat gazing out on the singularly quiet night. Twice during that time she heard Erskine come with soft footsteps, evidently to listen at her door.

"Mamma," he said, speaking low, but so distinctly that she knew he reasoned that if she were awake she would certainly hear him. It seemed to her that he must hear the throbbing of her heart as she waited. A wild desire possessed her to fling wide the door and bid him come in and listen while she said to him: "The woman you have taken to your heart, to love and cherish forever, is false to the truth, false to every sense of honor, false even to her own child!"

She clutched at the arms of her chair, to keep her, and held her breath that it make no sound.

Erskine went on tiptoe back to his room, and his mother, who had almost spent her physical strength, sank limply back into her chair. But before the clock struck again she had got to her knees. All the while she had been conscious of a strange reluctance about going to God with this trouble. Accustomed as she was, and had been ever since she became a praying woman, to taking all things, small as well as great, to Him, it had seemed strange even to herself that she held back.

Not that she had said that she would not pray, she had simply shrunken back with a half-frightened "Not yet, I am not ready yet; let me think." But she reached the moment when she understood that she must have help and must have it at once, and that only God could give it.

She knelt long; at first speaking no words, not thinking words. Then she broke into short, half-sobbing ejaculations: "Lord, show me the way. Christ, son of Mary, son of God, help me!" And then the habit of years asserted itself and the sorely shaken woman entered wholly within the refuge and poured out her soul in prayer.

When she arose from her knees, the rosy tints of a new day were beginning to flush the east. She drew her shades and went back to her bed and slept. Some things had been settled for her; she need not think about them any more.

The woman who a few hours later appeared at the breakfast table in a white morning dress and with her hair carefully arranged, showed little trace of her night's vigil, though her son regarded her searchingly.

"I am thankful to see you here," he said. "I was quite worried about you last night. It is so unusual not to meet you at dinner and have a little chat with you. You did not even give a fellow a chance to say good-night! I was sure that something was wrong." His wife laughed.

"Erskine cannot get away from the idea that he is his mother's nursemaid," she said lightly. "And he is a real 'Miss Nancy' for worrying. Such a night as he gave me, merely because you did not choose to come down to dinner! He must have trotted out to your door to listen twenty times, at least."

"Twice, anyway," said Erskine, gayly. "Never mind, though; she is all right this morning, and that is more than I dared to hope." But he watched her closely.

"What tired you so, mamma? Or rather, who did? Irene said you had company all the afternoon."

"Yes, an old acquaintance. I don't think you could guess who it was."

"Not at least without seeing her. Was she also an old acquaintance of mine?"

"I think you will remember her; at least you will, her brother. It was Miss Parker."

"'Miss Parker?' Not Mamie? How interesting! Why didn't you keep her to dinner? I should like to have met her. Is she 'Miss Parker' still, after all these years? That is rather surprising, isn't it? She must be thirty or more. And what about her brother? I haven't heard anything of him to speak of, since I left college."

"Who are these interesting people who seem to have just sprung into existence again?" Irene asked. "I have never heard of Mamie Parker, have I? Is she an old sweetheart of yours?"

"Hardly!" Erskine laughed carelessly. "There was a time during my college life that her brother and I were rather intimate; then we drifted apart; he was a good fellow, though. What about him, mamma?"

"Something that greatly surprised me. Had you supposed him to be of the material that makes missionaries? That is what he has become: a foreign missionary. He went out to China about seven years ago, purely in a commercial way. He represented a New York business house, but he carried letters of introduction to our missionaries located there, and became intimate with them and so interested in their work that, after a time, he gave up his business entirely and became a missionary teacher."

"Is it possible!" said Erskine. "I think he is the last one I should have chosen for such a future; from our class, I mean. Though he was a fine fellow with a big unselfish heart. Didn't I always insist upon that, mamma, in the days when you did not like him very well? Weren't there such days? I have almost forgotten."

"I don't think I considered him remarkable," Mrs. Burnham said. "Though I remember that Alice saw possibilities in him. She liked him for being so good to his sister."

"And he is really in China! How does his sister like that?"

"So well that she is going out to be with him for a year, and perhaps longer. She is in daily expectation of receiving a summons from a party of missionaries with whom she is to travel. She is very enthusiastic about it; sees ways in which she can further the work. I should not be at all surprised if she remained there and made it her life work."

Erskine Burnham looked curiously at his mother, as if to determine whether she was really in earnest, then threw back his head and laughed.

"Mamie Parker a missionary in China!" he exploded, "or anywhere else! my imagination isn't equal to such a flight as that."

"She has changed wonderfully, Erskine. At first I could not make myself believe that she was really the Mamie Parker we used to know. Yet as I studied her closely I could see a suggestion of the girlish face. She was pretty, you remember, but I did not think her face gave promise of the beauty it has now. However, she is more than beautiful. She is an educated cultivated woman."

"Educated?" Erskine repeated the word incredulously.

"She went back to school, Erskine, the winter after she visited her brother, and prepared for college. She is a Smith graduate, think of it! As for culture, I don't think I ever met a more perfect-appearing lady than she has become."

"Dear me!" said Irene with a but slightly suppressed yawn, "what a paragon she must be; I'm glad I didn't meet her. I detest paragons. Now, if you, sir, can stop talking about her long enough to consider it, have the goodness to tell me at what time I may expect you in town this afternoon? We are to be at the Durands' at five, remember. Don't you dare to tell me you must be excused, for I have simply set my heart on having you with me."

But Erskine could not so readily be made to forget his anxieties. He put off a direct answer to his wife, and followed his mother to her room to press his inquiries tenderly.

"Are you sure that you are all right this morning, and that it was only weariness which kept you so close a prisoner last night? There is something about you that I don't quite like; there are heavy rings under your eyes, and you are paler than usual. Did you sleep well?"

"Not very," she said after a moment's hesitation. "I was—restless."

He studied her face and spoke with tender reproach.

"Mommie, something troubles you. Am I not to know it?"

She had no recourse but to speak truth.

CHAPTER XIX

ALONE

She laid a tender motherly hand on his arm as she said:—

"Something has been troubling me, Erskine, something that I cannot explain, because there is a sense in which it is not my trouble at all, but has to do with others. For a time I was very much perplexed, but I have settled it now, what my share in it should be, so that it need not perplex me any more."

She knew that the truth was deceiving him, but it satisfied him. He believed that Mamie Parker's troubles, whatever they were, had been brought for his mother to share. His face cleared a little, but he felt it his duty to administer a loving admonition.

"Remember your one weakness, mamma; there was always in your nature a temptation to 'bear one another's burdens' too literally. If there is any way in which I can help without infringing on confidences, you will let me, of course?"

She was able to smile as she assured him that she would. Despite her night of vigil she felt strong. Her part had been revealed to her. She was to keep Irene's secret, to suffer and to act in her stead; and to shield her son's name and home as much as lay in her power. A miserable travesty of a home it looked to her; still, it was all he had, and for a time at least it could be kept sacred in Erskine's eyes. She had no faith in a perpetual concealment; such skeletons, she believed, were always unearthed sooner or later—often in unexpected and mysterious ways. How remarkable, for instance, it was that, of all the young women in the world who might have discovered and befriended the deserted child it should have been their old acquaintance Mamie Parker! Still, this morning, she could thank God that she need not be the one to unearth this secret.

Of course the child must be planned for—there was no danger that Ruth would forget her—but it had become very clear to her that nothing but disaster could result from an enforced acknowledgement of her by the mother at this late day. If Irene wanted her—if her heart had turned toward her child in the slightest, or, failing in heart, if her conscience had impelled her to make the least small effort to repair some of the mischief, then, indeed, Ruth would have braved public opinion, gossip, Erskine's pain and shame, everything to help her. And she could do it understandingly. Had not Ruth Erskine, away back in her girlhood, helped her father in his tardy right-doing?

It is true that, even at this late day, her face flushed with pain and shame over the thought of the manner in which she had done this, at first; still, she had done it. And later, had she not herself taken the initiative and opened the way for her husband to do his belated duty? Who could know better than she the cost of such effort? But there was one infinite difference between past experiences and present problems. Both her father and her husband, when the crucial test came, had a foundation of moral strength to build upon; while Irene—

Ruth Burnham knew that she had tried very hard to find some lighting up of the story. She had thoroughly probed Mamie Parker to discover whether or not through the years the mother had made some sign which proved that she at least knew of the continued existence of her daughter; but there had been absolutely no proof that she had ever thought of her six months' old baby again! Ruth had to turn quickly away from that subject as one that would not bear dwelling on. The idea that a mother had actually and deliberately abandoned her baby, roused such a sense of revolt in this woman's heart that there were times when she told herself that she could not breathe in the same house with such a creature.

Miss Parker herself had seemed able to appreciate this feeling. At least she had given no hint that she expected or hoped anything whatever from the mother, and frankly owned that she had avoided meeting her on occasions when there would have been opportunity. She had not felt, she said simply, that anything could be gained by coming in contact with her. And all her plea had been that Erskine's mother should in some way interest herself in the welfare of the lonely girl.

She was very lonely, now, more so by far than she used to be, Miss Parker had said in a voice that trembled. Then she had waited a few minutes to regain self-control before she explained that her mother had to a very great extent taken the place of mother to the little one.

"She used to spend her vacations with us," she said, "and mother fell into the habit of looking after her clothes and her comfort in every way, just as though she were a daughter; and the child loved mother with a devotion that is uncommon in one so young. Of course she cannot but miss her sadly."

"Have you lately lost your mother?" Ruth had inquired, and her tone had been so full of tender sympathy that Miss Parker had explained in detail how it was that she had only her brother left. That was why she was going out to him, so that they might be together, at least for a time, since they were all that was left of home.

Jim had not married; his sister sometimes feared that he never would. Didn't Mrs. Burnham think that was a calamity for a man?

"I used to think so," Ruth had replied, as one who did not realize that she was speaking aloud, and then she had started and flushed over the thought of what she might thus be revealing; and the flush had deepened as she remembered what this woman already knew of her son's wife. But Miss Parker had not once glanced in her direction, and made no sign that she had heard. She went on, quietly, talking about her brother. Men, she thought, were different in that respect from women. A woman need never marry in order to be comfortable, or to be cared for; but there were ways in which the average man was helpless and almost homeless without the one woman to care for him, selected from all the world. This was so different from the usual putting of the subject that Mrs. Burnham had felt impelled to smile. Yet as she looked at the beautiful woman opposite her she admitted that her brother's home would certainly be brightened by her presence. Still, it was a long way to go to make a home for a brother.

"Do you have any thought of remaining there," she had asked. "I mean, of making it a permanent home?"

Miss Parker did not know. She had not allowed herself to look ahead very far. There were so many changes in life that it did not seem wise to try to plan. She should like to remain there, like it very much, she believed; that is, if she could help in the work. She was sure that she could help Jim; at least, she could take care of him, and give him more time to do his work; and Jim was a success. Still, there were times when she was sorry that she had planned in this way, on Maybelle's account. Even now, if she could make a change, could delay a little, without incommoding her brother, she would do so; but Jim had made plans in view of her coming that would seriously inconvenience him if she did not go.

Yes, there had been changes, sad changes since her plans were made. Mr. Somerville, who was a frail man and hopelessly careless of himself, had contracted a cold, a few months ago, that had settled on his lungs; and it was now evident to all but that poor little girl that she would, before long, be fatherless.

Oh, she would be cared for, no doubt, so far as her body was concerned. She was at school, and it was a good school, as good, perhaps, as any of them. At least she, and her mother, had been at infinite pains to discover it; still, it was school, and not home, and poor Maybelle had never been quite happy there. The teachers were kind, but cold and unsympathetic. They did not understand the child, and they almost openly disapproved of her father. He went every day to see her, but the time was coming when he would no longer be able to do so, and she dreaded to think what Maybelle would do when this truth dawned upon her.

In these and many other ways had Miss Parker made it apparent to Mrs. Burnham that her hope lay in winning the woman who had been so much to her, to become this deserted and lonely child's friend and guardian.

This was the problem therefore which occupied Ruth Burnham's chief thought for a number of days following Miss Parker's visit. Only one decision with regard to it had been reached: that she would do what she could; but what that would be, she was unable to determine. Her way seemed hedged in with difficulties which had not occurred to her during those first awful hours. How, for instance, was she, a stranger, with no claim to other than a stranger's interest that she could press, to present herself before a young woman who was under the care of her own father, and beg to be taken as a friend and adviser?

Then, too, she shrank exceedingly from meeting the father; meeting and talking with a man who had been Irene's husband! his very presence on the earth seemed an insult to her son! What explanation could she possibly make to him as to her interest in his daughter? Would her name tell him anything? What did he know of the after history of the mother of his child? If he was acquainted with her present name, might he not look upon the coming of her husband's mother as an added insult? For, after all, he was a decent man, decent enough for a woman like Mamie Parker to acknowledge his acquaintance; and he had done what he could for his deserted child. She could not even find that he had been seriously to blame for the child's desertion; therefore he might well resent this tardy coming to his aid.

Going back step by step over her interview with Miss Parker, Ruth found that there were many questions which she had failed to ask; and among them was this important one as to the father's knowledge of Irene's present name and home. It seemed almost necessary to wait and write to Miss Parker before attempting anything. Yet she shrank morbidly from this; it seemed like opening the whole horror afresh.

If there were actual need on the part of the girl, such as could be met by money, her way would have been clearer. But of this she had thought at once, and Miss Parker had almost dignifiedly declined her help.

"Dear Mrs. Burnham, I consider it my privilege to look after Maybelle in all such ways; we have done it for years, mother and I together, and now it seems almost like her trust to me. It has been a real comfort to see that the child was provided with such little luxuries of the toilet, for instance, as I longed for and could not have. We were much straitened in my girlhood, and I have been living my life over again in this young girl; though she is much less silly than I was. I must not be deprived of this privilege, Mrs. Burnham; indeed I have her father's permission to do for her whatever I think wise; he trusts me fully; and I have no one else, now, to think about."

So that avenue seemed closed. Ruth, thinking about it almost irritably as the complications grew upon her, told herself that it would have been wiser for Mamie Parker to plan to stay away from China and attend to all the rest of it; she could do it better than any one else.

She wrote to Miss Parker at last, a careful letter, re-written several times lest it tell too much between lines.

That young woman had evidently taken it for granted that the Burnham family were supplied with the main facts in this tragedy, and had found it hard to rally from her astonishment at finding the mother in ignorance. Ruth knew that she believed that Erskine was not. She longed to tell her that this was false, yet held her pen. Did not this infringe upon her solemn covenant with God to shield her daughter-in-law as much as right would permit? Yet, was it right to let her son's good name be smirched unnecessarily in the eyes of this woman who had known him in his spotless youth?

At last she wrote this:—

"Since our interview I have been through a bitter experience trying to decide as to my duty in certain directions. I believe now that I have reached a decision, and feel that I am not called upon to tear down with my own hands the fair home which my son believes he has begun to build. He is God's own servant, and God will see to it that he understands all that he must understand. I believe that I may leave it with Him."

She waited eagerly for a reply to this letter; it came in the form of a telegram.

"I am to sail on Saturday. My poor little girl is alone. Father buried yesterday. Have written.

"M. M. Parker."

CHAPTER XX

THEY HATED MYSTERY

Mrs. Ruth Burnham was settled in a drawing-room car, surrounded by every comfort and luxury that money and modern ideas can furnish for a long journey; and her son Erskine stood looking down on her with a face only half satisfied.

It occurred to him as a matter of astonishment that, with the single exception of her one trip homeward, after her ministrations to Alice, and while he was abroad, his mother had not, since he could remember, taken a journey without him. And here she was, starting for New York, and planning for a stay of indefinite length, while he was remaining at home. He did not wholly like it.

"It does not seem quite right, mamma," he said, with a smile that had almost wistfulness in it. "I am not used to seeing you off, you know. It seems as though I should be going along to look after your comfort."

"You have already done that, Erskine; I am sure a queen could not be more carefully provided for."

"And you have really no idea when you are coming home?"

"I could not plan for it, dear. Your Aunt Flossy is a woman of many schemes, you know, and it is long since I visited her; not since you and I were there together, years ago."

"It was always 'you and I together,'" he said, discontentedly, as though he almost resented this sudden independence of him.

"And this other—person—whoever she is, you will not let her absorb you? I can see how she will wear you out, without me to manage for you. She is imperious and selfish, of course."

His mother smiled on him tenderly, and a little sadly. "How did you learn that, Erskine?"

"Oh, by intuition; or common sense. She would not expect an entire stranger to take a long and tiresome journey in her behalf if she were not."

"I don't think she knows anything about the journey, or the stranger, my son."

"Then it is all Miss Parker's fault?" and he frowned. "She has not grown like her brother; not as he used to be, at least. Why doesn't she stay at home and attend to her own affairs, since they are of so much importance? That sounds ugly, I know, but I don't like to lend you, mommie, indeed I don't. You belong to me; and besides, there seems to be an air of mystery about the whole matter, and I hate mystery; at least between us."

It was at that moment that the call of "all aboard" sounded, and Erskine gave his mother a hasty last kiss and made flying leaps toward the platform.

It was a relief to have him go. His mother also hated mystery; and despite her attempts at frankness, no one was more conscious than she of the part that she had not told.

She had shown Erskine the telegram and made at the time the very brief explanation which it had taken her hours to arrange.

"It is a protégé of Miss Parker's, Erskine, for whom she has bespoken my sympathy and help. The girl is quite alone, her father has just died; and since I have been long promising your Aunt Flossy, and they are in the same city, I think I ought to take this time for my visit."

"A protégé," Erskine had repeated with lifted eyebrows. "A relative? Is she responsible for her? How can one shift such responsibilities as that, especially upon a stranger?"

"She is not related to Miss Parker," his mother had replied, and was glad that at the moment she had been bending over a drawer, so that her burning face was partially hidden. If Erskine only knew whose responsibilities had been shifted! It was that thought which burned her face.

"She is not!" he had replied in an exclamatory tone. "Then why in the name of common sense should she,"—and then, his mother had determined what she would say further.

"Erskine,"—her face was still bent over that bureau drawer—"the peculiar circumstances connected with this child were explained to me by Miss Parker in confidence, and of course I cannot speak of them; further than to tell you that she considers the girl as a trust."

"Well," Erskine had said, after waiting a moment for more words that had not come, "I don't half like it, mamma. I am sure of that; and if it were not for your making this long-promised visit to Aunt Flossy, I should not consent to your going. As it is, rushing off at an hour's notice, in response to an ordinary telegram, as though somebody had a right to order you around, seems absurd. I shall write to Aunt Flossy not to let your heart run away with your judgment. I am really afraid you are being imposed upon, mamma. Remember, we know nothing about these Parkers."

After his mother had watched, with the nervous tremors with which one watches when all that one has is jumping from a moving train—until Erskine was lifting his hat to her from safe ground, and her train was gliding away from him, she drew a deep breath of relief; not only from that immediate tension, but all the hours which had preceded it. Every moment since the arrival of that telegram had been a nervous strain to her, because of the things that she must say, and the things that she must not say.

Irene, especially, had taxed her honesty and ingenuity to the utmost. From the first moment, the young woman had been curious and painstaking in trying to satisfy herself.

"The idea!" she would exclaim. "It seems to me that is asking a great deal of an old woman; and Erskine says this Miss Parker is only a passing acquaintance. What possible claim can she have on you? Why is she so interested in this girl? Do you understand it? It looks as though there was a love affair, somewhere, doesn't it? She is an old maid, of course. You can depend upon it that she was in love with that girl's father!"

There was a side to this woman which Ruth in her secret soul called coarse. So far as she knew, it was a phase of her character that was never exhibited to Erskine.

With her fine regard for truth, and her contempt of anything like subterfuge, Mrs. Burnham found it hard to satisfy the curious questioner, and yet keep back that part of the truth which she must not tell. She could not but be glad when the strain was over.

Not once had she mentioned the name of the girl. It had been a continual terror to her lest she should be asked it; but though Irene asked every possible question that might throw light on the mystery, she had been mercifully preserved from thinking of names. Mrs. Burnham had learned from Miss Parker that the first name, Maybelle, would reveal nothing; it had been chosen by the father for his still nameless child, months after the mother's desertion; and chosen for no better reason than that Baby had come in the month of May, and was a "little beauty." But the name of Somerville might at least have startled Irene, had she heard it; and her mother-in-law determined that she should not. Having resolved upon silence as the right course, the more absolute it could be, the better for all concerned.

So it was not until the train was fairly under way, speeding eastward at thirty miles an hour, that Ruth felt free to draw a long breath and rest her overstrained nerves. Her mind wandered back through the years, lured there by the thought of Flossy. It was years since they two had been alone together, but just at this time Flossy's husband had taken a hurried business trip abroad.

"It is really providential that I am at home," Flossy had written, in response to her old friend's letter, telling that she might soon visit her. "Evan wanted me to go with him, brief as his stay is to be; and I should have done so, but for the illness of a very dear friend who seemed to need me; to think that if I had gone, I might have missed you!"

Dear Flossy! what a rarely wise little woman she had become! astonishing them all, not by her sweetness,—they had always been sure of that,—but by her strength and skill as a Christian worker. No young woman left to herself in a dangerous world could have a safer, more helpful friend than Flossy Shipley Roberts. Yet Ruth, even as she thought this comforting thought, remembered that the duty thrust upon her of guarding the hateful secrets of others must prevent her from speaking plainly even to Flossy.

However, she found reticence with Flossy easier than it had been with Irene. Joyfully glad to get possession of her old friend was Mrs. Roberts, and athrob with eagerness to hear all that she had to tell her, and sympathetic about the minutest details; yet in nothing did she show her perfect breeding and rare tact more distinctly than in the questions that she did not ask, concerning things that Ruth did not choose to tell.

She told very little.

"You know, Flossy, I have been planning to come to you for a long, long time."

"I certainly do!" interrupted Flossy, with an air that obliged Ruth to stop and laugh.

"But the reason I am here just at this time is because a protégé of my friend—the young woman who sailed last week for China—has just lost her father and is alone in this great city, so far as relatives or very close friends are concerned, and I am commissioned to try to comfort her."

"And I know, dear Ruth, how certainly you will succeed," was Mrs. Roberts's comment and her only one.

A little later she asked: "Where do you find your charge, Ruth? Is she a young girl, did you say? Delightful! I hope you will let me help? Oh, no, I must not go with you on your first visit, of course. One new face at a time is enough for the poor child to meet."

Ruth blessed her in her heart for the delicate reserve which would not let her question even about the woman who had gone to China. After Irene's baldly put inference she shrank from trying to explain Miss Parker's interest in the girl.

It was on the morning after her arrival in town that Mrs. Burnham sat waiting in the reception room of a dignified, many-storied house, which, she told herself, had everywhere about it the unmistakable boarding-school air.

She had sent up her card, but was uncertain how much it would tell, or whether she should be allowed to see the person on whom she had called. As matters had turned out it seemed unfortunate that she had so long delayed her visit to Mrs. Roberts. If she could have been introduced here by Miss Parker in person, it might have been better for all concerned. As it was, she felt strangely out of place and embarrassed. She had not been able to decide just how she would account for her extreme interest in this stranger. It was especially embarrassing to remember that she must account for it even to the girl herself. While she waited, she went back in memory to that other waiting, in a boarding-house parlor, when she had called to see Mamie Parker. What eventful years had intervened, and what changes they had wrought! How mistaken she, Ruth Burnham, had been about many things, notably her estimate of Mamie Parker. Had she been able with prophetic insight to get a vision of the woman Mamie was to be, would it have made a difference, a radical difference with all their lives? Then she flushed to her temples as she remembered that such thoughts were almost an insult to her son.

Just then the door opened and there entered Madame Sternheim, the head of the "Young Ladies' Fashionable School."

Madame Sternheim was dignified and correct in every movement and word, and was as cold as ice.

Yes, Miss Somerville was with them, of course. Her poor father had left her in their charge, and a serious responsibility she found it. Oh, yes, Miss Parker, before she left, had spoken of some one by the name of—of Burnham—she referred to the card which she held in her hand—who might write, or be heard from in some way. She seemed not to be at all sure that any one would call.

Yes, certainly, the circumstances were peculiar and had been all the time. The poor father—it was by no means a pleasant thing to have to speak plainly of the dead, but it was sometimes necessary, and perhaps Mrs.—yes, thank you, Mrs. Burnham, knew that he was not in every respect the fit guardian for a young woman?

Oh, yes, Miss Parker had been most kind, most attentive; Miss Somerville owed her a deep debt of gratitude, certainly.

It seemed a strange—"Providence—shall we call it?" that took Miss Parker away to China at just the time when it would appear that her self-assumed charge needed her the most. She, Madame Sternheim, had never professed to understand the situation. Miss Parker, she believed, was not even remotely related to the girl, not even a relative of the relatives—was she? Yet her interest in the child and her father had been unaccountably deep. There had always seemed to her to be an air of mystery about the whole matter. Madame Sternheim did not like mystery; in fact she might say that she shrank from it. Did Mrs. Burnham understand that Miss Parker knew personally any of the family connection?

Ruth was angry with herself that she must blush and almost stammer over so simple a question.

No, that was what Madame Sternheim had been led to infer. The relatives were all in England, were they not? It seemed strange that the girl was not to go out to them; but then, her poor father—Had Mrs. Burnham been personally acquainted with the father? Well, she knew of him probably? which was perhaps quite enough. Miss Parker's unaccountable interest in him was beyond understanding, until one remembered that no one could tell on what the human heart would anchor, especially a woman's heart. She had never thought that Mr. Somerville was especially—but then he, poor man, was gone; they need not speak of such things now. And Miss Parker, too, was gone—to China! That was unaccountable. If love for the girl had been what had prompted her attentions all these years, why, the poor child was doubly in need of it now. She had been deeply attached to her father despite the fact that—

"Ah," Madame Sternheim broke off quickly, as the door slowly opened, to say:—

"Here she is, Mrs. Burnham, to speak for herself."

CHAPTER XXI

"A STUDY"

A tall, pale girl with delicate features and great brown eyes and a wealth of gold-brown hair.

"A study in black and white," was the phrase that floated through Ruth's mind as she looked at her. The girl was in deep mourning unrelieved even by a touch of white, and her face was intensely pale. Yet there was something about her, a nameless something, that claimed instant interest, and Mrs. Burnham, who, ever since she had heard of the girl's existence, had been struggling with an unreasonable desire to hate her, felt instantly drawn toward her. She felt rather than realized that, whatever might have been Irene's appearance in girlhood, the two had nothing in common now, for her eyes.

"I have heard your name," the pale girl said, much as she might have addressed a book agent, "but I did not know that you were coming to New York."

"My dear," broke in Madame Sternheim, reproof in her tone, "I am sure it is very kind in Mrs.—yes, Mrs. Burnham to take all this trouble for your sake. She tells me that she is not related to you in any way, and it is certainly quite unusual for strangers to be so kind."

"It is very kind," the girl said coldly, and stood irresolute apparently as to what she should do or say next; while Ruth, sorry for her and for herself and unreasonably annoyed with Madame Sternheim, was at a loss how to proceed.

The Madame came to her aid, addressing the young girl.

"Do be seated, my dear, and make yourself at least look comfortable." There was a strong emphasis laid upon the word "look" and the reproof in the tone was still marked, as she continued:—

"Mrs. Burnham will naturally want to have a talk with you, and learn what little you may be able to explain to her about this sad matter, although I am too fully aware that it will be very unsatisfactory." Then she turned to Ruth.

"With your permission, dear madam, I will retire and leave my charge in your care for the present. I assure you it is a great relief to me to find that there is some one willing to share with me this heavy responsibility."

The girl turned at this, and with slow, languid steps preceded the Madame to the door, which she held open for her to pass, and bowed respectfully as she did so. Then, waiting until a turn in the hall hid the lady from sight she carefully closed the door.

Ruth, meantime, was watching her with a half-terrified fascination. She was so calm, so self-possessed, so utterly without feeling of any sort, apparently. What was to be said to her? and what good could come in any way from that which now began to look like interference? She was not in the least prepared for the sudden change which the closing of that door seemed to make.

The girl turned with an impetuous movement and seemed to fly, rather than walk, over the space between them, and, flinging herself in a crushed little heap in front of her guest, hid her face on Mrs. Burnham's lap and burst into a passion of weeping.

"Poor little girl!" Ruth said softly, and laid her hand tenderly on the bowed head. There seemed no other word that could be spoken until the storm of weeping had in a degree subsided.

"Oh, do forgive me!" the child said, after a minute, but without raising her head. "I did not mean to cry, I meant to control myself; I thought I could, through it all, but I am so wretched! and she—she freezes me! she wants me to be resigned, and to remember how much better off I am than some other girls who have no one to look after them, and it doesn't help me one bit. I am so glad that you have come! You are Aunt Mamie's friend, so you can't be like Madame Sternheim; and you won't tell me that Aunt Mamie isn't related to me in the most distant degree and in the nature of things cannot be, will you? I can see that you are not like the Madame the least bit in the world, and I am glad, *glad*! Oh! I am a very wicked girl! I ought not to have said that; she is good, she is *very* good; and she is patient with my faults and follies; and yet—there are times when I almost hate her! Oh, dear! what will you think of me? I don't act like this very often; I don't cry often—I don't cry at all! but now I must, or I shall die!"

Then followed another outburst of passionate weeping.

"Cry as much as you want to, dear child," Ruth said. "It is only natural, and will do you good."

All the time her hand was moving over the tumbled masses of hair, making quiet, soothing passes.

After a little the girl sat up and brushed away the tears. "I can't think what made me," she said. "Only you reminded me of Aunt Mamie, and then—it all came back. I don't know what I am to do; it seems to me that I cannot live without her, but I have got to; and without—everybody. It does seem sometimes as though there was never another girl in the world so utterly alone; but Madame Sternheim says there are, hundreds of them, even in this city! I am so sorry for them all! I wish they could die and go to heaven. I wish I could, with papa. But Madame Sternheim says—" she stopped abruptly and struggled for self-control, and spoke almost fiercely.

"I won't tell you what she says about my father, nor think about it. It isn't true, and if it were, she—"

Ruth felt a curious feeling of indignation rising against Mamie Parker. How could she have deserted this child? so soon, at least, after her bereavement? Surely she needed her more than the brother did, who had been alone for years! Then came a great gust of shame and shook her heart. Why should Mamie Parker, a stranger, be expected to show compassion for this lonely girl when her own family, her own mother—But that would not bear thinking about.

"Poor little girl!" she said again, with infinite tenderness. "Will you take me for a friend? I will do the best I can to be a true one."

"Oh, thank you," the child said impulsively. "I am so glad, *so glad* for you! and only last night I thought I could never be glad about anything again! Aunt Mamie had to go, of course, at the time appointed. It isn't like other journeys, you know; they have to sail when they are told; missionaries do, I mean. That is,—oh, you understand. But Aunt Mamie felt very badly about leaving me; and she said she thought you would love me; but of course I couldn't see why you should. It isn't that I am not cared for, Mrs. Burnham. I have been with Madame Sternheim for six years and I am sure that I have every care and attention that a girl possibly could; she has always made that plain to me; but—She did not like papa, Mrs. Burnham. She never did; and she—almost spoke against him, even to me! Could a girl ever care very much for one who talked and felt as she did about the dearest, kindest, most loving papa that ever lived? oh!"

She clenched her hands, and the tears threatened to choke her; but she put them back with a strong will, and even faintly smiled.

"I shall not cry again," she said. "Madame thinks it is wicked. Mrs. Burnham, I wish you could have known my papa. He was—I mean he was not—oh, I don't know how to say it; and I am not sure that I want to say it, ever. He was good to me always; a girl like me couldn't have had a better father; and I don't know how to live in this world without him. It kills me to have to stay all the time among people who say always; 'Your poor father!' and shake their heads and look as though they could say volumes of ugly things about him if they chose. They shall not! I will not have people talking about my father! the dearest, the best! a great deal better than the self-righteous creatures made of icicles that they admire!"

Ruth was amazed at the suppressed fury of her tones, and at her eyes which, but a moment before dim with weeping, now blazed with indignation. Evidently the child had passed through a severe mental strain.

"Don't, dear," she said gently. "No one could be so cruel as to want to speak against your father. I am glad you love him so dearly; he can always help you. You will not want to disappoint him in any way, you know."

The girl looked at her searchingly as one startled. This was evidently a new thought; it took hold of her heart. A softened light came into her unusually expressive eyes and after a moment she said very gently:—

"No one ever said anything to me like that, before. It helps."

They made great strides toward intimacy even in that first morning. So great that when Ruth, pitying the girl's loneliness and evident dread of the people by whom she was surrounded, proposed that she send for her to come and take dinner with Mrs. Roberts and herself, she caught at the suggestion with an eagerness which showed what a relief it was to her; and then almost immediately demurred.

"But I ought not to presume in that way. I am certain the Madame will think so. Will not your friend think it very strange in me, a stranger, to intrude upon her home?"

"Wait until you see her," Ruth said, smiling. "Mrs. Roberts and I are very old friends, and I am almost as much at home in her house as I am in my own."

As she spoke, she felt a sudden stricture at her heart over those commonplace words. Was she not in these later days almost more at home in Flossy's house than in her own?

But Maybelle's face had gloomed over.

"I think I must not go, Mrs. Burnham," she said. "I suppose I ought not to wish, or even be willing to go; I am sure Madame Sternheim will be shocked at the idea. I am in deep mourning, you know, and my loss is so recent."

Unconsciously the child had imitated the prim decorum of her Mentor, and it had changed her entire face.

Ruth leaned forward impulsively and kissed her, while she spoke with a smile:—

"Dear child, be yourself, and not Madame Sternheim. Adopt me, will you, and let me attend to the decorum part, and all the rest. Mrs. Roberts is quite alone, save for me; her husband is away on a business trip, and her children have scattered for the vacation; so we shall be very quiet, we three; and there is no reason in the world why you should not come to us. I want you to know Mrs. Roberts; she is anxious to see you, and would have come with me this morning, if she had not thought it better that you and I should make each other's acquaintance first. As for you, you will love her the first time you look at her. Shall I speak to Madame Sternheim myself about it?"

When this was done, Madame Sternheim was discovered to be graciousness itself. She might be doubtful as to Mrs. Burnham's place in the world, her knowledge of people being limited and very local, but the name of Mrs. Evan Roberts called for instant approval, and to know that Mrs. Burnham was her friend and guest was sufficient passport for her. It was very kind and thoughtful in dear Mrs. Roberts, she was sure, to send for the poor child; and very like her too, if all that the Madame had heard concerning her was true. Did Mrs. Burnham know that her friend had the name of always doing the most delicate kindnesses that no one else would have thought of? She was really a wonderful woman? Madame Sternheim had long wanted to know her. They need not trouble to send the dear child home, she herself was going out this evening, and would have pleasure in calling for Miss Somerville at ten o'clock.

"Isn't it beautiful here?" Maybelle said, a few hours later, as she sank among the cushions of a "Sleepy Hollow" and feasted her beauty-loving eyes on the harmonies of Mrs. Roberts's living-room. "It is like a poem, or no, a picture; that is what it is like, Mrs. Burnham; one of papa's pictures. How he would have loved this room! He was always making sketches of sweet, dear, home rooms, and there was always a beautiful mother in them with a baby in her arms. I think my mother must have been very beautiful, for it was always the same face, and I know it was intended for mamma, though he never told me so; I could not talk with papa about her, ever, it made him cry. Don't you think it is dreadful to see a man cry? When I started the tears in his dear blue eyes, I always felt like a wretch! and for that reason I gave up trying to say anything about mamma, though I should so love to have heard every little thing about her. Papa must simply have adored her, but I have had to dream her out for myself. I have spent hours and hours over it, studying papa's sketches, you know, and trying to clothe them with flesh. I believe I know just how she looked. Sometimes she would grow so real to me that I almost expected her to hold out her arms and clasp me to them. I was a wee baby, you know, when mamma went away."

CHAPTER XXII

A LOYAL HEART

The friendship so strangely started between Mrs. Burnham and the girl thrust upon her conscience, grew apace. As Ruth had surmised, her old friend Flossy had lost none of her charm with young people, and she won Maybelle's fascinated interest from the first moment of their meeting; an interest that developed rapidly into love.

When Mrs. Roberts's young people came home—an event that Ruth, at least, had dreaded for Maybelle's sake—it was found that the charm was increased. Ruth, in writing to Erskine about them, which she did at some length, had added: "I might have saved you much of this description, by simply saying that the children are very like their mother. Even Erskine, tall and muscular as he is, a thorough boy in every sense of the word, and a manly one, yet has that indefinable indescribable charm about him that our little Flossy always had and always will have, should she live to be a hundred, bless her! what a blessing she would be to this old world if she should. Do you realize, dear, that he is your namesake, as well as mine? At first I was not sure that I wanted another Erskine,—there is but one to me, you know,—but Erskine Roberts is such a splendid repetition of the family name that we cannot but be proud of him."

But she gave no description of Maybelle, and mentioned her name as little as possible. She shrank almost painfully from the thought of writing about this girl to one who ought to be deeply interested in her,—as in the nature of the case Erskine should be if he knew,—and yet looked upon her as an intruder, almost resenting his mother's efforts in her behalf.

But if she kept silence about her to Erskine, she atoned for it in the amount of time and thought that she bestowed upon the child. As the weeks passed and she grew to better understand this child-woman with whom she had to deal, she found herself bestowing upon her a wealth of love and tenderness that she had not supposed any but her very own could call out. And her love was returned in royal measure. However much Maybelle might admire and love Mrs. Roberts and enjoy her son and daughters, she had given the wealth of her heart unreservedly to Mrs. Burnham. "Next to Aunt Mamie I love you best of all the world," she would declare as she patted Ruth's shoulder with a loving little touch that was peculiarly her own. "It ought always to be Aunt Mamie first, you know, because she—she *mothered* me all those years when I was hungry for a mother. Dear Mrs. Burnham, if she were your daughter and I could be your granddaughter, would not that be perfect? But that couldn't be, of course, for Aunt Mamie loved her own dear mother better than any other mother in the world; and she was a *dear*; I loved her very much, but—how many different kinds of love there can be in the same heart!" she broke off to say, with the air of a dreamy philosopher, "Different kinds of loves and different kinds of unloves, ever so many of them! the heart is a curious country, isn't it?"

By that time Mrs. Burnham had come to understand Miss Parker's absorbed interest in the girl, which continued unabated even amid the absorbing interests of a strange land. She wrote long loving letters to the child of her adoption, and long earnest ones to Mrs. Burnham about her.

"There have been times," she wrote, "when I have almost regretted that I left the dear girl all alone and came away out here where weeks must intervene before I can hear from her. I felt this especially after I found that my brother, although very glad indeed to welcome me, had made interests here about which I knew nothing, one that is to help make a home for him in the near future, so that so far as care and companionship are concerned he could have done very well without me. When I first began to understand the situation here, I was puzzled, and just a little bit troubled over the question why I had been allowed to come, or rather left to think that to come was the only right course, when apparently I was much more needed at home on that dear child's account, than here. But after reading Maybelle's letter I understood that it was in order to leave the way clear and plain for her to your dear heart; you can do so much more for her than I can ever hope to. How blissful the darling is over her new friendships and interests! I am glad that you have kidnapped her loyal little heart, just as I knew you would."

"Poor girl!" Mrs. Burnham said softly to herself after reading this letter. "She has one of those hungry hearts that Maybelle talks about; and she fancied that her brother could fill it, instead of being quite satisfied with his generous corner of it! I wonder if it can be possible that she cared for the child's father, as the Madame hints? That would account for—but there is nothing to be accounted for; one could not help loving Maybelle. I must tell Miss Parker that she is always to have the first place in that 'curious' heart, while I am enthroned as second. Dear simpleton!" Then, as the thought crossed her mind, not for the first time, that the one who should hold that first place might be named Erskine, the uneasy conviction shook her that in such event certain ugly truths would have to be revealed.

But she put the thought from her as soon as possible. She could not plan for the future, and for the present, Maybelle and Erskine Roberts were simply comrades heartily enjoying each other's society, as her own Erskine and Alice Warder had done, without apparently other thoughts than those shared with them by Marian Roberts, who was Erskine's twin.

Ruth wrote to Miss Parker that same evening, giving her a detailed account of one of her talks with Maybelle.

"You may well call hers a 'loyal heart,' my friend," she wrote. "You should hear the pathetic way in which the child talks about you by the hour! Yesterday she said to me:—

"'Sometimes I used to wish that I could call Aunt Mamie, mother. She is the only woman that I ever had such a thought about; I suppose it was because she came close enough to give me an idea of what a real mother would be. I mean to keep her always for my heart-mother. There can be heart-mothers, you know, and in some ways they are almost as dear as real ones. Oh, I wonder if you know how a girl like me sometimes longs and *longs* for a real mother! I think it is the only possession that I ever envied. Sometimes, Mrs. Burnham, I have been fiercely jealous for hours together, so that I almost hated the girls who chattered about their mothers. Wasn't that dreadful! Oh, I cannot think what would have become of me long before this, if I had not had Aunt Mamie.'"

Thus much Ruth Burnham wrote, and stayed her pen. Was it necessary for her to tell all this? To lay bare even to this woman, who knew so much, the depths of a suffering young heart, thereby revealing the magnitude of the mother's sin against it? And that mother was her daughter, her son's wife! She wanted to write it; there were times when she wanted to shout it out to all the world, just what manner of woman was being sheltered by her name and home. She knew that she would never do it, but ought not Mamie Parker who had mothered the child, to understand? She thought long, she shed a few struggling tears that seemed to burn her face; the hurt at her heart was too deep for tears, and then she hid her face on the writing table and talked with God.

The end of it was that she tore the sheet across and threw the fragments into her grate. And wrote again:—

"You may well call hers a 'loyal heart,' my friend; she loves with a depth that seems to me unusual in one so young; and she has enthroned you at her heart's very centre. I want to say, just here, that I do not think she overestimates what you have done for her; I believe you have saved her to herself."

Meanwhile, the days that Mrs. Burnham, without any definite planning, had thought might be given to her visit lengthened into weeks, and still she lingered in the East.

Erskine was astonished, was bewildered, was half indignant, yet she set no date for the home-going. One reason for this was the fact that Mr. Roberts's stay abroad, which was to have been very brief, had been much lengthened by unexpected business complications, and his wife was begging her old friend to stay with her until his return. But of course there was no real excuse for this, as she had her children and multitudes of home friends about her. The real reason was that Ruth could not decide to leave

Maybelle. The girl clung to her with an ever increasing abandon to the joy of having for her very own one who knew how to be in every sense of the word motherly. Certainly she was nearer real happiness than her confused life had ever been before. From being one whom some of her schoolmates pitied and patronized because she seemed to have no friends of her own except a somewhat doubtful father, she became almost an object of envy.

All of the girls at Madame Sternheim's knew Mrs. Evan Roberts by reputation; and highly exaggerated stories of her house and her friends and her lavish expenditures for certain of them, were afloat in the school. But it chanced that Maybelle was the first one of the school girls who had entered the charmed circle of Mrs. Roberts's friendships.

When it became known that she was being sent for three or four times a week to take dinner with the Roberts family, that she went on Tuesdays to luncheon, that she spent most of her Saturdays and Sundays in the same choice home, interest in her comings and goings became marked. Then, when she began slowly, and almost reluctantly it must be admitted, to choose out some especially lonely or homesick or timid girl to take with her to dine at Mrs. Roberts's, her popularity knew no bounds.

Madame Sternheim, too, during these days was gracious almost beyond recognition. It was not that the good woman had not meant to be gracious always; she had been faithful to her duty as she saw it, and poor Maybelle, who confessed that she had hours of almost hating her, had in reality very much for which to thank her.

But Madame Sternheim was very human indeed, and the daughter of a poor artist father with a questionable past and a doubtful future, whose only friend, apparently, was a very fine young woman, it is true, but a woman without family and with no reasonable way of accounting for her interest in the girl, and nothing to show how soon the interest might cease—for that matter she had already gone away off to China for no reason in particular, unless it was to be well rid of her charge now that the father was gone—was one person, and a girl who had apparently been adopted into the inner circle of Mrs. Roberts's family was quite another; especially now that the poor father had been respectably buried and all doubtful or uncomfortable things could be forgotten. Madame Sternheim was relieved and pleased and hopeful. She liked to have Mrs. Roberts's carriage stand before her door waiting for Maybelle. She liked to say to certain of her patrons:—

"Oh, the coachman is used to waiting; our dear Maybelle is almost certain to be tardy, but then she is so much at home at Mrs. Roberts's house that she can take all sorts of liberties. Oh, yes, she dines there several times a week and often takes some of her classmates with her. Dear Mrs. Roberts welcomes my girls to her home as though she were their elder sister. What a charming woman she is! Really when one comes to know her intimately, one feels that the half has not been told concerning her."

And Maybelle was blossoming under this reign of love. Her cheeks were rounding out a little and taking on a touch of color, and her eyes were growing less sad. She had by no means forgotten her grief nor put aside the thought of her father. On the contrary, she liked nothing better than to talk of him by the hour to a sympathetic listener, while to be allowed to talk about her mother, was to give free vent to the one pent-up passion of her life.

It was to Mrs. Burnham that she talked most freely, though Mrs. Roberts's young people were sympathetic, and Erskine, especially, liked nothing better than to hear long stories about the artist and his method of dealing with a picture.

"He made them up," Maybelle would say, "composed them, you know, or made a plot, as you do when you write a story for your college paper. The picture grew, just as a story does. 'That's an idea!' papa would say, when I was sitting meekly enough beside him, telling him some story of my day. 'That's a look I never saw before, let me get it,

Maysie'—that was one of his dear names for me, he had dozens of them—and he would seize palette and brush and work for a few minutes as hard as he could, then sit back and gaze at me and think, and I knew that a new picture was born and would have to be watched over and nourished and developed. It was very interesting."

"Yes, indeed! he painted me a hundred times and in a hundred different ways, but they did him no good; he never would try to sell them, nor even show them. They are all boxed up with our other things and stored; Aunt Mamie took charge of them. He told her they were never to be sold. I think it was because my mother's picture was always mixed in with them, and he could not bear to sell her. He used to make pictures of me, sometimes, that he said were like mamma. There would be just little hints of me about them, not a likeness of me at all, but a beautiful girl, and the tears would come into papa's dear eyes when he looked at her, and he would say softly, 'It is her image.'"

When Maybelle talked in this way to Ruth, she once or twice said wistfully:—

"It must be beautiful to be loved in the way that my father loved my mother." But Erskine Roberts never heard any words of this kind.

CHAPTER XXIII

PUZZLING QUESTIONS

"This is lovely!" said Maybelle, as she drew the curtains, and pushed her sewing chair closer to Mrs. Burnham's. "Isn't it nice to be alone together? Erskine wanted me to go with them to the rehearsal and act as prompter, but I told him I was going to follow the promptings of my own heart and stay with you, especially since his mother must also be away. If we lived all alone in a dear little home, you and I, I could take care of you all the time."

"I am afraid I should need something besides lovely rooms and pretty sewing," Mrs. Burnham said laughingly.

"Yes, indeed! but I could do them; all sorts of things. I used to do things for Mrs. Parker, and for papa when he would let me. I was always coaxing papa to have a little bit of a house just large enough for us two, and let me take charge of it; I knew I could; I could learn, you know, and Mrs. Parker taught me a great many things; but he never would. Poor papa! he didn't want a home; he said that he had one once, and he wanted it to live in his memory forever. He meant that time—before mamma died. Do you think it is like most men to be so constant to a memory?"

"I do not know," Mrs. Burnham said, with an effort. She never knew what to say to Maybelle when she was in this mood. It was impossible to join in the talk about a dead mother, and not feel herself a hypocrite. But Maybelle was already on another theme.

"Dear Mrs. Burnham, I am glad we are alone to-night. There are matters about which I want to talk with you.

"Do you know, I have been treated always like a little girl? and it seems to me that the time has come for me to begin to be a woman. I used to try to get papa to tell me about his affairs, but he never would. During those last dreadful days, all he would tell me was that he had left everything to Aunt Mamie, and I was to do just as she said. But I have a feeling that papa was poor; and that he just made enough by his pictures to support us, perhaps not always that; I have thought lately that perhaps a great many of my nice things and—and opportunities, came through Aunt Mamie. Madame Sternheim has dropped hints more than once that have made me believe so. And now,—don't you think I ought to know all about it, and be making plans to support myself?"

"My dear!" was all that Ruth could say, in an almost dismayed tone. Maybelle's future and her connection with it were more puzzling to Erskine Burnham's mother than they could possibly be to this child. The earnest young voice went on:—

"I wrote to Aunt Mamie just how I felt, but she cannot see it as I do. She says that she is alone in the world, that money is the only thing she has enough of, and that papa gave me to her to take care of. She does not understand why I should not be quite happy over such an arrangement; but dear Mrs. Burnham, I am sure you do. It is not that I do not love to belong to her, I mean to, always; and sometimes I cannot sleep for the joy of thinking that she loves me so dearly; I can't think why she does. But don't you think that a self-respecting girl wants to support herself just as soon as she possibly can, unless she has a father and mother who can do it as well as not, and want to?"

This also was a sore and embarrassing phase of the subject to poor Ruth. Oh, to be able to say to her that her mother, her own mother, was in a position to cover for her every need that money could supply and that the man who now stood in the place of father to her would insist upon so much tardy justice—if he knew of her existence! Yet Ruth's common sense told her that even though there were no terrible reasons for silence for the sake of others, the hardest blow that could be given to a girl like Maybelle would be to destroy her beautiful illusions of her mother with the base truth. That mother of sacred memory, alive, well, living in ease and luxury and ignoring her as utterly as though she had never been born! Could such a cruel blow as that be borne! Yet any words that this much-tried woman could arrange in reply to the appeal just made, seemed false. She hesitated, and knew that her face was flushing under the girl's earnest gaze. At last, she said the only words there seemed left for her to say.

"My dear, I am a little bit on both sides of this question. I certainly sympathize with your view, and on general principles should agree with you. But the circumstances are peculiar this time." And as she said the words she felt like a hypocrite; how peculiar they were, that poor child had not the least idea! "Miss Parker is, as she says, practically alone in the world. Her brother's marriage is a coming event; then he will not need her any more, in the special sense in which she can help him now, and he does not need her money, for he has plenty of his own. Their father discovered a gold mine, you know, as well as one of another metal, almost more valuable than gold. So, if Miss Parker wants to spend a little of her surplus money upon you, because she loves you, ought you not to please her in this, and be governed by her advice, at least for the present? When you are older, and especially when Miss Parker returns home, which I think she will do before very long, probably some plans can be made that will please you both. Cannot you wait, dear?"

Maybelle sat thoughtful for a moment, then she drew a long sigh.

"I suppose I must," she said. "Indeed, there is no other way for me at present; only—I am to graduate, you know, in a few days, and I thought—but of course I ought not, contrary to Aunt Mamie's wishes. But I do not know what she wants me to do for the summer. She has not seemed to remember it. I have always spent the summer vacations with her."

"You are not to forecast anxieties about the summer," Mrs. Burnham said, trying to make her voice sound cheery and free from all anxiety, though it struck her like a physical pain, the fact that she could not say to this girl who was growing dearer to her with every passing day, "Come home with me, child, of course;" that she could never invite her to her home, and could never explain to her why she must not. She must simply be silent and trust to Maybelle's shrewd guessing that there were reasons why this new friend of hers did not feel at home in her own home, and was not at liberty to take her friends there.

It was true that summer was upon them, and the air of the boarding school was athrob with the plans of eager girls getting ready for the home-going. Maybelle was almost the only one who had not some sort of home to plan for. And yet Maybelle was to graduate! If only Mrs. Burnham could say to her, "Come, we will make home together, and you may do for me all that your heart prompts." There were hours when she was tempted to do something of the kind. But her words to Maybelle revealed none of her pain.

"There are lovely schemes maturing for the summer. 'Good times,' my dear, and unlike the illustrious Gloriana McQuirk you are 'in 'em.' I am not to divulge them before the appointed hour, but I empower you to say to those envious schoolgirls that your summer plans are a delicious secret even from yourself, being locked in the heart of that blessed little schemer, Mrs. Roberts."

Maybelle's face was still serious, but, after a moment, she laughed softly.

"I am the strangest girl!" she said. "I don't think there can be another girl in the world who lives my kind of life. I have not what Madame Sternheim calls a 'relative' this side heaven to care what becomes of me, and I have the dearest company of people, on whom, according to Madame again, I have not the shadow of a claim, who never weary of doing for me! What more, for instance, could you and that dear Mrs. Roberts and those girls and boys of hers do for me, even though I had that potent charm, some of 'the same blood' in my veins? And yet, do you know, selfish creature that I am, the Madame has so instilled her principles into me that if I only had a sister or brother of my very own to love and care for, I think I could give up joyfully all other luxuries."

"Are you not forgetting your aunts in England, my dear?"

Maybelle shook her head and spoke resolutely. "I want to forget them; I do not claim them as aunts of mine." Then, in response to Ruth's look that might have meant reproach, she added:—

"They did not like mamma, Mrs. Burnham, and they were not good to her. Papa told me as much as that. He said she was young, and away from all her home friends and unhappy, and they led her a hard life. Papa could not help feeling hard toward them for that. It was the reason why he never went to England again after Grandmother died. He took me to see Grandmother, did you know that? But she did not seem like a grandmother. She wasn't *dear*, you know, and sweet, like the grandmothers in stories, and in real life too,—some of the girls at school have lovely ones,—but mine was stately and cold. She and my two aunts used to talk about mamma right before me.

"'She looks like *her*,' one of them said, with a strong emphasis on the 'her' a contemptuous emphasis it seemed to me. And the other aunt replied, 'But she isn't like her in disposition, apparently.' Then Grandmother said quickly, 'Heaven forbid!' Could one love people who talked in that way before a child about her dear dead mother? Not that they meant me to understand," she added thoughtfully, after a moment, as one who must do full justice even to one's enemies. "I don't think they did; they were the kind of people who think that a child is deaf and blind and stupid. I understood hints and shrugs of the shoulders and curls of the lip and exclamations a great deal better than they thought I did. I have no relatives, dear Mrs. Burnham, that I care for, but I have friends whom I love with every bit of me. May I ask just one little question?—and you need not answer it if it is part of the secret. Do the summer plans include you? Because if they don't, and there could be a way for me to have you for just a little piece of the summer, I—"

The tremble in her voice had grown so marked that she stopped abruptly. She looked up, after a minute, with her eyes swimming in tears, and said with a queer little attempt at a laugh:—

"I'm not going to cry, Mrs. Burnham, don't you be afraid. And I'm not going to be selfish and babyish; I mean to be just as glad and happy and grateful as I can be, even though you have to be away from me all summer long."

It was just at that moment that Ruth resolved upon yielding to Flossy's entreaties and spending at least part of the summer with them at their new seaside cottage, which was to be a surprise to all the young people, Maybelle included. Erskine expected her at home, but what were Erskine's needs compared to this deserted child's?—and the child clung to her. But she would not tell Maybelle, not just yet; so she spoke lightly, commending the child's resolve to count her mercies, and then admonishing her that she had better also count her stitches, as she was making a mistake in the row she was crocheting.

There was a thoughtful silence on the part of both for a few minutes, then Maybelle spoke again in what Mrs. Burnham called her grown-up tone.

"There is one strange question I have wanted to ask of somebody for a long time. I tried to talk to Erskine about it without letting him know that it was really a question in my mind; but Erskine is like all boys, very wise and very positive, without being always able to give a reason for what he believes."

"Which means," said Ruth, smiling, "that Erskine did not agree with you."

"Well, he didn't," and Maybelle stopped to laugh at herself; then spoke earnestly.

"That is, so far as I may be said to have an opinion on that subject; I am not sure what I think, or at least I do not know why I think it. Mrs. Burnham, do Christian people ever pray for their dead? And if they do not, why not? Does the Bible say we must not? I have tried to find something in the Bible about it, and I could not."

Ruth was much startled. This was very different from the question she had expected. The young people argued vigorously upon every live question of the day, not excepting interesting theological points, but this was out of the regular line. While she considered just how best to answer it, Maybelle explained.

"I suppose that seems to you a strange question; young people do not often discuss such things, I suppose; but it interests me very much because I have such a longing, sometimes, to pray for mamma, that I can hardly keep her name from my lips; yet I thought perhaps it was wrong. I began to have that feeling almost as soon as Aunt Mamie taught me to pray. I had said my prayers before that time; papa taught me to say: 'Now I lay me down to sleep,' and 'Bless thy little lamb to-night.' I used to like to say them, but I did not understand what praying really was, until long after that time. But when Aunt Mamie made it plain to me, and my heart took hold of the fact that I was really talking with God, and that I could talk to Him about papa, and in that way help him, I cannot tell you how glad I was! And then, very soon, I wanted to put mamma in."

Nothing that the girl had said had ever startled Ruth as much as this. Was there a woman living who needed prayer more than this child's mother? Yet how could she counsel her daughter to pray for her?

CHAPTER XXIV

AN ALLY

"I do not know that there is any 'thus saith the Lord,' against your wish, my dear," she said at last, in a hesitating tone, "but the inference from all gospel teaching seems to be that this life is the time for prayer."

Maybelle gave a disappointed sigh.

"I should think people would study into it," she said, "and find out if they might. It makes such an awful blank in one's praying to suddenly leave out a name that has been on one's lips and in one's heart for years."

Then Ruth knew that the child was thinking of her father, and that she must move very carefully in trying to comfort her.

"I did not have that feeling about my father, Maybelle dear, nor about my husband. On the contrary I had an almost joyful realization that they were beyond the need for prayer—were where they could make no mistakes, where the mistakes of others could never harm them any more, and where they would be forever in the presence of the Lord. What could one possibly ask more for them?"

Maybelle was silent for several minutes, and her eyes were soft with unshed tears. Then she spoke gently:—

"What a lovely thought! thank you."

After a moment she began again, earnestly.

"Mrs. Burnham, there is something I want you to know. What I am sure that Madame Sternheim thinks about my papa isn't true. Papa learned how to pray; and every afternoon during those last few weeks, he and I used to read in the Bible together, and pray. And the last time I saw him he told me that, although he had wasted his life, and been in every way a different man from what he ought to have been, God had forgiven him, and was going to take him home. He wasn't a bad man, ever, Mrs. Burnham; at least—well, I know he did some wrong things, but he was good in many ways. He had a very low estimate of himself, though, and those were the words he said. I shall never forget the last sentence he ever spoke; I can often close my eyes and seem to hear his dear voice with its note of exultation, 'It is wonderful, but I am going *home*!' He used to speak that word 'home' in a peculiar manner; his voice seemed to linger over it lovingly, like a caress. He had no home, you know, after mamma went away."

This was Maybelle's way of speaking of death; but the woman, who realized how literally the phrase "went away" applied to this child's mother, could never hear it without an inward shudder. Her own eyes had dimmed with tears as she listened to this pathetic and yet gracious close of a wasted life. Then she acted upon a sudden resolution.

"Maybelle, dear, there is one person for whom I want you to pray with all your soul; that is my son's wife."

"Your daughter?" said Maybelle, lingering over the word as a sweet sound, yet with a hint of surprise in her tone, as though she might almost ask, "Why should any woman so blessed as she need praying for?" But what she added was:—

"I should love to pray for her. Tell me about her, please. She must be a very happy woman to have the right to call you 'mother.' What is it you want me to ask for her? Of course she is a Christian?"

"She is a member of the church," said Ruth. "But I do not think she knows the Lord Jesus in the way that you and I know Him, or that she loves and serves Him."

"Oh!" said Maybelle, and that single mono-syllable from her lips meant much. Surprise, regret, pity, resolve, were all expressed in it.

Ruth made haste to finish what she had resolved to say.

"And she needs to know Him; oh! she needs it more than most women do. If she could come, even now, into intimate fellowship with the Lord Jesus Christ, it would make an infinite difference, not only with her life, but in the lives of others. There are others who—" She stopped abruptly; excitement was getting the better of discretion. She must have a care what she said. After a moment she spoke with less intensity.

"I hope you will pray, too, for Erskine. For my son, I mean." For Maybelle had made a little startled movement at the mention of this name, and turned great wondering eyes upon her.

"My son's name is Erskine, you remember. He is my only one, dear, the only treasure that I ever had; for years and years he has been all that I have; and I cry out so for God's best for him! He is a Christian, a good, true Christian man; he is everything that to other people seems desirable; but—"

"I think I know what you mean," Maybelle said gently. "I know that there can be degrees in living religion. Sometimes I think I know that fact better than any other; I have had so many illustrations of it in my life. It must be hard for him that his wife does not always think just as he does in this. At least I should think it would be very hard indeed for married people not to be as one in such matters."

"Yes," said Ruth, "it is very hard." Then she turned suddenly to a radically different subject, with the conviction strong upon her that she could talk no more about Erskine and Irene without saying what would be better left unsaid.

But she had secured a wonderful ally in Maybelle. The girl knew how to pray, and her faith was as the faith of a little child: simple, and literal, and firm. She became intensely interested in Mrs. Burnham's daughter-in-law. She asked many questions about her, sometimes making remarks, in her ignorance, that wrung Ruth's heart.

"I think I love her," she said one day. "There are times when I feel a curious yearning tenderness for her, as though I must put my arms about her and kiss her. It seems strange, doesn't it, when I have never seen her? I do not love a great many people; of course I like ever so many, but this feeling that I have is different. Still, I suppose it is the way one feels toward those for whom one prays, definitely and daily. Isn't it?"

"Perhaps," said Ruth, unable to add another word, and turning away her face so that the child could not see what it might express. If only Irene had loved *her*!

One noticeable feature of this time was that Maybelle began to speak confidently regarding the answer to her prayers.

"You will tell me when your daughter truly begins to serve Jesus Christ, won't you?" she said. "I think I should like to know it, soon, because it changes the tone of one's prayers, don't you think, as soon as one for whom you have been asking just this, recognizes Jesus Christ and begins to be acquainted with Him?"

"You speak very confidently, dear," Ruth could not help saying. "Do you always feel quite sure that the people for whom you pray will 'recognize' Jesus Christ?"

"Not always," the girl said thoughtfully. "I cannot be sure, because they may keep on refusing to let Him in, and of course He will not force an entrance. When I was a little girl, I thought that was very strange. I wondered why God did not *make* people love and serve Him, whether they wanted to, or not. But when I grew old enough to realize what love really is, I knew better; for what is enforced service worth? and as for enforced *love*, that couldn't be. But sometimes the feeling comes to me that the one for whom I am asking, will let him in; and I have it now."

And then Mrs. Burnham began to desire exceedingly that this girl should pray mightily for her son. More than all things else, more even than that the rags of his outward respectability—as regarded his home—might be preserved to him, did she long for his entire consecration to God. She knew only too well that, despite his strict integrity and his firm adherence to the letter of his faith, the world was gripping him with a mighty hold. She knew, too, how insidiously and how surely Irene's views, and Irene's feelings, and Irene's wishes were slipping in between him and that entirely consecrated life which would hold him safe above all the world's allurements.

It was not that he was markedly different in word or deed from what his early manhood had promised. It was rather that he had not grown, spiritually, with the passing years; and of late years, since his marriage, his mother could detect a backward movement, as of one drifting downstream imperceptibly to himself, and losing force. There were times when she felt almost jealous of the hold which her daughter-in-law had taken upon the heart of this girl who believed as well as prayed.

"You will not forget my Erskine?" she said one day when they had been talking about it.

"Oh, no!" Maybelle said quickly. "No, indeed! How could I, dear Mrs. Burnham, when he is your son, and you asked me to pray for him? I never forget him; but after all, it isn't so important, you know."

"Why not?" The mother was almost indignant. From her standpoint nothing in life seemed quite so important as that Erskine should be the kind of Christian that the Lord wanted.

"Why, because," said the child, wonderingly, "he *belongs*, you know, and—won't the dear Lord take care of his own? But it is different with her,—why, she may not let Him!"

There was the most peculiar emphasis of that word "belongs"; and almost infinite dismay expressed by the last phrase. Maybelle was a literalist. She believed that when the Lord said, "Ye *will not* come unto me that ye might have life," he meant that it was quite within man's power to refuse it.

But from that hour Ruth's heart was quieter concerning her son, and she prayed in stronger faith. Erskine "belonged" and she could trust the Lord to take care of His own. It seemed strange, but the child was really helping the Christian of mature years. "Except ye become as little children," she repeated to her heart with a grateful smile. Maybelle's faith was as the faith of a little child; that was what made it so strong.

The plans for the summer matured and, to the joy of all concerned, Mrs. Burnham was carried a willing captive to the new seaside home; and, on one pretext or another, lingered there from week to week. The young people were fertile in schemes, and vied with one another in pretexts to hold her just a few days more.

"You cannot surely go until after the fourteenth!" and "Why, we must have you for the twenty-first, anyway!"

Meantime, Erskine was growing almost indignant, at least on paper. His final argument was put with lawyer-like directness.

"It seems to be true that you have ceased to care for your son, but perhaps the advent of your grandson will move you. Erskine Burnham, Junior, arrived at four this morning, as I have already announced to you by telegram, and is in excellent health and spirits, and very desirous of beholding the face of his grandmother; I might remark, in passing, that his father and mother sympathize with him in this desire, save that the cruel grandmother seems to be quite dead to all natural affection. We are hoping that to have a grandson will be something so unnatural as to arouse her desires for home."

But if he could have seen his mother during that first hour after the despatch reached her, he would have been deeply pained as well as puzzled. Did ever grandmother take such triumphant news in such strange fashion before? She was alone in her room, and she let the paper drop away from her while she hid her face in her hands and shook as though in an ague chill. Her grandson! yes, but Irene's son! born of such a mother into this dangerous, sin-stricken world! to be trained by such a mother! and her fair and lovely daughter an outlaw at this moment from her mother's home and heart! How would it be possible for a boy with such an inheritance as such a mother would give him, to escape the snares that would assuredly be set for him? Great waves of pain seemed to have this woman in its clutches, as she lived over again her own young motherhood, and thought of all that it had meant to her, and contrasted herself with that other mother; and remembered that she was the mother of Erskine Burnham's son.

But by degrees saner thoughts began to come. Heredity was not everything, she reminded herself; and even according to it its full place, had not the boy a father? The thought of Maybelle in this connection helped to quiet her. Was ever sweeter, purer, more lovable girl born of woman than she? And was not that same woman her mother? What of heredity here?

But the girl was deserted by her mother, and mercifully preserved from such training as she would have given. What was that promise? "When my father and mother forsake me, then the Lord will take me up." Had not the Lord made good this word? If only this little new boy, her grandson, could—And then Ruth turned in stern repellence from herself. What was this that she was thinking! Could not God take care of his own?

But she must go home, of course she must go home now, at once. But she did not. One of Mrs. Roberts's flock fell ill, and before noon of the following day was very seriously, even desperately ill, and there followed a long, hard battle with disease; and Ruth, who had lingered for her pleasure, apparently, could not of course leave them now, when for the first time there was opportunity to be of real service. The sick one, even after the battle was fought, was slow in convalescing, and the mother was worn, and Ruth could see that she held a place in this home that no one else just then could fill, and she stayed.

So it came to pass that the summer was gone, and the Roberts household was established in town again, and Maybelle was entered at Madame Sternheim's for a year of graduate work, before the Burnham carriage waited at the station for the belated grandmother, and her son paced the station platform more eager and impatient for his mother than it seemed to him he had ever been in his life before, and his son was two months old that day.

CHAPTER XXV

A CRISIS

"Do you think I will ever let you go away from us again?" This was Erskine Burnham's word to his mother when he had her all to himself in the carriage. His arms were about her, and he was kissing eyes and nose and hair after the fashion of his childhood.

"Such a wicked, wicked grandmother! Does she think she deserves the most beautiful, most intelligent grandson that ever drew breath?"

Throughout that drive they were very gay; both of them covered under the semblance of merrymaking, the deep feeling that neither wished just then to express.

Only once, as the carriage turned in at the familiar gateway, did Erskine trust himself to a tender word:—

"O mommie, mommie! do you suppose you know anything about how a boy feels to get his mother again?"

"My boy!" she began, but her voice broke, and she could not utter another word. And then the carriage drew up before the side entrance, and Erskine became very busy with the bags and wraps, and believed that his mother's emotion was the natural feeling of a grandmother on coming into her possession.

The weeks that immediately followed were very far from happy ones, although one member of the family circle was doing her utmost in the interests of peace.

Ruth Burnham had not lingered for months away from her home simply from dread of facing the situation; nor yet on account entirely of the young girl whom she had taken to her heart; there had been underneath these, a determined purpose to leave those two quite to themselves; to try the effect upon Irene of relieving her for a time of her mother-in-law's daily presence. It is true she had not planned just how long she could do this—she had not been sure when she went away that it could be done, save for a few days; but she had allowed herself to be apparently swayed by every passing reason for delay, despite Erskine's evident bewilderment over such action, with an end in view which had to do with that solemn self-sacrifice she had made. It remained to be seen whether this phase of it had been of any avail.

At first, Irene was gracious, or tried to be; but in all her apparent sweetness, and sometimes even attempts at deference, there was a curious little undertone sting, which made Ruth feel constrained, and always uncertain what to say or do next.

But the baby, toward whom her sore heart turned with a hunger that was almost pain, was as fair and sweet a creation as ever came from the thought of God. So like his father—in the eyes of the grandmother, that there were moments when she could shut herself up alone with him and live her mother-joy over again.

Not many of them; her time with him was literally counted by moments, and grew more and more uncertain each passing day.

Ruth had schooled herself to see at least indifference on the part of the mother toward her child, and had planned how she would try to atone for such unutterable loss by making him the very centre of her own life. But behold! instead of anything like indifference, Irene developed a love for the child so passionate, so fierce, indeed, that it suggested the instinct of wild animals, instead of cultivated motherhood.

Moreover, the poor mother was jealous of even the nurse who lavished loving nonsense upon her baby, and intensely jealous of the grandmother, for whom the baby, even thus early in his life, began to exhibit a perverse fondness.

The entire situation was a surprise, and, it must be admitted, an added blow to Ruth. Instead of being able to rejoice that the maternal instinct had been at last awakened in this woman, she was dismayed and heartsick over it. If Irene meant to begin thus early to keep the boy under her constant care and surveillance, what hope was there for his future?

She awakened to the fact that she had been counting upon this mother's fondness for all sorts of social functions, and expecting to see her enter with zest upon her former care-free life, thus making it possible for the baby to be much under his grandmother's supervision. She had planned prematurely. Irene seemed to have forgotten society; she never walked, or drove, without her baby; she kept him with her during all his waking moments, and apparently lived for the purpose of warding off the attentions of, especially, his grandmother.

In vain did Ruth try, by utmost deference to the mother's superior claim, by never presuming to offer even a suggestion as to the child's care, to disarm the intense dislike that Irene could not help showing—a dislike of having her even notice the child.

So marked was this condition of things becoming to the servants that Ruth, beyond measure distressed and bewildered, stayed much of the time in her own room, and considered and abandoned a dozen schemes for going away again. The difficulty was to make any movement that would not excite Erskine's suspicion; for Erskine, being a man and a very busy one, continued to be what Irene once told him he was, "as blind as a bat." He was a very proud, glad father, prepared to believe that his son was the sweetest, brightest, most beautiful baby who ever blessed the earth with his presence, and he was unequivocally and blissfully happy at seeing that baby in his grandmother's arms. In rejoicing over her home-coming, and in delighting over the thought of having his son grow up in daily intimacy with her, he said "we" as heartily and jubilantly as though certain that Irene shared his happiness, and it is certain that he so believed.

"We have learned one lesson, anyway," he said gayly, as they sat together one evening after dinner. "That is that we mustn't let you get away from home again very soon. A mother who has no conception of when it is time to come home must not be allowed her freedom. Do you think we have forgiven you already for those months of indifference to us? What was the charm, mommie? You have never told us. The truth is, you have told us very little about that long visit. Irene used to be sure that there was some attraction that you did not reveal. Have you made her confess, Irene?"

Irene made a feint of joining in his gayety, and said something about not thinking it worth while to attempt what he had failed in accomplishing.

"Well," Erskine said, after a moment, puzzled and a trifle hurt because his mother did not seem to join heartily in the nonsense, "there is one comfort; I am not afraid of her deserting us again. Erskine Burnham, Junior, is an attraction that will hold, even though his father's power seems to have waned."

It was by random sentences like these, that Ruth was made to realize how difficult it would be to get away again.

As the days passed and the situation grew more and more strained, the mother's only comfort was that Erskine did not understand it. How should he? The claims of business pressed every day more heavily upon him. From being the younger partner in a great legal firm, as his decided ability became known, he had risen steadily, until responsibilities as well as honors had been thrust upon him, and he was now a recognized power in his profession. This meant very close attention to business, and he had scarcely any time that he could call his own.

How could he know, and, after a little, the resolute mother asked herself why he should ever know that when he left his beautiful home each morning for his long, busy day in town, he left jealousy and suspicion and unreasoning aversion behind him?

"I think she hates me," Ruth said to herself as she sat in her room with folded hands and listened to the vigorous protests of the boy across the hall, and knew that she, his grandmother, who loved every hair of his dear golden head, must hold herself from going to him. "I am sure she hates me, and the feeling grows stronger every day. Oh, what shall I do? what can I do! How is one to endure such a state of things for a lifetime? I am not an old woman. I may have to stay here for years and years! If I could *only* get through with it all and go to my home!"

It was not often that she indulged herself in such moods, and she felt always distinctly self-condemned when they were allowed to take hold of her. She had never been one to indulge herself in what her old friend Eurie Mitchell used to characterize as "useless whining"; and it would be beneath the mature Christian to allow it.

But a crisis was at hand. Erskine surprised his family one afternoon by coming home several hours earlier than usual.

"I ran away!" was his gay announcement as he found his wife and mother in the living-room. They had been entertaining a caller who had asked first for Ruth, and then had insisted upon seeing the young mother and the baby.

"Such tiresome people!" Irene had said impatiently. "Forever trying to pry into my affairs! I wish they would at least let me have my baby in peace."

But she had ordered the nurse to bring him down to her in a few minutes, for the callers were Erskine's friends of long standing, and she knew that he meant them to be treated with all deference.

"This is great luck to find you both here," Erskine said. "It will save time. I escaped from the office on purpose to enjoy a drive with my family. It is just the day for Boy Junior," and he tossed the delighted baby in his arms as he spoke. "It is as balmy as spring. Why, this is a spring month, isn't it? I had forgotten. Get ready, beloveds, and we shall have time for a glimpse of the bay before the sun sets."

"Oh, no!" said Irene, hastily. "Not today, Erskine; I don't want to go. You can take mother, and baby and I will stay at home."

Erskine looked surprised and troubled.

"Why is that, dear? I planned on purpose for you. I don't think you get out enough in this sweet spring air. I could not help noticing how pale and worn you looked this morning. Don't you think so, mamma? Come, dearest, it will do you good; and I have so little time nowadays for driving with you. I have been planning all the morning to get away."

"I don't want to go," Irene said fretfully. But her husband took no notice of the words.

"We'll go on a lark!" he explained to the delighted baby. "Father and mother and grandmother and grandson. How does that sound, my boy? I feel like a boy myself to-day. You and the little boy may have the back seat, mommie, and your big girl and boy will sit in front, and drive. Don't you want to drive, Irene? The horses are in fine spirit, just as you like them to feel when you have the reins.

"Here, nurse," as that young woman appeared at the moment in the doorway. "Put this young man into driving attire, while the ladies are getting on their wraps. We mustn't waste another minute of this glorious sunshine."

But at this point the baby asserted himself. The nurse had taken him from his father's arms and was moving toward the door; as he passed Ruth, he made a quick, unexpected spring in her direction, and had not her arms been quick and her grasp firm, there might have been an accident. As it was, he cuddled in her embrace with a gurgle of happiness.

"You young scamp!" said the proud father, with a relieved laugh. "You knew where you meant to land, didn't you? Showed excellent taste, too. He is becoming to you, mommie. You look young enough to-day to be mistaken for his mother. Doesn't she, Irene?"

For Ruth's cheeks had flushed like a girl's, and her heart was beating swiftly under the baby's caresses. She bent her head over the golden one, and murmured some incoherent sentence, while she hid eyes that were filled with tears. It was so rare a thing in these days to get a chance to cuddle that baby!

And then Irene spoke, in a tone of voice that her husband had rarely heard:—

"Rebecca, I did not ring for you. Go away; I will bring the baby myself. I *wish* you wouldn't! I don't want him kissed nor fondled. Give him to me."

This last, addressed to Ruth, in a tone so sharp and a manner so rude that Erskine in unbounded astonishment said:—

"Irene!"

Just that word, but not as she had ever before heard it spoken.

"I don't care!" she said. "Let her leave my baby alone. I don't want her to touch him, and I won't have it! I *won't*! I say!"

Her voice had risen almost to a scream.

Rebecca had disappeared with the swiftness with which this woman's servants generally obeyed her commands, and Ruth, putting the baby without a word into his amazed father's arms, fled away also.

CHAPTER XXVI

A STRANGE CHANGE

There was no driving out that day; the Burnham horses were remanded to the stable with no other explanation to their astonished care taker than that the ladies had decided not to go out.

When Ruth, distressed and bewildered as to what course to take, obeyed the tardy summons to dinner, she found a stranger in the dining room whom Erskine introduced as a member of the Severn law firm, from town, who had come out for a business conference. Would she be kind enough to take Irene's place at table? His wife, he explained to the guest, was the victim of a severe headache and must be excused.

Throughout the dinner Erskine was thoughtful for and courteously attentive to his mother; but of course there was no opportunity for a personal word. When at last he excused himself for a business conference and took his guest to the library, Ruth stood where he had left her, irresolute and distressed. Under normal conditions the proper and natural thing for a mother whose daughter was suffering with headache would be to go to her with sympathetic inquiries and offers of help. Should she attempt this? Would Erskine think it the right step for her to take? She feared that she knew only too well how Irene would receive her; but no matter. The question was, What did Erskine want? What did he think about it all? Did he blame her for the strange exhibition he had seen that afternoon? True, it was not more than she had endured before, but it was a strange experience to Erskine, and it would be only natural for him to think that his wife must have had strong provocation, in order to make such an outburst possible. If he thought that,—if he blamed her in any way, how would it be possible ever to undeceive him? Wait—ought she to undeceive him? Ought she even to exonerate herself? Could she expect any man to take sides against his wife? What a horrible question! Could she want him to do such a thing even for her? Oh, the misery of it all! That she and her son had reached the hour when they could not explain to each other!

Only one thing seemed certain. She must go away somewhere, and speedily. It must now be apparent even to Erskine that they could not continue longer in this way of living.

She crept back to her room, at last, and sat in the darkness with hands closely clasped, so closely that the diamond of her engagement ring cut into the flesh. She listened for words from across the hall, or for movements. She went over and over and over the miserable scene of the afternoon; she listened for Erskine, and wondered if he would stop at her room, and was afraid to have him come.

It was late when he came upstairs very quietly and paused at his mother's door and listened; and she was breathlessly still. Then he went on, to his own rooms; and Ruth, physically exhausted, went to her bed, and, in the course of time, fell asleep, not having been able to come to any decision as to what she could do.

The gray dawn of another day was beginning to make faint shadows in the room, when a knock at her door awakened her, and Erskine entered.

Was she awake? he inquired anxiously. It was too bad to disturb her rest, but he must. Irene was ill, very ill. Nurse was with her, and the baby had awakened and was crying. Might he bring him to her, and could she care for him until they could plan how to manage?

Even in that moment of haste and anxiety Ruth detected in her son's voice a kind of solemn relief, almost of satisfaction, and read its meaning. It was as if he had said:—

"Irene is violently ill, is not herself, indeed, and probably has not been for a long time. It is plain that she was not responsible for what she said or did yesterday." His mother could understand that even such an explanation, sad as it was, was balm to his soul. She sprang up and began to dress in haste, while she answered him. Of course she would care for Baby; bring him at once; or wait, she would go for him herself.

"Go back to Irene," she commanded. "She may be needing you this minute; and you needn't think of Baby again." How glad her hungry arms were to enfold him, even at such price, she would have been almost ashamed to have had known.

In this manner the dreaded day broke for them; with all embarrassments forgotten and all programmes of possible action swept away. Irene was desperately ill. Rebecca, the baby's nurse, who was a graduate of a training school, and had done hospital service, admitted that it looked like what she called "a case." She was willing to transfer her attentions entirely to the mother, until other arrangements could be made.

Then began in the Burnham household a new and strange but very busy life. With incredible promptness the house took on that indescribable and distinctly felt change which serious illness brings in its train. All ordinary routine was suspended. The eight o'clock car for which Erskine was almost as sure to be ready as the sun was to rise at a given moment, halted at the corner for passengers as usual, but went on without him. He came down to breakfast at any hour when he could best get away from Irene, and sometimes stood in the doorway, coffee cup in hand, ready for a summons; for Irene was as imperious in her delirium as she had been in health. The house seemed to be in the hands of physicians and nurses. As the illness had from the first assumed a serious form, a trained nurse had been at once secured, but it proved necessary for Rebecca, also, to be in almost constant attendance. This placed the baby entirely in the care of his grandmother, whose thankful and devoted service was his at any hour of the day or night. While the machinery of all the rest of the house was more or less thrown out of gear, the people taking their meals at any hour that chanced to be convenient for them, and ordering all their movements with a view to the sick room, Erskine Burnham junior went on his serene and methodical way. He was bathed and dressed and breakfasted at his usual hours; he went out in his carriage at the given time; he sat on the porch in the sunshine at just such and such periods, and was in every respect as serene and sunny and well-cared-for a baby as though his mother was not lying upstairs making a desperate fight for life.

This state of things lasted for about three weeks; then the alarming character of the illness subsided, and by degrees, the long, slow period of convalescence was entered upon, and the house adjusted itself again to changed conditions.

In kitchen and dining room something like routine could once more be carried out; and Erskine began to think of business, and even to get away to his office for an hour or two each day.

By and by the closely drawn shades below stairs were raised, and flowers began to appear in the vases.

But in Baby Erskine's apartments his grandmother still reigned supreme. The special trained nurse had departed, and Rebecca had sole charge of the patient. A young nurse girl had been secured at the first, to help with the care of baby, under Ruth's supervision, and she was proving herself a comfort.

Altogether, these days, full of responsibilities though they were, and not without some anxieties, held much comfort and even happiness for Ruth. Erskine's baby was in her care, and as often as she chose was in her arms; she could fondle him as she would, without fear of reproof. She could bathe and rub and clothe the perfect little body, she could curl the lovely golden rings of hair about her fingers, she could catch him up in a transport of bliss and kiss his lovely little neck and dimpled chin and exquisite arms, and in a thousand tender mother-ways rest her heart upon him.

And the baby lavished love without measure upon her, and clung to her when any attempt was made to take him away, and made wild little demonstrations of delight at her approach; and all day she was happy.

It was only at night when he lay in his crib near her bedside, sleeping quietly, that the spectre of the near future came and sat with her and set her heart to quivering. The days were passing swiftly; each one was bringing nearer the hour when she must give back her treasure and banish herself. Where? She did not know; she had not been able to decide. Somewhere with Maybelle, if that could be brought about; only—What could be said to Erskine?

Was it absolutely necessary? Was it possible that this very serious illness, whose outcome much of the time had been more than doubtful, had wrought changes in Irene? Sometimes it almost seemed to her that such was the case; and yet it might be only physical weakness that made the difference.

Daily now, by the doctor's advice, Baby was taken to his mother's room for a few minutes. At first, Ruth sent the little maid with him, and avoided going in at the same time, lest the baby's demonstrations of delight over her would annoy his mother. But one morning as she was passing through the hall with Baby in her arms, the door of the sick room opened, and Rebecca called:—

"Mrs. Burnham, will you please bring Baby here a minute? His mother wants to see him."

So Ruth turned at once and carried him to the bedside, where he, being in genial mood, chose to smile upon and coo at his mother.

"He grows rapidly, doesn't he?" Irene said, and it was the first remark she had volunteered, directed to her mother-in-law.

Ruth had seen her twice a day ever since there had been any admittance for other than those in constant attendance, but her visits had necessarily been very brief, and there had been no attempt at conversation.

"Yes, indeed!" she made haste to say. "He is growing finely; you will be astonished to find how strong he is, and he seems to be perfectly well."

"He does you credit." His mother's tone was listlessness personified. Ruth, looking at her closely, began to realize that some strange change which seemed not to be accounted for by illness had come upon Irene. It was not simply that the fierceness of her love for her child was gone, and almost if not quite indifference taken its place, physical weakness might account for that; but there was an indescribable something about her that seemed to Ruth like a surrender, as one who had made a fierce fight and been worsted in the battle and had given up. The troubled grandmother thought it all over after she and baby were back in his room. She could not but fear that a new distress was coming upon them. What if Irene were that abnormal creature, a woman who could not continue to love a child, even her own! There was no fear that she would again desert it, her evident and unfailing, even increasing passion for her husband would hold her, this time, to her home; but— could the misery of it be borne, if this baby must grow up under the control of an unloving mother? She strained him to her so suddenly and so closely that he rebelled, and got off a lovely jargon of talk in protest.

She went back, later, to Irene's room, carrying the baby who was in a flutter of delight over just the joy of living. It did not seem possible that one could look at him without loving him. She could not help wanting to test Irene and see if her interest in him had indeed waned.

She smiled languidly on him, and suffered Ruth to place him on the couch beside her, although she said:—

"Two visits in one morning! Hasn't he been here before?"

"He was so sweet in his new dress," Ruth explained, "that I thought his mamma ought to see him while it was fresh." Then she began to rehearse some of his pretty baby ways, making a distinct effort to awaken in his mother's heart a sense of pride in her child. Irene listened vaguely, as one who only half heard. Suddenly she made an impatient movement.

"Here," she said, "take your baby. He is so full of life that the very sight of him wearies me. Take him away."

Ruth's heart sank. Better the fiercest, unreasoning passion of love and jealousy than this!

Others beside herself began to notice and be puzzled and troubled by this change in the patient. Rebecca, the nurse, expressed her mind to Ruth in anxious whispers.

"Doesn't it seem queer to you, ma'am, that she doesn't notice baby more? and he growing so smart and cunning! You know how she was just bound up in the child, and couldn't seem to think of anything else?"

"It is because she is still so weak that she cannot yet think connectedly about anything," Ruth replied with a confidence that she was far from feeling. "You noticed, didn't you, that she said he was so full of life it wearied her to look at him?"

But the nurse who had received hospital training, shook her head and whispered again:—

"It isn't right, ma'am, somehow. I'm no croaker but I've seen lots of sick folks and I don't think things are going just right with her. If I were Mr. Burnham, I should want another doctor to see her, or—something."

Then came Erskine, his face troubled.

"Mamma, did you ever see any one get well as slowly as Irene does? It almost seems to me as though she is weaker to-day than she was two weeks ago; and she seems to take less and less notice of Baby. Last night when I heard him laughing, I asked her if she did not want me to bring him for a little good-night visit, and she said: 'No, I don't want him. I've given him up!'"

His voice broke with the last word, but he waited for his mother to say something encouraging; and she had only the merest commonplaces.

"She has been very ill, Erskine, and I suppose we must be patient. She cannot be expected to be interested in anything while she is still so weak."

"Mamma, you don't think—" and then Ruth was glad that the baby cried, and she had to go to him, without waiting to tell what she thought.

CHAPTER XXVII

A RETROGRADE MOVEMENT

Erskine, once roused, could not rest. He came to his mother on the next evening, his face more troubled than before.

"Mamma, I had a long talk with the doctor this morning. He is not satisfied with the present state of things. He admits that for some days there has been a retrograde movement. He has been watching very closely and has become convinced that there is some mental disturbance, a heavy mental strain of some kind that must be removed before medicine will be of any use. Now what possible mental strain could Irene have!

"I told the doctor that before we were married, she went through very trying experiences, and lost her nearest relative while she was alone in a foreign country; but that time was long past, of course, and there had been absolutely nothing since, to trouble her."

His mother's start of dismay at hearing the doctor's word, and the flushing of her face did not escape him, and he added almost sternly:—

"Mother, are you keeping something from me that I ought to know?"

For a moment she did not know how to answer him. Then her mind cleared and she spoke quietly:—

"I am doing right, Erskine; I have no secrets of my own from you. I have heard of some things that I can conceive of as troubling Irene, but she did not confide them to me, and I have no right to talk about them even to you; especially as I can think of no good, but rather harm, to result."

He turned from her abruptly. She could see that he was not only sorely perplexed but hurt; in his hour of deepest need his mother seemed to have failed him.

It was a bitter hour for her. Yet she felt that she must be right. Would any one but a fiend go to Erskine now with the story of his wife's long years of living a lie! If her duty elsewhere were but as clear as this! Could it be that this was what was preying upon Irene and causing that retrograde movement? Had her long-sluggish conscience awakened at last? Was she perhaps ignorant of the fate of her daughter? Was she afraid that her former husband was still living, and that he and Erskine might, sometime, meet? Who could tell what questions of horror and terror were struggling in her tired brain and wearing out her weakened body?

Ought she—the woman who knew the whole dread story, knew many details that the sick one did not—ought she to be the surgeon to probe that wound? To be able to talk about it all might help. And yet—who could tell? The knowledge that her husband's mother knew every detail of that life which had been so carefully hidden from them, might be the last shock to that already overcharged brain.

Oh, to be sure of her duty! She told herself that she would perform it at any cost, she would shrink from nothing, now, if she could but be sure of the way. Well, why should she not be sure? Where was her Father? What was that promise: "Thine ears shall hear a word behind thee saying: 'This is the way, walk ye in it.'"

Sleep did not come to her that night, but perhaps she was given a strength that was better. She spent much of the time on her knees beside the quietly sleeping baby; and though, when morning came, she was not sure which way she was to turn that day, "whether to the right hand or the left," she found her mind repeating the words: "In quietness and confidence shall be your strength."

The day passed without marked changes of any sort. Erskine comforted himself with the belief that Irene was a trifle stronger. He told his mother that Dr. Sutherland was coming out to see her on the following day. The great nerve specialist could not get away from the city before that time. Irene heard of his expected visit with the same air of indifference that she had exhibited toward all things of late. She lay very quiet most of the day, and at evening made no objection whatever to Erskine's going to an important conference with his firm.

No sooner was he gone than she herself proposed that Rebecca go at that time to the kitchen to superintend the making of a new kind of food for her, instead of waiting until morning.

"I might want to try it in the night," she said, "and I don't need any further attention at present. Mother will stay with me."

This looked like deliberate planning. Irene had never before, of her own will, arranged to spend five minutes alone with her mother-in-law. That astonished woman while hastening to agree to the proposition, made a swift mental claim upon the promise: "Thine ears shall hear a word behind thee saying, This is the way."

It was Irene who began conversation as soon as the door closed after Rebecca. But the topic she chose was a new astonishment.

"I have been thinking about those two step-daughters of yours, Seraph and Minta. You must have lived a strange life with them."

Ruth turned surprised eyes upon her.

"I did not suppose that you had ever heard of the girls," she said. "Erskine was so young when they left us that I thought he scarcely remembered them."

"Oh, he remembers them very well. He has told me some things; but it was Mrs. Portland from whom I received their connected history. She was here for two months while you were away, and was quite intimate with me; she ran in often, and liked nothing better than to talk about you and those two girls."

Now Mrs. Portland was an old resident of the neighborhood who had known Judge Burnham and his daughters before Ruth had heard of their existence. What she could reveal of their history if she chose, would leave nothing for another to tell. The question was, Why had their story interested this sick woman? Or rather, why was it being brought forward just now?

"It seems strange that they both came back to you to die, doesn't it?"

This was certainly a strange way of putting it! Ruth hesitated how to reply. At last, she said:—

"Seraph never left home, you know; and poor Minta was glad to return to it. She had been through a very bitter experience."

"Yes, I heard about it. You have had all sorts of experiences yourself, haven't you? And to conclude with a good-for-nothing daughter-in-law seems too bad!"

Surprise and almost consternation held Ruth silent. This was so utterly unlike any sentence that she had expected! Irene's tone expressed both sympathy and regret. Ruth decided to pass it off lightly. She laughed a little in a way that was intended to express good cheer, as she said:—

"You are not to find fault with my daughter-in-law, if you please! I allow no one to do that."

"That is because you are not acquainted with her yourself. You don't know anything about her. You think you do, but you are mistaken."

There was no excitement in her tone; there was even no indication that she had a personal interest in the conversation; it seemed to be a mere statement of fact.

Ruth's swift thought took hold of the promise and heard the voice: "This is the way." She spoke with quiet firmness.

"I know all about her; I know a great deal more than she thinks I do."

Irene moved on her pillow so as to get a more direct view of the other's face as she asked:—

"What do you mean?"

"Just that, dear. I know much more than you think, and have known it for a long time."

"You don't know what I mean," the tone was still impersonal, "but I am going to tell you. You think I was a widow when I married your son. I was not." She raised herself slightly on one elbow as she spoke, using more strength than she had exerted since her illness. Ruth came swiftly over to her and slipped a supporting arm under her as she said:—

"Don't try to raise yourself up, Irene, and I wouldn't talk any more. I know all that you want to tell me. You were a divorced wife, and your husband was living; but he has since died. You see I understand all about it."

Irene's eyes fairly pierced her with their keenness; still, her voice betrayed no emotion.

"You knew it all the time?" she said.

"I have known it for a very long time, Irene. Don't talk any more; it is time for your medicine now, and after it you must be very quiet, you know."

Irene was as one who had not heard.

"You do not know the worst," she said, still speaking as though her words were about some one else; but she was deathly pale. "There was a child."

Ruth hurriedly wet a cloth in a restorative and bathed her face, while she spoke low and soothingly, as to a child.

"Yes, I know; there was a dear little girl, who is a young woman now,—one of the sweetest, dearest girls in the world. I know her and love her. Irene, for Erskine's sake, won't you try to be careful!"

For Irene had pushed the soothing hand away and was making a fierce effort to raise herself to a sitting posture, and her eyes looked to Ruth for the first time like Maybelle's.

Ruth hurried her words.

"I know all that you want to say; you must lie quiet and let me talk. I am sure there must have been strong provocation, and you were very young; I know how bitterly you must have regretted it all."

"You cannot know that, at least," she said. "There is no need for what you call future punishment, I have had mine here; and I have hated you for fear you would find me out. How long have you known it?"

"For a long time, many months. Irene, I *cannot* let you talk or think about it now. Won't you try to put it all away for to-night? There is nothing, you see, that you need to tell me."

The great solemn eyes that Maybelle's were like when she was troubled were fixed upon Ruth.

"Could you put it away?" she asked. "It has never been away from me for a moment, the fear that Erskine would—would—"

A convulsive shiver ran through her frame, as of one in physical pain.

"Oh!" said Ruth, in terror, "this is all wrong! If you are worse, Erskine will never forgive me."

Irene made a visible effort to control herself, and lay with closed eyes, and motionless, allowing Ruth to bathe her face and make hot applications to her hands and feet. After a little, she spoke, quietly enough.

"I will talk quietly, but you must let me talk, now. I have kept it to myself just as long as I can. Since Baby came, my life has been a daily terror. Will you tell me how you came to know about me, and why you have not told Erskine? I am sure you have not, but I do not understand why."

"Because," said Ruth, solemnly, "Jesus Christ, to whom I belong, told me not to do so. It is your secret, Irene, yours and His. You must let Him tell you what to do with it."

Irene gazed at her. "You are a strange woman," she said at last, "a very strange woman; but you are good, and I have not understood you. I am sorry that I hated you. If I had understood, it might have been—different. I thought you would find it out, sometime, women always do, and I hated you for that; I dreaded you, you know. Every letter that came from you while you were away made me faint and sick because of what might be in it. I was afraid to have Erskine come home at night because of what he might have heard; and I was afraid to have him go away again in the morning for fear it would be the last time he would kiss me."

"Poor child!" The words were wrung from Ruth's heart,—the first words of real tenderness that she had ever spoken to this woman.

Again there came that strange new look into Irene's eyes.

"I'm sorry that I hated you."—*Page 354.*

"You are a good woman," she said slowly. "I am sorry that I hated you. Let me talk now, and tell you about it. I have got to! I ought not to have married that man; I never pretended even to him that I loved him. I married to get rid of dulness and restraint, and to go to Europe. I was a young fool! I got rid of nothing, and instead of feeling only indifference for him I learned to hate him. He was a drunkard, and I hated him for that. Then—I did not like the baby. You can't quite control your horror of that, can you? I don't wonder, now that I have learned what mother-love really is. I could almost hate myself for having such a feeling. You think a mother couldn't—but she can. I turned from the child, just as I had from the father, in disgust. Even so early in her life she looked like him, and I hated him. He was a weak man, and I never had any patience with weakness. Sometimes he was maudlin and loving, and then I hated him worst of all. One day I went away from him and stayed away. That was all I did. Oh, yes, I got a divorce; that was because I hated his name. At first I meant to do something for the child, I didn't know what,—he worshipped the baby,—and then I heard that it died; and I did not know until years afterward that it lived; but it was too late then to do anything. By that time I had met Erskine and discovered what love really meant. Oh, to think how I have loved him! and I have struggled and planned and lied to keep his love! I have even prayed to keep it! and now it is all over!"

"Irene," said her listener, firmly. "If you persist in talking, I shall have to send for Erskine. You must swallow this sedative and then lie still and let me talk. I will say in just a minute all I want to, and then we will both be quiet and you will try to sleep, for Erskine's sake. It isn't all over; it is just beginning. We cannot undo the past, but we can make another thing of the present—and the future. I promise you, before God, and call on Him to witness, that I will never by word or look reveal to Erskine one word of what we have said or of what I know, unless you tell me to do so. When you are well and strong again, you will decide how much or how little you want to tell him. God will show you what is right and you will want to do right; I am sure of it. And we will love each other, you and I, and help each other. Two women who love one man as you and I love Erskine Burnham should be very much to each other. Now I am not going to say another word."

She bent her head and kissed the sick woman on her forehead—her first voluntary caress.

Irene, who had closed her eyes and was death-like in her stillness, opened them again and looked steadily at her. Then she said with slow conviction in her tones:—

"You are a good woman."

CHAPTER XXVIII

"SOMETHING HAD HAPPENED"

But Ruth Burnham went to her room that night in a tumult of pain and self-reproach keener than she had felt for years.

As plainly as though a book had been opened before her, and a solemn unseen figure had pointed to the page, she read the story of her failure.

She had tried to be good to this woman, she had been outwardly patient with her faults, she had been long suffering, she had been silent over wrongs—she had effaced herself in a thousand ways, but she had been as cold as ice. There had been nothing in her face or voice to invite the confidence of this younger, weaker woman. There had been nothing in her daily attitude toward her to suggest the love and sympathy of Christ.

She cried to Him for forgiveness, for the privilege of beginning again, for wisdom to know just how to do it. And then she prayed for Irene in a way that, with all her trying, she had not been able to do before.

It came to her while on her knees that she would tell Irene of Maybelle's beautiful faith and daily praying for her mother, without knowing that it was her mother.

Were the child's prayers being answered? Was this strange new mood of Irene's part of the answer?

But they could not be brought together, that mother and daughter, not now—it was too late. How could they? What explanation of her existence, of their intense interest in her, could be given to Erskine? Would Irene ever be intensely interested in Maybelle? Could she do other than shrink from her now, after all these strange years?

Oh! there were depths to this trouble that she must not try to touch. But one thing was plain: she must help Irene. Whatever would do that, at whatever sacrifice, must be done.

The next day, that in some way Ruth had thought would be an eventful one, passed in even unusual quiet. Irene seemed less restless than usual, and lay much of the time with closed eyes. The great specialist came out to see her, and there was a long interview, and a long conference afterward with the attending physician, but they kept their own counsel. All that the family knew was that in the main they agreed, and the specialist wished to withhold his final opinion until he saw the patient again after thirty-six hours.

In the evening Irene roused herself from what had for several hours been almost a stupor, to ask Erskine if he could give the entire evening to her, and if they could be quite alone.

"Yes, indeed," he said with a brave attempt at gayety. "We will banish them all, even Rebecca, and I will be doctor and head nurse and errand boy combined. See that you get a good sleep, Rebecca, and you need not come until I ring for you."

To Ruth this arrangement was somewhat of a disappointment. She had hoped that Irene would want to see her for a few minutes; there were questions that it would seem as though she must want to ask, and there were things that Ruth felt might help her, if she were told them. But Irene gave no hint that she even remembered what had passed between them, save that, as Ruth went to bid her good-night, she made a movement with her hand to draw her down and murmured:—

"You are a good woman."

Erskine held the door open for his mother to pass, then followed her into the hall.

"Mamma, don't you think Irene has seemed a little better to-day, more quiet? And she took a good deal of notice of Baby this afternoon."

There was such a wistful note in his voice that his mother's eyes filled with tears; she longed to comfort him, and realized that she did not know how.

She was wakeful and alert during the first part of the night, ready for some emergency which she feared, without knowing just why. But toward morning she slept heavily, and was wakened by the sunshine and the prattle of Baby's voice in his crib at her bedside.

She dressed hurriedly, still with that vague impression upon her that something had happened or was about to happen. In the hall was Erskine, standing with folded arms gazing out of the window; gazing at nothing. The first glimpse she had of him she knew that something had already happened. His face was gray, not white, with a pallor that was unnatural and startling; he gave her a strange impression of having grown suddenly old— years older than he had been the night before. And he looked strangely like his father.

"Erskine," his mother said, alarmed, and hurried toward him.

He turned at once, lifting a warning finger.

"Hush!" he said; "I think she is sleeping. She has been very quiet since midnight."

Then he went without another word into his dressing-room and closed the door.

It was a strange long day. The patient lay quiet, not sleeping all the time, but like one too weak and too indifferent to life to move. The house was kept very still; although noises did not seem to disturb the sick one, the different members of the household conversed in mono-syllables and in whispers when they met.

Ruth kept the baby out all day in the lovely soft summer air, and he was happy. When a tear rolled once or twice down the cheeks of his grandmother, he kissed her lovingly, and patted her face with his soft hand. The specialist came again, but he did not stay long, and Ruth, who could not leave her charge at the time, did not know what he said. No one came to her with any word. One of the maids told her that Mr. Burnham was sitting beside his wife, and had not left her room for hours.

The afternoon shadows were growing long, and Ruth was explaining to the baby that it was almost time for him to go to his little bed, and that she did not know whether mamma could kiss him good-night or not, when Rebecca, her face swollen with weeping, crossed the lawn and touched her arm.

"May I take Baby, ma'am? The doctor said perhaps you would want to go to Mr. Burnham. He went into his dressing-room and closed his door, and the doctor thinks perhaps you might help him; he was awfully pale."

"Is any thing wrong?" Ruth asked hurriedly, as she rose up to give her charge into Rebecca's arms. "Is she worse?"

But Rebecca was crying. "Oh, ma'am," she said, "she just slipped away! it was awfully sudden for him! the doctor told him she might live for hours, I heard him."

"Rebecca, she is not *dead*!"

"She just stopped breathing, ma'am, and that was all. Mr. Burnham was sitting close to her where he has been sitting 'most all day, and she didn't look any different to me. I thought she was asleep; but he looked up suddenly at the doctor, poor man, with *such a face*! I never shall forget it! and the doctor said:—

"'Yes, she is gone.'"

And then Rebecca, who had not loved her mistress devotedly in life, broke into bitter weeping.

Ruth was like one paralyzed. She stood gazing at the girl as though unable to move. It was not Erskine's grief so much as her own consternation that held her. It seemed to her impossible that Irene was dead! With all her thinking, and her foreboding, she had not thought of that. She had felt on the eve of a great calamity, but it had not been death. Erskine's gray, pale face that morning had not suggested such trouble. Instead, she had worried herself all day long with the possibilities connected with that evening conference; of what Irene had told him, and how he had borne it and what he would feel must be done.

She went to Erskine at last, utterly in doubt what to say to him. He was in his private study with his head bowed on the desk. He did not notice his mother's entrance by so much as a movement. She went over to him and laid her hand gently on the brown curly locks, with a caressing movement familiar to him from childhood. He put out a hand and drew her to him, but neither of them spoke a word.

A tender memory of the long ago came to Ruth. She was back in the days of Erskine's childhood, she was in that very study which had been his father's, with her head bowed in anguish on her husband's desk, while he lay in the room below dressed for the grave. Her little boy stood beside her, a longing desire upon him to comfort his mother; and half frightened because she cried.

"Mamma," he had said at last, hesitatingly, "Mamma, does God sometimes make a mistake?" It had come to her like a voice of tender reproof from God himself, and had helped her as nothing else did. Long afterward she had told the boy about it, and it had become a sacred memory to them both.

"Erskine," she said at last, speaking very tenderly;—

"Does God sometimes make a mistake?"

His strong frame shook. "O mother!" he said. "*O mother!*" and lifted tearless eyes to her face. How old he looked, and haggard! How like to his father his face had grown!

Just then there came one of those commonplace interruptions from which in times of mortal stress we shrink away. The intrusive world knocked at his door with its questions, and thrust duties and responsibilities upon him.

Did Mr. Burnham wish this, or that, or the other? Could Dr. Cartwright speak to him a moment? It was a matter of importance. Would he see Miss Stuart for just a minute about a telegram?

It was harrowing. His mother's heart ached for him. The interruptions to his grief seemed impertinent and trivial, and those who were nearest to him deplored them as they always do, without realizing that the commonplaces of life are often salvation to desperate souls.

Erskine rose up to meet the demands upon him, putting back with stern hand all outward exhibition of his misery save that which his face told for him.

He gave careful attention to the thousand details that pressed upon him. He planned and arranged and carried out, when necessary, saving his mother all the burdens possible, but it seemed to her that he avoided seeing her alone.

It was not until Irene's body had been lying for an entire week in the family burial ground that Erskine came to his mother's room one afternoon and asked if she were engaged.

"Only with Baby," she said eagerly. "Come in, Erskine, and see how sweet he is. You haven't seen him since morning."

He took the child in his arms and studied his face intently, smiling over his pretty motions in a grave, absent-minded way; then he gave him back with a question:—

"Can you banish him, mamma, for a little while? I want to talk with you."

"Yes, indeed," she said. "Rebecca can take him for a walk. I will have him ready in a few minutes."

He watched the process of robing and kissing, with eyes that seemed not to see; and that troubled his mother, they were so full of pain.

When the baby was gone, and Ruth had closed the doors leading into other rooms and seated herself near to him, he seemed to have forgotten that he wanted to talk.

His eyes were fixed on the far-away hills that towered skyward, and were snow-capped; and yet she was not sure that he saw them.

"Mother," he said at last, "she told me you were a good woman, and it is true. I have always been able to anchor to you. We have trusted each other utterly, you and I, and spoken plainly to each other; we must always do so. You have something to tell me. Will you begin at the beginning and let me have all that you know? Don't try to spare me, please; I want the whole. O mother! If I had only known long ago, it might have been— different."

There was no reply that she could make to this.

After a moment, he said again: "You know that I am not blaming you, don't you? It was what I might have expected of you, what you did; she thought it was wonderful. But if she could only have trusted me!"

"Will you tell me the whole, mamma? Irene told me to ask you; she said you would not tell it without her word. I mean about the man, and—the child; all the details. How did you hear of it all, and when?"

He hesitated over the simple words, his face flushing painfully. Ruth hurried her speech to save him further effort.

"Do you remember, Erskine, when our old acquaintance Mamie Parker called upon me? It was then that I heard the story."

He made a gesture of astonishment.

"Mamie Parker! Is it possible that she is mixed up in our family matters?"

"She found the little girl without other care than a father could give, and interested herself in her, and loved her. She has been thus far in the child's life as dear and wise a friend as a girl could have."

Then she began at the beginning and gave in minutest detail the whole story, as it had come to her at first, and as she had since lived it with Maybelle.

Erskine's amazement at the discovery that the young girl to whom his mother had been summoned by telegram, and for whom she had cared ever since, was the one whose life-story he was now hearing, was only equalled by his pain in it all. But after the first dismayed exclamation he sat like a statue, his face partially hidden by his hand, interrupting neither by question nor comment.

Ruth purposely made her story long that he might have time to get the control of himself; and she tried to make Maybelle's loveliness of heart and mind and person glow before him; under the spell of the thought that it would all be less terrible to him, if he could realize that his dead wife's strange conduct had not ruined the young life.

CHAPTER XXIX

RENUNCIATION

When she stopped speaking because there was nothing more to be told, they sat for a little in utter silence.

When at last Erskine spoke in a low, carefully controlled voice, he asked the very last question that his mother expected.

"How soon do you think she could come to us?"

"Who?" Ruth's astonishment blurred for the moment her penetration.

"Mother! whom could I mean? The child. She must be sent for; she must come at once; or, at least as soon as a suitable escort can be secured. Would she come? And would she stay, do you think? I mean would she stay willingly? Oh, mamma, surely you will help me!"

"Erskine, dear boy, what do you want to do?"

"My duty." He withdrew his shielding hand and his pallid lips made an effort to smile; then grew grave again, taking almost stern lines.

"She is my wife's daughter; and as such I stand now in the place of father to her. As fully as it is possible for me to do so, now, I want to fill that place. To provide for her, to take care of her in any and every way that she may need care; to have my home hers as fully as it is our little son's." His voice broke there, and for a moment he was still. Then he went on.

"You said you loved her; it would not be unpleasant to you to have her here, would it?"

Then his mother found her voice.

"Erskine, Maybelle has a place in my heart second only to Baby's, and I would like so much to have her with me, that at one time I tried to plan a little home where we could be together. But—do you realize the situation, do you think? We cannot live entirely to ourselves, you know, we have friends; and we have neighbors who ask questions. If Maybelle comes to us, to remain, what is to be said to them?"

"The truth, mamma; never anything but truth. She is my wife's daughter by a former marriage, the half-sister of my boy."

"Erskine, dear son, I must hurt you, I am afraid; but do you realize what the truth will be to the child? She loves her dead father with such love as I believe few girls give, and she cherishes in her inmost heart an ideal mother who has been invested with more than human qualities; if you could hear her talk about that dear, dead mother, you would understand."

He had shielded his face again, and was quiet so long, that it seemed to her she could not bear it. At last he spoke, huskily but with firmness.

"I understand, mamma, more than you think; at least I believe I realize something of her feeling; but—I cannot help it. Truth must be spoken; the real must take the place of the ideal. Isn't it so in all our lives? I promised her dead mother that it should be so. It was perhaps a morbid feeling,—some might think so,—but in any case, she felt it; she said that she could not die without my promise that the truth should be made plain to the girl, and that she should be told the very words that her mother said, at the last. And I believe she was right," he added firmly after another moment of silence, "I will speak only truth about it all, so help me God."

Never was summons more joyfully received on the part of a young girl than the one that called Maybelle to the distant home of her newest and, as she phrased it, "almost" her best friend.

The night preceding her departure she spent with the Roberts family, where together they went over the situation as they understood it, for Erskine Roberts's benefit.

That young man had just arrived for a few days' vacation and could not be said to approve of the new plans.

"Why is Aunt Ruth in such terrific haste?" he grumbled. "She has never mentioned a visit to you before this, has she?"

"No," said Maybelle, her bright face shading for a moment. "She never said a word about it; but you know it is all very different now. She is alone; I mean there is no other woman, and there is a dear baby to be thought about; I don't positively know, but I cannot help hoping that she needs me."

Maybelle's tones had become so jubilant that they made Erskine gloomy and sarcastic.

"For nurse girl you mean, I suppose," he said savagely. "And if that delightful arrangement should be found convenient for them, I suppose you would stay on indefinitely?"

"Erskine," said his mother, smiling, "don't be a bear! she hasn't promised to stay forever."

Then Maybelle, her color much heightened, tried to explain further. "The reason for such haste is so I can have one of Mr. Burnham's partners for an escort. It was found that he had to come East on a hurried business trip, and of course it was an unusual opportunity."

"I should hope so!" grumbled the discontented youth. "And who is there to escort you back? I'll venture they haven't planned for that!" Then suddenly he bent toward the girl, ostensibly for the purpose of returning to her the letter that had dropped to the floor, and spoke for her ear alone.

"I'll tell you how we will manage that, Maybelle. I will come for you myself, if you will let me. Will you let me?"

A vivid crimson mounted to the very forehead of the fair-faced girl, and she seemed at a loss how to reply; but she certainly had not been troubled by his appeal whatever it was, so the indulgent mother slipped away and left the young people to themselves.

"Am I to tell her, Erskine?" Ruth had asked her son, on the day that she was to go to the station to meet Maybelle. He shook his head.

"No, mamma, no, I will not make it harder for you than is necessary. Yes, I know only too well how surely you would do everything for me if you could; but—I have assumed an obligation, and I do not mean to shirk it in the slightest particular. Do not tell her anything save that you wanted her—that is true, is it not?" he broke off to ask anxiously. "Then, in the evening, when she has had time to become somewhat rested from her journey, send her to me in my library and I will manage the rest."

How he managed it, or what took place during that interview which must have been strangely tragic some of the time, Ruth never fully knew. She asked no questions, and what her son and the girl revealed to her in scraps and detached expressions afterward, suggested a confidence so sacred that even she must not invade it.

She had known by the start and the swift look of pain which swept over Erskine's face when he first met Maybelle at the dinner table, that the girl in her radiant beauty suggested his dead wife. To Ruth there was a strange unlikeness to the face that she had not loved; but her heart was able to understand how Irene had been to one whom she had loved, nay worshipped, as she had her husband, a very different being, living a life solely for him, and leaving a memory that the fair girl could awaken.

Maybelle was all but overwhelmed with astonishment and a sweet timidity when Ruth told her that Erskine wanted to see her for a little while in his library.

"Not alone!" she said. "Without you, I mean? Oh! Am I not almost afraid? I mean, I shall not know what to say to him. It is all so recent, you see. I can see his beautiful character shining through his sorrow; dear Mrs. Burnham, I admire him almost as much as even his mother could wish, but I can see that a great crushing sorrow is heavy upon him, and a girl like me does not know how to touch such wounds without hurting. Does he mean to talk to me about her, do you think? Does he know that I loved her and prayed for her all the time? Oh, dear friend, don't you think he wants you too?"

Ruth kissed her tenderly, solemnly, and put her away from her. "No, dear," she said gently. "He wants to see you quite alone. He has something to tell you. You will know what to say after you have heard him; God will show you."

She closed the door after the slowly moving, half-reluctant, serious girl, and sat alone. It came to her vaguely, as one used to sacrifice, that here was another. She must sit alone with folded hands while another, and she a young girl upon whom he had never before set eyes, went down with her son into the depths of human pain. Was it always so? Was that forever the lot of motherhood, to stand aside and have some one else touch the deepest life of her children, whether in joy or pain?

The interview was long, very long. Sometimes it seemed to the waiting mother that she could not endure the strain; that she must go to that closed room and discover for herself what those two were saying to torture each other. But at last, the door across the hall opened and Maybelle came with swift feet and knelt in front of her, hid her face in the older woman's lap, and broke into a passion of weeping.

At first Ruth let the storm of pain roll on unchecked, only touching the bowed head with soothing hand and murmuring:—

"Poor child! dear little girl!"

But the girl cried on, and on, as though she would never stop, her whole slight frame shaken with the force of her sorrow.

Across the hall Ruth could hear the steady tread of her son's footsteps as he paced back and forth, fighting his battle alone. Should his mother go and try to comfort him? But this motherless one was clinging to her.

"Maybelle," she said at last, "is it a hopeless grief? Is there no One who can help?"

Then the girl made a desperate effort to control herself. She reached for Ruth's hand and gripped it in her young, strong one. Then, after another moment, she spoke:—

"Forgive me. I did not mean to hurt you; I did not mean to cry at all; I said that I would not; but it was all so new, so—O mamma, mamma!"

The head, which had been raised a little, went down again; and the exceeding bitterness of that last wailing cry of renunciation Ruth never forgot. She had grace to be thankful that the mother was not there to hear it.

But the violence of the storm was over, at least so far as its outward exhibition was concerned. In a few minutes more the girl spoke quietly enough.

"He is very, very good. I did not know that any—just human being could be so good. And he spoke tenderly all the time of—of my mother. I could feel in his voice the sound of his great love for her. My poor, poor mother!"

Later, after much had been said and there had been silence between them for a few minutes, she spoke suddenly:—

"He asked me to call him 'father,' he said he wanted it." Ruth could not suppress a little start of surprise and—was it pain? In all her hours of thinking over this whole tragedy, trying to plan how all things would be, she had not thought of this. Yet it was like Erskine; the utmost atonement that he could make, in word as well as deed, would be made.

"What did you say in reply?" she asked the waiting girl.

"I said that I would try to do in all things just as he advised. I could not do less, Mrs. Burnham; he is very good. I told him about my own dear papa, and that I should always, *always* love and honor him as I had reason to; and he was good about that, too; he said that the way I felt about him was not only natural but it was right, and that he honored me for it. Then he spoke of Baby Erskine and called him my little brother; and that broke my heart. I have so longed to have some one of my very own. Mrs. Burnham, do you think perhaps that—that papa understands about it all, and would want me to—"

She seemed unable to express her thought in words, but Ruth understood it, and the yearning wistfulness in the child's voice was not to be resisted. The older woman put aside her own pain to comfort and counsel this girl who had certainly in strange ways been thrust upon her care.

A thought of comfort came to her, that, after a little hesitation, she gave to the girl.

"Maybelle dear, if you call my son 'father,' what name does that give to me as my rightful possession?"

She had her reward. There was a moment's wondering thought, then a flush of surprise and a wave of radiance swept over the expressive face. She spoke the word in a whisper, almost a reverent one, yet the syllables were like a caress, and thrilled with joy:—

"'Grandmother'! Oh! do you mean it? that I may?" And then the caresses that Ruth received were almost as sweet as any that she was waiting for Baby Erskine to voluntarily bestow upon her.

CHAPTER XXX

"TWO, AND TWO, AND TWO"

It took but a little while for the Burnham household to settle down quietly to routine living; so easily, after all, does human nature adjust itself to tremendous strains and changes. Maybelle fitted into her place as though she had always been an acknowledged daughter of the house, come home after long absence. And the neighbors, even those morbidly curious ones, of which there are always a few in every community, took kindly to the new order of things and to the bright-faced stranger who rode and drove and walked and appeared in church with Erskine and his mother, and was introduced with punctilious care as "My wife's daughter, Miss Somerville."

They could not help, even from the first, saying kind and complimentary things about the beautiful young face, and after a few days of wonderment and conjecture they arranged their own story—with a very meagre array of facts to build upon—quite to their satisfaction.

"Oh, yes, I knew she was a widow when he married her; but I never heard of a child."

"Well, he married abroad, don't you know, and I suppose the girl just stayed on, with her relatives. Her mother must have been a mere child when she was first married; though this girl is very young, and Mrs. Burnham was probably older than she looked; for that matter, don't you know, I always said that she looked older than her husband? I suppose the girl has lived abroad all her life; that's what makes her look different, some way, from American girls, though her mother was born in this country, she told me so. Still, the girl would have English ways, of course, always living there. Did you hear her say the other day that the Somerville brothers, great English bankers that Ned Lake was asking her about, were her uncles?"

"It seems hard that the poor girl couldn't have been with her mother before she died," said one whose interests ran naturally in other channels than those of ages and pedigrees.

"Yes, it does," chimed in another home-keeping and home-loving matron, "but then her death was awfully sudden. Erskine's mother told me that they had no idea of her dying up to the very day; and I guess the girl has been separated from her a good deal. I have heard somewhere, and I am sure I don't remember where, that there was a fuss of some sort in the family. Probably her first husband's people didn't like the idea of her going into society and marrying again, especially marrying an American; English people are queer about some things, I have heard; I suppose they held on to the girl as long as they could."

Thus, with supposition and surmise, and a stray fact now and then, and vague remembrances, the story was worked over and shaped and pieced until it suited them. Meantime, the Burnham family went quietly on its way, having no confidants, and, while they spoke only truth when they spoke at all, judging it not necessary to tell the whole truth to any.

So quiet and peace settled once more upon Ruth Burnham's home, and it was proved again, as it often is, that a new grave in the family burial ground is more productive of peace than a life has been.

Erskine was habitually grave, and his mother told herself sorrowfully that sin, not death, had permanently shadowed his life. But by degrees his gravity took on a cheerful tone, and Baby Erskine, whom at first he had almost shunned, became a never failing source of comfort to him.

As for Maybelle, no grown-up daughter was ever more devoted to a father's interests than she became. She hovered about his home life with an air of sweet, grave deference, ministering to his tastes with unlimited thoughtfulness and tact, until from being to him an infliction for whose comfort he must be thoughtful from a sense of duty, she became first an interest, and then almost a necessity. The neighbors said how lovely it was in her to take her mother's place so beautifully.

Then, of course, there were some to say that they shouldn't wonder if she should succeed at last in comforting him entirely for his loss. Wouldn't it be romantic if he should marry her! Of course she was really not related to him at all, and great difference in age was much more common than it used to be. For that matter, Erskine Burnham was still a young man. For their part, they agreed almost to a woman, that it would be a nice idea—

But all that was before they made the acquaintance of Erskine Roberts. That young man was true to his word, and in the course of time came across the continent. That he came after Maybelle, as he had said he would, was perfectly obvious, but he did not take her back with him, as at one time he had tried to plan to do.

He had two more years to spend at the theological seminary, and during those two years it had been agreed by all concerned that Maybelle was to continue to bless her new home with her presence.

Erskine Roberts was one of the very few to whom the whole situation had been fully and carefully explained. Not only Maybelle, but Ruth herself had written the story, both to Erskine, and his mother; and then, when his namesake came out to them, the other Erskine had him into his private room one evening, and as he believed was his duty toward the man who was to make Maybelle his wife, went down with him into the lowest depths of his life tragedy. And Erskine Roberts, who had been half angry with the man ever since he had heard the strange story—though he admitted all the time to his secret soul that Erskine Burnham had been in no wise to blame, went over loyally and royally to his side, and said to Ruth while his honest eyes filmed with something like tears and his voice was husky:—

"Aunt Ruth, it must be a grand thing for a mother to have a son like that man across the hall. If I can be half like him in true nobility, my mother will have reason to be proud."

And he even admitted to Maybelle that, since he could not have her to himself yet awhile, he was glad that that man who was worthy that she should call him father was to have the comfort of her.

It was noticeable to themselves that they said very little about the mother. Poor mother! she had forfeited her right to be talked of in the tender and reverent way that Maybelle would have talked, or with the passion of longing for something had, and lost, that used to mark her words to Ruth. She said that word "mamma" no more; the tone in which she used to speak it had been peculiar, and had marked it as set apart for a special and sacred use. Evidently it meant more to her than the word "mother," or at least meant something different. Now, in speaking to Ruth, she said always: "My mother," and said it in a hesitating, half-deprecating tone, almost as if she must apologize for her.

It was not that the girl was bitter; on the contrary she was markedly tender of her mother's memory and pitiful toward her.

Ruth, with the reflex influence of this upon her, found herself searching for all the lovable qualities in Irene that she could by any possibility recall, and by degrees it appeared that death was having its inevitable and gracious influence over hearts, softening the past and casting a halo of excusing pity over that which had at the time seemed unpardonable. But her daughter never again said in a passion of exquisite tenderness: "My mamma!"

She had learned to say "father," and used the word with a shy grace that was fascinating; she had learned also what was of far more consequence: to have the utmost respect for and faith in the man to whom she gave the title. Respect deepened steadily into love, and he became indeed "father" to her, in her very thought. Yet she never put into the word the throbbing love that had shone in the words "My papa!"

They were a peaceful household, with a fair and steadily increasing measure of happiness. "Baby Erskine," as they still called him and probably would, his father said, until he was ready for college, lived his beautiful, carefully ordered life, blossoming into all the graces and sweetnesses of judiciously trained and sheltered childhood, and being familiarized with all the sweet interests and excitements that belong to a baby beloved. His first tooth, his first step, his first definite word were as eagerly watched for and as joyously heralded as though a fond mother had been there to lead. Never had child a more devoted sister and admirer and willing slave than Maybelle; and no words ever expressed more exultant pride and joy than those in which she introduced him to transient guests: "My little brother."

She labored patiently by the hour to teach the boy to shout "Papa!" as soon as he caught a glimpse from the window of the man who would presently ride him upstairs on his proud shoulder; but they never tried to train the baby lips to say "mamma."

"I am glad," said Maybelle one day, breaking suddenly into speech in a way she had, over a train of thought, the steps by which she had reached it being kept to herself: "I am glad that he will always have the dearest and wisest of grandmothers close at hand."

Ruth smiled indulgently.

"By inference," she said, "I am led to believe that you are speaking of Baby Erskine and his grandmother, and am duly grateful for the compliment, but the last remark you made was about the climbing roses on the south porch. Am I to be told or simply be left to imagine the steps by which you reached from rosebuds to Baby Erskine?"

Maybelle laughed softly. "The transition was not so very great, dear doting grandmother! Confess that you think so." Then, the color deepening a little in her face, she added:—

"I was thinking, dear, of our home here, and of the coming changes, and of other—possibilities. To be entirely frank, I thought of a possible second mother for Baby Erskine. Father is still so young that one cannot help thinking sometimes of possibilities. And then, even though I want you so much, I could not help being glad that in any such event you would be close to Baby Erskine."

Ruth held from outward notice any hint of the sudden stricture at her heart over these quiet words, and said cheerfully:—

"The near at hand probabilities are crowding us so hard just now, darling, that I don't think we have room for remote possibilities; let us leave the unknown future, dear child, to One who knows."

It was true that the coming changes were almost beginning to crowd upon them. The climbing rose bushes over the south porch were even thus early thinking of budding;

which meant that June and Flossy Roberts and her family would be with them in two months more.

Time had flown on swift wing after all. It hardly seemed possible that the young man, who had seemed to begin his theological studies but yesterday, was already receiving letters addressed to "The Reverend Erskine Shipley Roberts!"

One shadow Maybelle had, and Ruth understood it well, although it was rarely mentioned between them. Erskine Burnham, the very soul of unselfish thoughtfulness for others, had yet held with unaccountable tenacity to one strange feeling. He shrank with evident pain from the thought of Mamie Parker's presence in the house. She had returned from China early in the previous year, and Maybelle's first eager hope that "Aunt Mamie would come to them at once" for a stay of indefinite length had been wonderingly put aside upon the discovery that "father" apparently shrank from even the mention of her name.

He made a painful effort to explain to his mother.

"Of course, mamma, I do not mean for one moment to stand in the way of anything that you and Maybelle really want, and I do not know that I can explain to you why I feel as I do; but—she is associated, painfully associated, as you know, with that which is like the bitterness of death to me. And I cannot—We will not talk about it, mamma."

Ruth understood and was sorry for the morbid strain which it revealed. She made earnest effort to combat it, not vigorously but with suggestive sentences as occasion offered. It hurt her that Erskine should allow so comparatively small a matter to retard his progress. He had not only gone bravely through his peculiar trial, but had made a distinct advance in his spiritual life. Maybelle's constant prayer for him had assuredly been answered. The Lord Christ had, manifestly, a stronger grip on his personality than ever before. All the details of business and literary life were learning from day to day that they were not to be masters but servants to this man, and that One was his Master.

But this sore spot which could not be touched without pain, his mother felt sure would continue to burn as long as he hid it away. If he could know Mamie Parker as she now was, it was almost certain that the sting of pain and shame which her name suggested would lose its power.

But Maybelle felt sure that Aunt Mamie would never come unless invited by the host.

"And I can't want her to, grandmother, much as I long to see her, so long as her presence is not quite comfortable to father."

So the grandmother bided her time, and spoke her occasional earnest words.

"In short, mamma," Erskine said one morning, turning from the window where he had been standing a silent listener to what she had to say, "In short, mamma, you are ashamed of your son, are you not? And I don't wonder; he is rather ashamed of himself. You have been very patient, you and Maybelle, but this whole thing must cease. Of course the child must have her friend with her. Invite her, mamma, in my name, to come at once and remain through the season. I want it to be so. I do, indeed, now that I have settled it; make Maybelle understand that I do."

After he had left the room he turned back to say pointedly:—

"Of course, mamma, it will not be necessary for me to see very much of her; but I shall try to do my duty as host."

She saw how hard it was for him, but she rejoiced with all her heart at this triumph over the morbid strain.

And Mamie Parker came; and was met in due form by her host and treated in every respect as became an honored guest.

There came an evening when Ruth sat alone by the open window of her room. She had turned out the lights, for the room was flooded with moonlight. It outlined distinctly the little white bed in an alcove opening from her room, where her darling lay sleeping. She had just been in to look at him, and had resisted the temptation to kiss once more the fair cheeks flushed with healthy sleep. Downstairs in the little reception room she knew that Maybelle and Erskine Roberts were saying a few last words together; the girl and the boy who, to-morrow, would begin together the mystery of manhood and womanhood, "until death did them part." From time to time she could hear Maybelle's soft laughter float out on the quiet air; they were very happy together, those two.

From one of the guest chambers near at hand the murmur of voices came to her occasionally. It was growing late, and most of the guests had retired early to make ready by rest for the excitements of the morrow; but sleep had evidently not come yet to Flossy and her husband. They were talking softly. They were happy together, those two. Downstairs on the long vine-covered south porch two people were walking; the murmur of their voices as they walked and talked came up to her, Mamie Parker's voice, and Erskine's. And the mother knew, almost as well as though she could hear the words, some of the things they were saying to each other.

"Mommie," her son had said but a little while before as he bent over and kissed his boy, and then turned and put both arms about her and kissed her, using the old name that of late had almost dropped away from him:—

"Mommie, can you give me your blessing and wish me Godspeed?"

She had not pretended to misunderstand him. She had known for days, it almost seemed to her that she had known before he did, the trend that his life was taking. There had been no word between them, but Erskine had told her once, that he believed she knew his thoughts almost as soon as they were born, and he seemed to take her knowledge for granted.

She was glad that she had controlled her voice, and that her answer had been quick and free:—

"Yes, indeed, my son; God bless and prosper you."

She knew he would be prospered. At least a woman knows a woman's heart. They would be happy together, they two.

Two, and two, and two, everywhere! the youth and maiden, the mature man and woman, the father and mother who were smiling together over their son's espousals, always "they two."

It had been "they two" once with her. And again, and for many years, mother and son; but now—It seemed for a moment to the lonely woman as though the whole world beside was paired and wedded and only herself left desolate. She pressed her hands firmly against the balls of her closed eyes. Should she let one tear mar this night of her son's new joy?

And then, tenderly, like drops of balm upon an aching wound, came the echo in her soul of an old, *old* pledge: "With everlasting loving-kindness will I have mercy on thee, said the Lord, thy Redeemer... I will betroth thee unto me in faithfulness."

"I am a happy woman," she said aloud, in a quiet voice; "I am blessed in my home, and in my—children, and in the abiding presence of my Lord."

Manufactured by Amazon.ca
Bolton, ON